JUN - - 2024

WANDER LOST

LAURA MARTIN

HARPER

An Imprint of HarperCollinsPublishers

ALSO BY LAURA MARTIN

The Monster Missions

Glitch

Hoax for Hire

Float
Vanishing Act

Edge of Extinction #1: The Ark Plan
Edge of Extinction #2: Code Name Flood

Library of Congress Control Number: 2023919954
ISBN 978-0-06-332621-7

Typography by Julia Tyler
24 25 26 27 28 LBC 5 4 3 2 1
First Edition

*For the four blessings that call me
mom. This one is for you guys.*

Life is more fun if you play games.
—Roald Dahl

ONE

The way I see it, there are two ways your life can fall apart: slowly or all at once. Slowly seemed better—you'd get a bit of a warning before things spiraled out of control. It's like the way roller coasters do that really slow climb, so you can mentally prepare yourself for the drop that's coming.

My life didn't fall apart that way. It went from fine to not fine in a matter of minutes. It was like being on an elevator going up when suddenly the cable snapped and the floor dropped out. No warning. No lead-up. Just snap. Swoosh. Splat. Or maybe it was more like a shark attack, where you're swimming along peacefully, minding your own business, and then you lose a leg.

The bottom dropped out on our first day of seventh grade at a brand-new school. Our mom had dropped my twin brother, Nash, and me off the way she always dropped us off at school, like she was pulling into the final lap at the Indy 500. Some moms rolled into the drop-off line all perfect hair, Starbucks, and smiles. Our mom was perpetually late and usually still had hot rollers in her hair when she pulled in with less than a minute to spare. We'd gotten very good at launching ourselves from a still-moving car over the years. Most of the time Nash stuck the landing, but I was much more likely to have to use the tuck-and-roll method. It wasn't exactly the best impression to make at a new school, but we'd been to so many new schools by this point that it was just par for the course.

New beginnings were supposed to be exciting, but I hated them. I'd always hated them, but I think I hated the start of a new school year most of all. While all the other kids my age were buying their school supplies to put in their new backpack next to their carefully chosen first-day-of-school outfit, I was usually off sulking somewhere my mom couldn't find me. I'd end up wearing whatever random T-shirt I grabbed that morning, and it was always a surprise to open my backpack and pull out the supplies my mom had purchased. Blue binder with Superman on it? Interesting choice, Mom. I hated it, but you can't exactly complain when you flat-out refused to attend the shopping trip. She told me that one of these days she was going to purposefully buy me the ugliest supplies she could find, bonus points for items with chickens on the front. Not your typical purchase for a twelve-year-old boy, but again, I couldn't exactly complain. I'd just have to rock the poultry-themed gear for the entire school year, come what may.

Instead, I usually just got a duplicate of whatever Nash had carefully chosen, only in a different color. If he picked out a red folder with stripes, then you could bet that I had a blue folder with stripes. It was a twin thing, the same-item-in-a-different-color phenomenon. My mom had dressed us that way too until we were about nine and realized we could say no. Maybe we should have figured that out earlier, but Nash and I tried to keep the peace with our mom. That's what you did when your mom was a few cards short of a full deck. Nash didn't like it when I said that about her, though, so we usually just described her as quirky and left it at that. Although it feels a lot like describing King Kong as a moody monkey, but whatever.

The day had been a normal one—well, as normal as the seventh grade could get. A kid had gotten his head stuck in his locker on a dare, and another girl went to the office with a pretty epic bloody nose, but normal other than that. We'd had no idea our life was about to change when we'd walked out of the big double doors for the pickup line that afternoon. I remember sweating as I stood on the curb next to Nash in the hooded sweatshirt that had seemed like a good idea this morning when it was cold but was now a small personal oven in Indiana's 90-degree heat. My mom had told me to put a T-shirt under it in case I got hot, and I'd argued with her and insisted on doing it my way. So now I was pretending that I wasn't dying of heatstroke while fully intending to act like I wasn't regretting my decision when she pulled in. If she ever pulled in.

"Why is she late?" I asked Nash as I rolled my shoulders under the weight of my backpack. It had barely zipped over the math workbook, social studies book, and the brick our new science teacher had passed off as a textbook. If homework on the first day was any indicator of what the seventh grade was going to be like, I was going to see if I could get sent back to sixth. Weirdly enough, Nash's backpack looked even more stuffed than mine, which was odd, considering we had most of the same classes.

"Relax, Rhett," Nash said with a dismissive wave of his hand. He looked incredibly relaxed in his green polo shirt and cargo shorts. He'd pulled out a baseball hat and shoved it onto his head so that his dark hair curled up around the back in the humidity.

"I'm very relaxed," I snapped.

4

"No," Nash said. "You're actually twitchier than normal, and that's really saying something."

"Why does your backpack look like you're smuggling home a Saint Bernard inside it?" I asked, purposefully changing the subject.

"Because I am," Nash said, his face completely deadpan. "His name is Herman, and he's got gas." I snorted despite myself. Nash glanced around the deserted parking lot of our new middle school and then leaned in conspiratorially. "Actually," he said. "The media specialist, Mrs. Elmhurst, let me borrow something."

I leaned in and whispered back, matching his secret agent tone exactly. "Was it a book?"

Nash laughed and then shook his head. He slipped his backpack off, letting it land on the pavement with a weird jangling noise.

"Guess again," he said.

"A Saint Bernard that swallowed someone's keys?" I said. With one more glance around the parking lot, Nash unzipped his bag, and I saw a bulky rectangular box with thick black lettering down the side. I crouched down to inspect the game and raised my eyebrows at my twin, who smirked back.

"I know," he said. "I'm a rebel."

"You do realize that if literally anyone heard you say that about a board game, we'd be labeled the dorkiest of dorks for the rest of our middle school careers, right?" I said.

"You realize that you're already the president of that particular club, right?" he retorted, and I gave him a sharp jab with my elbow. I decided not to comment on the club he'd be president of, even though I could think of a couple of doozies. The truth was that I'd missed Nash today, sarcasm and all. This was the second year that Nash and I had been separated for most of our classes, and I hadn't liked it one bit. Just like our previous school, this one believed in splitting up siblings. So while we had most of the same classes, we attended them at different times of the day. I hated it. Maybe it was a twin thing, but I never really felt complete if Nash wasn't right next to me, and the thought of navigating yet another brand-new school without him sitting shotgun was one I was having a hard time swallowing. I shook off that thought before looking down at the box just barely visible among the jumble of textbooks and papers he'd crammed into his backpack. He'd always been the braver, more reckless twin, but this was pushing it even for him. Our mom wasn't exactly someone you messed with, and she was going to pull up any minute.

"A board game?" I said. "Really? You know the rules."

Nash nodded. "Duh," he said. "I *did* grow up in the

6

same house as you."

"Sometimes I wonder about that," I muttered under my breath as I slid the innocent-looking box out a fraction of an inch so I could get a better look. My fingertips tingled, and I let the box go so I could clench my hands into fists. "You should bring it back before Mom gets here," I said, my voice tight. "I bet Mrs. Elmhurst is still there. You can turn it back in, and Mom will never have to know. If she gets here while you're gone, I'll just tell her that you really had to go to the bathroom."

"Chicken," Nash said. "Seriously, were you born without a backbone?"

"Don't call me that," I said. "I just don't feel like getting grounded on our first day. I mean, the president of the dorks has responsibilities, you know." It went without saying that I'd go down for this if Nash got caught. Mom had always treated punishments as a package deal since apparently our primary job was to keep one another out of trouble. From the outside that probably seemed incredibly unfair, but twins had a special responsibility for each other. At least that's what Mom always said, but again, Mom was quirky.

"Well, after the first day, Mom will have gotten to Mrs. Elmhurst, and we'll never be allowed to check out a board game again," Nash pointed out. "She may even get them taken out of the media center like she did at Montgomery." I nodded, remembering how Montgomery Elementary had sported row upon row of sad, empty wooden shelves where board games used to be. They'd been placed in a special locked closet that the media specialist would open when a kid wanted to check out a game. Of course, that kid wasn't allowed to be us. She'd given us more than one side-eye over the whole debacle, probably wondering what weird religion we belonged to that forbade Monopoly. There was no religion, though. There was just our mother. As immovable as stone on the subject, she'd made it clear from the moment we were born that we were not to play a board game under any circumstances. Ever. It was a rule that I'd never really cared about. Board games weren't anything exciting, after all. All my friends played video games, and the board game thing had just been a weird blip on my radar over the years. Nash, however, had had a hard time letting it go and had asked over and over again over the years why we weren't allowed to play them. Mom had refused to engage, simply informing Nash that she knew what was best for her boys, and that we should trust her judgment. It was the same reasoning she gave for forcing us to eat our broccoli at dinner and brush our teeth, and it had honestly taken longer than it should have for us to figure out that it was a weird rule.

"That's kind of odd, actually," I said, cocking my head as I pulled my eyes off the game to survey the very empty parking lot.

"What is?" Nash said.

"That she didn't get to Mrs. Elmhurst already. I just figured it would have been her first call after dropping us off this morning."

"Maybe she's losing her touch?" Nash said, sounding hopeful. I nodded, but my stomach had an uncomfortable queasiness to it that I didn't think had anything to do with the contraband board game Nash had in his bag. Something was off about this situation, but I couldn't quite put my finger on it.

"Or maybe she's just losing her sense of time?" Nash said, pulling me from my musings. "I mean, it's almost four thirty. Where in the world is she? Should we go back to the office and call her?"

"Maybe," I said. But at that moment the door to the school opened behind us and our new principal, Mr. Jeffers, poked his head out. He spotted us almost immediately, which, considering we were the only kids still standing in the deserted parking lot, wasn't that hard.

"Benson twins?" he called, and we both nodded. "Come back inside," he said, flapping his hand at us. For a half second, I was annoyed to be addressed as the *Benson twins*. My annoyance was replaced with uneasiness as I registered the look on Mr. Jeffers's face.

"Uh-oh," Nash said, and I tried to swallow the tennis-ball-sized lump that had somehow lodged itself in my throat. Behind Mr. Jeffers stood the school guidance counselor, and if his face hadn't given away that something had happened, her presence definitely did. They only called in the big guns when things were really bad.

"What are the odds that they just found out I borrowed a board game?" Nash whispered under his breath.

"I have a feeling we have bigger problems than that board game," I said.

TWO

"I'm sorry, boys," Mr. Jeffers said with a helpless shrug as we sat in front of his large, cluttered desk a few minutes later. "I know just as much as you know. Your grandfather called here about a half hour ago to tell us that your mom's been in a car accident and wouldn't be able to pick you up today. He said that we were to bring you inside and keep you safe until he got here."

"Our grandfather," I repeated, even though I'd heard him perfectly well the first time. I thought that maybe if I just repeated the phrase enough it would eventually start to make sense. It didn't. The phrase "your mom's been in a car accident" didn't make any sense either, but my initial panic over that had faded slightly. Mr. Jeffers had been assured that Mom was in stable condition, which sounded like a good thing.

"You *do* have a grandfather, don't you?" Mr. Jeffers said, checking the two large files on his desk with our names on them.

"We do," Nash said slowly, glancing over at me, and I wondered if he was considering telling Mr. Jeffers that we hadn't seen our grandfather in years. That the last time we'd seen him, he'd been in a giant argument with our mom, and she'd stormed off with us, yelling at him that he'd never see us again. I gave my head the slightest of shakes and he blinked twice, which meant he'd gotten the message. We didn't have any kind of secret twin language like you hear about sometimes, but we had gotten really good at wordless communication over the years. Nash dipped his chin slightly before cocking his head to the right. He was asking me what I thought about all this. I shook my head slightly again, rolling my shoulders inside my sweat-damp hoodie. I was just as confused as he was. Nash nodded, and I glanced back at Mr. Jeffers to see him watching us with one eyebrow raised. He shot a look at the overly friendly guidance counselor, Mrs. Anderson, who, as far as I could tell, was just there for moral support and to smile with too many teeth. She sat in the corner holding a Kleenex box and seeming more than a little disappointed that we hadn't burst into tears so she could offer them to us. They both looked so puzzled

12

that I almost laughed despite the stress I felt rolling up from inside my chest.

Wordless communication was one of the last hold-overs from elementary school that Nash and I had these days. We'd always been a pretty well-oiled machine, Nash and I, but ever since we'd hit middle school last year things hadn't been quite the same. At home we were the same as we'd always been, but at school I could feel Nash pulling away from me. For the first time in our lives, we didn't have joint friends. Before, Nash and I had always been a package deal, so it didn't matter that I was the quiet to Nash's loud. If you were friends with Nash, you got me too. Two for the price of one. Now, just like last year, he was going to have friends I'd never even talked to. It had driven me crazy the year before when he'd tell a funny story about something Mike had done, and I'd spend the whole next day trying to figure out which of the kids in the hallway was crazy enough to glue his entire text-book to his desk. I'd figured it out, but only because Mike had escalated things and glued a lunch box to the front door of the school. I'd been a little hopeful that seventh grade would be different, but after one day it was painfully obvious that this year was going to play out just like the last. I sighed. Nash's new life made me feel left behind somehow. Forgotten. Like a toy he'd outgrown and discarded in the corner to collect dust. Now, though, sitting in Mr. Jeffers's office as the bottom fell out of the elevator, the last year seemed to disappear, and we were a united front. The same united front we'd been every time our mom had interrogated us for one dumb thing or another.

The thought of our mom forced me back to the mess at hand, and I glanced over at Nash at the same time that he glanced over at me. His lips were pulled into a tight line, and his eyes looked wide and worried. I wondered if my face looked just like his, or if it was completely blank, like everything inside me had been turned off momentarily and nothing had started to reboot yet. My emotions had frozen inside my chest like a jumble of razor-sharp blocks of ice. I knew that if I focused on them long enough to let them melt, the pain and the panic over Mom being in an accident would drown me, so I let them stay frozen, for now. I couldn't afford to drown now, not yet, because something had just occurred to me. If Mom was incapacitated—and based off what Mrs. Anderson and Mr. Jeffers had explained about the car accident she'd apparently had this morning, she was—we didn't have anyone else. Our dad had died of a heart attack before we were even born, and our mom was an only child. I had a vision of the state deciding to take Nash and me into custody until our mom was better, and I felt a chill go down my spine. That was an unknown quantity I wasn't ready for. Grandpa Benson wasn't much more known, but he was family and that had to count for something, didn't it? The fact that we had the same last name should have probably made me feel better, but it didn't. Mom had kept her maiden name of Benson for convenience, and she'd given the same name to us instead of giving us our father's last name of Thormendean. I was never sure if it was to avoid the mouthful of a last name or because she wanted to avoid the pain of saying his name over and over again for the rest of her life. Either way, the fact that we were all Bensons probably made the paperwork for this whole mess a lot easier for the school.

"How soon will our grandpa be here?" I asked. "He lives in southern Indiana." I said that statement with way more confidence than I felt. I had a vague notion that our grandfather lived south, somewhere, but for all I knew he could have moved since we'd seen him.

We'd only met him one time, when our mom had driven us to the backwoods of Indiana. I didn't remember much of the visit, except that he'd handed us both our very first Twinkie, and we'd been delighted with the cellophane-wrapped log of overly processed cake. I also remembered them arguing. Five-year-old Nash had been busy flipping over rocks in front of the cabin and exclaiming over the bugs he found underneath, but I'd always been one of those annoyingly perceptive kids who liked to eavesdrop on their grown-ups. You could learn a lot of stuff that way, like where the Halloween candy was stashed and why Mom was frowning so hard her forehead wrinkled.

So I'd stood next to Nash as he flipped over rocks, my eyes pointed down at the dirt where tiny white grubs squirmed and roly-poly bugs curled themselves into little balls in a panic, and I'd listened. Our mom was mad about something, but my grandpa had been madder. At least, he'd taken less care with keeping his voice down and his tone neutral. It was something about us, about teaching us something or protecting us from something, it wasn't exactly clear. But what was clear was that they disagreed in a big, big way on how it should be handled.

The visit ended with my mom grabbing both of our arms and dragging us back to her car. Nash had cried, pitching a tomato-colored fit because he'd wanted to bring home the giant black beetle he'd found, but my mom hadn't listened. She'd pried the bug out of his hand and dropped it unceremoniously in the dirt on the side of the road before forcing him into his car seat. He'd kicked and screamed and cried, and I could still remember her angry, tight face as she forced those buckles shut across his chest. Parents hated bad behavior on a good day, but if you acted up with an audience, watch out. I had buckled my own car seat and looked over at the man we'd just met, our grandfather, as he stood on the small drooping porch of his cabin. He was watching my mom struggle with Nash, his arms crossed over his chest in disapproval. He'd walked toward our car as my mom backed out, and for a second I thought he was going to try to stop us. Instead he'd stooped down to pick up Nash's mangled beetle and slipped it into his pocket. We'd never seen him again.

My stomach rumbled, and I was surprised to realize that normal things like hunger could just carry on during a crisis. I'd have thought my stomach would have been frozen just like the rest of my panic about Mom, but nope. My breath hitched in my chest as I imagined where she was at this moment, and images of hospital beds and beeping monitors flooded my brain. For a second I thought I was going to lose the very fragile grip I had on myself, but I managed to push the thoughts back down into my chest with the rest of the pieces of me that had frozen the moment Mr. Jeffers had started talking. I bit my lip, wondering if I'd even recognize my grandfather when he arrived. I had a vague recollection of someone tall, but I'd been pretty little the last time I'd seen him, so that wasn't really saying much.

It took our grandfather two hours to get to school. It was well past six o'clock when a battered blue truck rolled into the school parking lot, and Mr. Jeffers let out a sigh of relief. We were almost off his hands and out of his office, and he wasn't even going to attempt to hide just how happy that made him. Mrs. Anderson set down her Kleenex box, looking disappointed. Mr. Jeffers ushered us out the front door of the middle school we'd only attended for one day, Mrs. Anderson at our heels, and it felt a bit like two prison wardens taking their resident criminals out for some air. I swallowed hard, my eyes glued to the truck as it made its way across the parking lot. Questions were flashing across my brain in a loop like one of those electronic signs they always put up in front of churches and pizza parlors. Was our mom okay? What were her injuries? Why couldn't we see her? Could we talk to her soon? What exactly was the plan for us? Did anyone even have one? Or was everyone just winging this thing and hoping for the best? How long would we be staying with the grandfather we'd met a grand total of one time? What did he even look like? At least that last question was answered the moment our grandfather stepped out of his truck.

Grandpa Benson was tall, and I mean really tall. The kind of tall that usually made people do a double take and wonder if you were once a professional athlete. He unfolded himself from his truck like a puppet getting out of a box, and stood up to look down at Mr. Jeffers, who, up until about five seconds ago, I would have considered tall too. Now he was short. Bummer for him.

Our grandfather's hair was almost completely white with streaks of gray here and there, and so long that he had it tied back in a low ponytail with what appeared to be a shoelace. His face had the weathered leather look of someone who'd never worn sunscreen a day in his life, and he was wearing a pair of tired blue jeans with a wash-worn denim shirt tucked into them. I'd heard Nash call that look a denim tuxedo once, but on our grandfather, it seemed to fit somehow. His feet were encased in a pair of gray snakeskin cowboy boots that looked older than the truck, and as I took this all in, I realized that I recognized him. Or maybe I just recognized something of my mom in his sharp brown eyes and long, straight nose. This was our grandpa, even if he did look like he'd just stepped out of a John Wayne movie.

He looked from Nash to me and back again and nodded his head. "Boys," he said in greeting before turning his attention to Mr. Jeffers. "Thanks for watching over them until I could get here."

"Not a problem," Mr. Jeffers said. "Can I see your ID, please?" Our grandfather looked surprised by the request but nodded and produced a worn leather wallet from his back pocket roughly the size of a deck of cards. He flipped it open and handed it to Mr. Jeffers, who took it, nodded, and returned it. The two men turned their backs on us, and I felt Mrs. Anderson place what was probably supposed to be a calming hand on each of our shoulders. Her hands were cold and clammy and reminded me of dead fish, but I ignored the sensation as I watched Mr. Jeffers and my grandfather talk quietly, wishing I could hear what was being said.

Finally, Mr. Jeffers stepped back, now talking loud enough for his voice to carry over to us. "Please update us on how Mrs. Benson is doing," he said. Our grandfather gave a quick nod, and then opened his truck door and stood aside so we could climb in. It was one of those old bench seat models without a back seat so that one of us was going to have to sit shoulder to shoulder with him as he drove. I hesitated, not wanting that particular privilege, but Nash gave me an impatient shove from behind that sent me stumbling into the truck. I climbed in, followed by Nash, and we both struggled to fit our backpacks into the space between us and the dash since the floor of the truck was full of what looked like a giant furry rug. Mr. Jeffers noticed our struggle and cleared his throat.

"Um, boys?" he said expectantly. When we just stared at him blankly, he shifted uncomfortably from foot to foot, and glanced over at Mrs. Anderson as though looking for moral support. She produced a small packet of tissues from her pocket unhelpfully, and he sighed, turning back to us. "If you have any textbooks from school, I'd like to take those now. I'll return them when you come back, but just in case . . ." He let those last words dangle, and I felt a small shiver of goose bumps ripple down my arms. There was something about his face that made it clear that he didn't think we were coming back. I'd been so wrapped up with the news about Mom that I hadn't realized that if we were going to be staying with our grandfather, we wouldn't be making the trek back to Harrison Middle School.

Reluctantly I unzipped my bag and handed over the textbooks. Mr. Jeffers took them and turned to Nash, who hesitated for a second before unzipping his own bag. He pulled out the board game, and I saw our grandpa's eyebrows rise in surprise. He must know about our mom's board game rules. Nash's face fell in disappointment, and a surge of annoyance flashed through me. How in the world could he still care about a stupid board game in light of what was currently happening? Nash could sometimes get tunnel vision when it came to some goal he wanted to achieve, and usually I admired that about my twin. Now, watching the way he stared longingly after the game in Mr. Jeffers's hands, it made me want to smack him. I settled for a not-so-subtle jab in the ribs with my elbow.

Nash and I had only come this close to successfully playing a board game one other time. We'd been allowed to attend a birthday party held at a trampoline park, and Nash had managed to land wrong and sprain an ankle. Being his twin, I'd felt obligated to go with him to see the facility director, who had a stash of those useless ice packs that you had to pop and shake but never really got cold. While he was calling our mom to let her know about the injury, Nash had spotted a small stash of board games on a shelf in the guy's office. He'd slipped one out and innocently asked if we could play it until our mom got there to pick us up. Of course, he'd said yes. We'd gotten the game board out, feeling like criminals, and were just setting up our pieces when the birthday boy's mom had walked in to see where we'd gone. She'd spotted the game and immediately whisked it away from us. Our mom had explained her bizarre rule to this mom, even though we shouldn't have been anywhere near a board game at a trampoline park. That was our mom, thorough to a fault. She always had a backup plan for her backup plan and behind her plan B was plan C, D, E, and probably Z. That thought snapped me back to the present and our stranger of a grandfather. Somehow, I'd never pictured him being the plan B.

THREE

Mr. Jeffers stood on the curb, his arms piled high with homework we'd never do and a board game we'd never play, and attempted to wave as our grandfather climbed into the driver's seat. The truck grumbled a bit when he turned the key before finally coming to life with a disagreeable rattle. He pulled out of the parking lot as Nash and I sat in stunned silence, our deflated backpacks still held in front of us like shields. He flicked on the ancient-looking radio, and Kenny Chesney started singing about living on the beach. I glanced out the window as we passed the Dairy Queen and the library. We'd been in this town for about three months, and it had almost started to feel like home. Mom was restless. She hated staying anywhere for very long, and back in the days when she used to homeschool us, we'd lived somewhere new every few months. She'd thrown in the homeschooling towel in third grade when math got tricky, and we'd been allowed to attend a public school. Nash had loved it and thrived on all the people and noise and smells. I'd begged Mom to homeschool us again.

I was so focused on staring out the window that I almost didn't notice when the massive furry rug under our feet shifted and sat up. Nash yelped in surprise, yanking his feet up onto the truck's seat. I froze as the rug opened its eyes and turned to look at us.

"What is *that*?!" Nash said.

"That's Chief," our grandpa said, reaching a hand over to ruffle the massive dog's ears.

"Are you sure it's not a bear?" Nash asked.

"Hi, Chief," I said, reaching out a tentative hand so that the dog could snuffle it wetly.

"Saint Bernard?" I said, thinking of the innocent joke I'd made just hours ago before our world had turned itself on its head.

Grandpa Benson shrugged. "Maybe. Maybe a bit of mountain dog, maybe a bit of German shepard."

"I get the mountain part," Nash said, his legs still pulled in tight to his chest.

"Not a dog person?" Grandpa said.

"Oh no, I'm a dog person," Nash said. "But that, sir, is a horse." I couldn't help it, I laughed. I'm not sure if

25

it was the look on Nash's face or the way he was trying unsuccessfully to keep his feet on the seat while still holding his backpack, or even the utter absurdity of the entire situation, but I felt tears streaming down my face as I tried to stifle the laugh with my hand.

"It wasn't that funny," Nash muttered as Chief lay back down, once again looking exactly like a big fur rug someone had rolled up and thrown onto the floor of the truck. My laughter stopped when I noticed that we'd turned right to merge onto the highway instead of left to go to our house.

"Wait," I said. "Don't we have to at least stop at home for our clothes?"

Our grandfather shook his head. "Nope," he said.

"What do you mean 'nope'?" I said. "We have to go home!" I'd been banking on home. Somehow, I felt like if we could just punch in our garage code and walk into our rental's small kitchen, everything would be okay. Mom would be there and tell us this whole thing was just some big mistake, or she'd have left us a note or something.

"We need our clothes, and our stuff," Nash said, echoing me.

"I got your stuff," he said, jerking his head toward the back of the truck. We both turned to peer out the small window and saw two familiar duffel bags, one red, one blue, in the back.

"You went to our house?" I said. "And you packed for us?" This seemed absurd and entirely too personal considering he knew exactly nothing about us.

"Sure did," he said with a nod.

"Like? Underwear and toothbrush and everything?" I said.

Our grandfather nodded again without taking his eyes off the road, and Nash and I shared a flabbergasted look.

"No way!" Nash said, shaking his head. "That's too weird. How would you even have a key?"

"Didn't need a key," Grandpa said, and I heard Nash grind his teeth. Getting information out of our grandfather felt a lot like trying to pry open a tin can with a toothpick.

I was about to ask him how he'd somehow known our garage code when Nash gasped and sat bolt upright in his seat. I jumped in surprise at the sound and Grandpa jerked a little, which sent the truck wobbling across the center line before he corrected it.

"What is it?" Grandpa snapped, whipping his head left and right as though trying to spot an incoming air missile.

"Geronimo!" Nash said. "We can't leave Geronimo!"

"What's a Geronimo?" Grandpa said, his voice sharp. "And he better be worth almost giving me a heart attack!"

"Geronimo Jones the Third is my guinea pig," Nash said. "We can't leave him at the house. He'll die!" I immediately pictured Nash's little brown-and-black pet, which looked a lot like a furry potato. He'd gotten him for his birthday two years ago after the first two Geronimos had died very unfortunate deaths. There was a reason he was named Geronimo Jones the Third. Nash routinely plopped him on the counter with some lettuce while we were doing our homework and he'd sit there chewing and staring at us like he was plotting something. He wasn't my pet, but even I had gotten attached to the fuzzy little guy. Nash was right, Geronimo couldn't go more than a day without someone cleaning his cage and feeding him.

"Oh, the fat rat," Grandpa said, and reached over to open the glove box in front of Nash's knees. It popped open and inside was a very confused-looking Geronimo Jones.

"You put a guinea pig in the glove box!" Nash said in horror as he leaned forward to snatch Geronimo. To our grandfather's credit, it was a big glove box, and he'd even thrown some of Geronimo's hay inside. Geronimo seemed less impressed.

"Now that's taken care of, we should probably eat the frog," our grandfather said.

"Eat the frog?" I repeated in disgust. "What?! Why

are we eating a frog?" Nash just made a gagging noise, taking his eyes off Geronimo to look at our grandfather in wide-eyed alarm.

Our grandfather snorted, and I saw the first hint of a smile on his wrinkled face. It softened the harshness of it, and I saw a bit of my mom in the way his eyes crinkled up at the sides. "It's just a phrase, boys. Relax. 'Eat the frog' means to get the worst part of your day over with. If you have to eat a frog on a Tuesday, it's better to wake up and eat it than let it hang over your head for the entire day."

"Who has to eat a frog on a Tuesday?" I muttered, but our grandfather ignored me.

"Okay," Nash said. "So what's the worst part of this day you want to get over with?"

His question made me shift uneasily in my seat, and Chief flicked an ear at me in annoyance.

"Questions," he said. "I am not a big fan of questions, and I have a feeling you two have a few for me."

I nodded as I thought about telling him that might just be the understatement of the year. All the questions in my head swarmed forward at once, and I wasn't sure where to start. I glanced over at Nash for help, but he'd returned his attention to checking Geronimo for any glove box–induced injuries now that the threat of eating an amphibian was apparently off the table. I bit my lip and glanced back at the stranger next to me, which was awkward because I was practically sitting in his armpit. He had a concerned look on his face that was a dead ringer for our mom's look, and the hairs along my neck suddenly prickled to attention.

"What's going on with Mom?" Nash asked, taking the words out of my mouth before I could say them. "Is she okay?"

He drove in silence for a second and then heaved a sigh. "Yes and no," he said.

"Well, thanks for clearing that up," Nash muttered.

"How bad was the accident?" I pushed. "Was she hurt?"

"I think she's fine, for now," he said, and my eye twitched.

"What do you mean, 'for now'?" Nash said, snapping his head up. "What kind of grandpa says 'for now' like that?" Our grandfather opened his mouth to say something, but once Nash got on a roll, he tended to stay on a roll. "Also, what exactly are we supposed to call you? Grandpa? Grandfather? Gramps?" Now it was our grandpa's eye that did the twitch, and I wondered if having your two grandsons suddenly land in your lap was just as stressful as getting a surprise grandfather.

"What do you want to call me?" he said slowly. "Aren't grandkids the ones that decide that?"

"I mean, maybe?" I said. I knew that some of my classmates called their grandparents all sorts of strange names, usually because they couldn't say grandma or grandpa as a baby and their improvised gibberish had stuck. We, however, were twelve. There was no way we were going to come up with some cutesy mispronunciation, and besides, that felt a little too personal for a guy we barely knew.

"Well," our grandfather finally said, clearing his throat. "My friends called me Ace."

"Called? Past tense?" I asked. He just nodded without giving us any more of an explanation. I got the feeling that I was going to have to get used to that particular character trait.

"I guess that works," I said. "So, um, Ace? Can you please tell us what's going on? We need to know what happened to our mom. Can we go see her?"

"We'll see her soon," Ace said.

"Oh," I said, slightly surprised. "Great. How far is the drive?"

"She can't be reached that way," he said, "but we'll get to her one way or another."

"Um, what?" Nash said.

"I can't explain it any more than that," he said. "Next question."

"Okay . . ." I said, glancing at Nash for help, but

he'd turned his attention back to Geronimo. The "fat rat," as our grandfather had called him, was munching happily on an apple Nash had dug out of his backpack, apparently not at all traumatized by his time in the glove box.

"So," I said, my brain churning. "If we aren't going home, and we aren't headed to see our mom, where are we going?"

"I'm bringing you two home with me until we get this mess sorted out," Ace said.

"Your house," I repeated as a foggy picture of a cabin in the woods pushed its way up through my memories.

"Where exactly is your house?" Nash said, looking up from Geronimo.

"South," Ace said.

"Thanks," Nash muttered, "super helpful." Ace must not have heard him, though, because he just kept driving, his eyes on the road. I finally gave up peppering him with questions and sat back to watch the road. Everything about this felt off, and I needed a second to try to wrap my brain around things.

We pulled off the main highway and onto a gravel road before I'd even begun to figure out how we were going to handle the mess we were in. That gravel road turned into another gravel road, which turned into yet another gravel road, until I was so turned around that I knew I'd never be able to find my way back to the highway if I tried. Our grandfather, Ace, just kept turning at cornfields and bean fields, and with the exception of a random herd of cows that we passed, it all looked pretty much the same. He took one final turn down a dirt road that wound through a thick patch of trees before stopping in front of a log cabin–style house. He immediately climbed out, but Nash and I sat there for a second, staring. It was old, with a wide, covered front porch that was sagging in the middle, and a shiny tin roof that looked like a newer addition to the whole thing. A stack of wood leaned haphazardly against one side, while raised garden beds sat on the other.

I wondered if Nash's memories of the place were solidifying just like mine. We'd been here before, and somehow that made me feel a tiny bit better. Nash was clutching Geronimo so tight that the guinea pig was squeaking in alarm, and I reached over to loosen Nash's grip before the tiny animal decided to bite him. Instead, Geronimo bit me.

"Hey!" I cried, jerking my hand back in surprise. Everything that happened next felt like it was happening in slow motion. Our grandfather grabbed me around the neck and shoulders and pulled me out of the seat. This maneuver would have worked well except I was still belted into the truck, so it just made my torso go flying backward while my legs remained strapped in. I heard him mutter something before unbuckling me, and then Nash and I were both being hauled out of the truck and onto the hard-packed dirt. I hit with a thump that made my brain rattle inside my head, and Nash grunted as Geronimo Jones went flying through the air to land somewhere in the bushes.

We stayed like that for a second, splayed out on our backs in the dirt next to the truck, our grandfather crouched over us like a mountain lion on high alert.

"What was that?" Nash said, attempting to sit up. Ace's hand shot out and shoved him back down into the dirt, and it would have been funny if I hadn't been so freaked out. Our grandfather turned his head slowly, looking from the right to the left and then back again, and I felt the hairs on the back of my neck stand up. Another few terrifying heartbeats passed and then he stood up, brushing off his jeans before extending a hand to each of us. We took it, allowing ourselves to be helped up out of the dirt.

"Um, everything okay?" Nash said as he inspected a new scrape on his elbow.

"I think so," Ace said before turning to me. "Why did you holler like that?"

"Me?" I said, confused for a moment before I remembered what had happened in the seconds before we were yanked out of the truck. I held up my hand, where there were two tiny puncture marks. "Geronimo bit me." Ace's face twisted in annoyance, and Nash whipped his head around. "Wait! Where did he go?!" He went charging off into the grass, and Ace ran a frustrated hand through his hair, making it puff out from his ponytail. We watched as Nash clambered around in the underbrush, calling for Geronimo.

"So," I said, glancing at our grandfather out of the corner of my eye. "What did you *think* I yelled for?"

He shot me a quick look before turning his attention back to Nash and shrugging.

"No, seriously," I said. "This is Indiana. The most dangerous thing that lives here is a grumpy raccoon."

To my surprise, Ace snorted and cracked a smile, and I felt my insides loosen just a bit. The smile disappeared quickly, and Ace's face got serious again. "The things I worry about aren't native to Indiana," he said just as Nash held Geronimo Jones up in the air in triumph. Geronimo Jones proceeded to bite him too, since apparently flying through the air wasn't high on his list of enjoyable pursuits. Also, if I was honest, Geronimo Jones was kind of a jerk.

"Let's go," Ace said, and I turned to see our duffel bags slung over his shoulders. Nash came up beside me, sucking on his bleeding finger.

"Where's Geronimo?" I asked, glancing around.

"Back in the glove box," Nash said. "He needed some time to think about what he did." He jerked his chin at Ace's retreating figure. "Are we supposed to follow him?"

"Do you see any other options?" I said, hopeful that maybe I was missing something.

"Nope," Nash said. He strode after our grandfather and bounded up the rickety steps of the cabin. I glanced back at the truck, wondering if maybe I should keep Geronimo Jones company, but then sighed and followed.

FOUR

The cabin consisted of four small, cramped rooms, and Nash and I stood in the doorway taking it all in for a second. The main part of the house was a living room–kitchen combination with an ancient threadbare plaid sofa backed up against one wall. The kitchen had a refrigerator and one of those old-fashioned sinks that stretch out on either side like a countertop. The stove, or what I thought must be the stove, sat like a hunched old man in the corner. An honest-to-goodness smoke pipe protruded from its back and ran up the wall before exiting the cabin.

The walls of the cabin were bare except for a faded family picture. It drew me in like a magnet, and suddenly I found myself standing in front of it, looking at an image of a younger, smiling version of my mother. She was wearing jeans and a button-down shirt with the sleeves rolled up to the elbow. She was tucked securely under the arm of our grandfather, who, despite looking much younger in the picture, still looked stoic and weathered. Next to them stood a boy wearing a white polo, his hands shoved into the pockets of a pair of dark blue jeans. Beside him stood a bright-eyed woman who I assumed was our grandmother. Mom had told us that when she was around our age her mom had died of cancer, and I glanced back at my mom, wondering how old she'd been in this picture. Maybe eleven? Her life was about to change forever, and she'd had no idea. I could sympathize.

"You boys will be over here," Ace said, and we turned to see him standing in an open doorway. We peeked inside to see a bunk bed tucked in a corner beside a desk and a worn leather chair.

"I assume you two are fine sharing a room," he said.

"We're twins," Nash said. "We used to share underwear."

"Right," Ace said with a gruff nod. "Why don't you get unpacked. I'll be in the office."

He shut the door behind himself, and I sat down in the chair. It let out a puff of dust on impact, and I sneezed, wondering when was the last time this room had been cleaned. I ran a hand over the desk and watched as my palm cut a clean path through a thick layer of dust. If that was any indication, the answer was maybe never.

"I don't think he was planning on us coming here," I said.

"So you don't think this was a very sloppy kid-napping?" Nash said. "Because that option crossed my mind."

"Same," I said. "But Mom put him as our only emergency contact, which means she trusts him. And I don't think Mr. Jeffers would lie about her being in the hospital." I swallowed hard, and then glanced over at him. "Do you think she's okay?"

Nash shrugged. "I think she's alive." I bit my lip, trying not to let his nonchalance bother me. It was a show, a front, a way of throwing up a hedge of protection around himself so that the outside world would never know how badly he was hurting. He'd started it about the same time we'd started the sixth grade, and I still wasn't used to being on the other side of that hedge.

"Well, that's something," I said. "Do we unpack?"

Nash glanced around at the desk, chair, and bunk bed. "Into what?" he said. "There isn't a dresser or a closet." After a quick climb up the top bunk, we discovered that it had a large wooden cubby built into the back. It took all of two seconds to cram our duffel bags into it. That accomplished, we went in search of our grandfather's office.

It wasn't hard to find. The office sat right off the kitchen and, just like the rest of the house, the walls, ceiling, and floor were all made of a dark wood. I expected to find Ace in there, but it was a relief that he wasn't. We both took a step inside to take the place in, and goose bumps immediately erupted up the back of my neck.

In the middle of the room sat a curved half-circle desk with a bushy fern perched on one corner, but the most interesting feature of the room was the wall-to-wall glass bookcases behind it. Although *bookcases* might not be the correct word since there wasn't a single book in them. Behind the thick glass was the oddest jumble of stuff I'd ever seen. Glass jars containing large hunks of cracked-open geodes, the skull of a horse, bugs the size of birds splayed out and tacked on to old rounds of wood, an old boot with bright red laces and tiny windows cut into its leather, a curved sword, a double-headed axe, a stuffed owl, four jars of what looked like gems of various sizes and cuts, a large sealed jug with twisted plants growing inside it, and the oddities went on and on. Oddities, jars, and strange knickknacks weren't the only things on the shelves; in fact, the primary items were board games. Stacks upon stacks of board games. I took a step forward to put my hand on the thick glass, not quite believing my eyes.

"Whoa," Nash said, and I nodded as I scanned the names written in different-colored fonts across the boxes. My palm was tingling like my hand had somehow fallen asleep, but I barely noticed. The one thing we'd been kept from our entire lives was stockpiled in our grandfather's house. Why? I walked slowly down the case, my hand never leaving the glass. I took in the games wedged in between everything from a moss-covered globe to a taxidermy jackalope, trying to have this odd collection make sense.

It took me a second, but I quickly realized that I didn't recognize a single game. I knew I wasn't well versed in board games, but I hadn't been living under a rock. Even I knew about games like Candy Land or Monopoly, but those were conspicuously absent. I kept scanning the shelves, but I never spotted even a single game that I'd heard of. Instead, there were names like Blinky Bonk, Fuzzle Brain, Bug Bonanza, Wacky Wizards, Castle Chaos Fatal Fairy Tales, Treasure Hunt, Mornings with Monsters, and Pillage. I reached a hand out to the door of the case and gave its tarnished brass knob a tug, wanting to see some of the games up close. My arm jerked uselessly; the bookcase door was locked. Nash had apparently had the same idea as me, and I looked down the long case to see him tugging at a different door.

"Well, that didn't take long," said a voice behind us, and we both jumped guiltily and whirled to face our grandfather.

"Sorry!" I said. "We were looking for you."

"Not looking very hard," Ace said, walking around his desk to take a seat in the cracked leather wingback.

"Um," Nash said, turning from Ace to the giant locked case and back again. "I think I'm confused."

"You have a right to be confused," Ace said. He steepled his fingers together and considered us over the top of them.

"So, Mom obviously didn't get her aversion to games from you?" I said.

"Tell me about your mom's aversion," he said with a jerk of his chin toward the two sagging green velvet chairs opposite him. We sat down. Nash slumped back in his chair, one leg pulled under him and his arms crossed over his chest. I perched on the edge of my chair like I might need to leave in a hurry. A quick glance at Nash made it clear that I was going to have to do the talking.

"She wouldn't let us play them," I said. "Ever. We never had any in the house, and if we went to someone else's house, which didn't happen very often, she made sure there weren't any games there either."

"It wasn't a big deal," Nash said. "Board games are boring. Lame." I thought about pointing out to him that he'd had a board game stashed in his backpack earlier that day but didn't. Let Nash play the tough guy.

"It was a bigger deal when we were younger," I said. "But now everyone just plays video games or stuff on their phones. It's not like our friends were getting together for big epic board game parties that we weren't invited to."

"You mentioned video games and phones," Ace said. "Did your mom let you play those?"

Nash and I shared a look, and I wondered how much we should tell.

"She did," Nash said carefully. "For a while. But then they became a bit of a problem."

"How so?" Ace pressed, and my face flushed red. I was the problem. Nash was just being nice by not saying that.

"We had a game console for two years," I said. "Mom gave it to us one Christmas after I begged."

"Where was the problem?" Ace said.

"I didn't want to leave the basement," I said. "I stopped hanging out with friends. I quit the baseball team. I lost weight because I didn't want to stop play- ing to eat, and I stopped sleeping so I could play more. So she got rid of it."

"He was addicted," Nash said.

"And you weren't?" Ace said.

Nash shook his head. "I liked it well enough, but there was other stuff I'd rather do."

"There was nothing I'd rather do," I said with a sigh. My fingers twitched reflexively, and I clasped them into a tight fist and then released. The video game thing was a sore spot for me. When my mom had finally pulled the plug, I'd felt like she'd taken away my reason for breathing. It had taken a while to come out of it, and if I was honest, I was still struggling. You didn't have to worry about making friends without your twin in a video game. You didn't have to worry about becoming the president of the losers' club or how you'd do in your baseball game. In a video game you were a winner, and I'd gotten hooked on that feeling. Even if it wasn't real.

"Interesting," Ace said, and his tone annoyed me.

"Why do we have to tell you all this stuff when you haven't told us anything yet?" Nash said.

"Yeah," I said, mirroring Nash's crossed-arm pose.

"We will discuss this tomorrow," Ace said as he stood up. "It's well past time for dinner, and you two need your sleep." He headed out of the office and into the small kitchen, where we heard the rattle and clatter of pans being put on the stove.

Nash glanced over at me. "Do you think he'll ever actually tell us anything?"

"I have no idea," I said. "But I'm starving, so right now food sounds almost better than information."

With one last glance at the locked shelves, we headed into the kitchen to see what Ace was putting together for dinner. The antique cuckoo clock on the wall showed that it was almost nine, and I yawned so wide my jaw cracked. Dinner proved to be cheeseburgers with a pan of oven-baked French fries, and it tasted like heaven. The day had been a whopper, and we crawled into bed in a state of stupefied exhaustion.

Nash seemed to start snoring the moment his head hit the pillow, and I felt sleep weighing my own body down, but I fought it. I needed a minute of space to think. The second I let my guard down, my mom-shaped worries all came rushing front and center, demanding my attention. A tear I hadn't even realized was there slid out of the corner of my eye to run down my cheek and settle uncomfortably in my ear. My mom had always known when I'd been crying, which wasn't really a big talent since my entire face tended to turn bright red and puffy. She'd lay a cool hand on my cheek, look me in the eye, and promise me that I was going to be just fine. That whatever hardship or unfairness or pain I was in would pass. That I'd survived every single one of my hard days, and that was a pretty impressive track record. I sniffed, wishing I knew exactly where she was, wishing I could talk to her doctor, find out all her medical details even if I had no idea what any of it meant. I wished I could lay a hand on her cheek and tell her it was all going to be okay.

I squeezed my eyes shut and debated waking Nash up as even more tears found their way into my ears. When we were little, we were what my mom called sympathy criers. If he cried, I cried. It didn't matter that he was the one with the bee sting or the scraped knee. We'd grown out of that, though, and I wondered when exactly it had happened. My brain felt like a tangle of spaghetti with thoughts all looped and knotted around one another, and I started to wonder if I'd ever actually fall asleep or if I'd just lie there in the dark, exhausted, but with spaghetti where brains should be for the rest of my life. Then I fell asleep.

It turned out that falling asleep wasn't the problem— it was staying asleep. I woke up a handful of times, disoriented and confused, before I finally sat up and rubbed my eyes in search of a clock. To my surprise it wasn't even midnight yet. I was about to turn over and attempt to go back to sleep when I heard a noise. It sounded like a high-pitched squeak. I rolled over the edge of the bunk to give Nash's head a sharp tap.

"What?" he groaned, peering up at me in the dark.

"Listen," I said. He sat up, and together we waited in the darkness. The sound came again, but this time it was more of a whine than a squeak.

"Geronimo?" Nash said. "Do you think we can hear him all the way in here?"

"You left him in the glove box?"

"Left, forgot, same thing," Nash said. "He'll be fine." The sound came again, and we both froze.

"That's no guinea pig," I said. "Should we go check it out?" I was secretly hoping that Nash was going to tell me to stop being weird and go back to sleep. Instead, he climbed out of bed and I followed.

FIVE

The floorboards creaked creepily under our feet as we made our way through the living room. I thought about pointing out to Nash that this was what all the stupid characters in scary movies did, and it usually didn't end well, but my voice was stuck inside my throat. The light in Ace's office was on, spilling a warm yellow puddle out into the living room. The sound came again.

"That's coming from the office, isn't it," Nash whispered. I nodded, and together we crept toward the door and peered inside. At first glance I thought the office was empty. The brass light on the desk was on, throwing the loaded shelves behind it into sharp relief. On the corner of the desk was one of the board game boxes, its cover displaying a massive crocodile with its mouth cranked open to reveal the game's title in gold lettering between its teeth. It took me a second to spot the horse on the desk. In my defense, that's not where you usually find horses.

Standing no more than two feet, roughly the size of a small dog, stood a perfectly proportioned gray stallion. He was munching quite happily on the fern perched on the corner of Ace's desk and every now and then he would stomp a tiny hooved foot on the wood top with a sharp click. He ripped out a large mouthful of the fern and shook his head, mane flopping to let out a high-pitched whinny. That was the noise we'd heard. I was so flabbergasted by the tiny horse that it took me a second to notice the woman sitting behind the desk.

Like the horse, she was tiny at less than a foot in height, and sat reclined with her white button boots propped up on the arm of the chair. She'd bolstered herself up with what looked like a few of the plaid cushions from the couch, and they wobbled precariously as she paged through what looked like a small paper booklet of some sort, turning it this way and that before leaning in to squint at the black print. She shook her head, making the severe bun of curly fire-engine-red hair bob unhappily. She was wearing what looked like a bright red old-fashioned bathing suit that contrasted strikingly with her pale freckled skin.

"Are you seeing what I'm seeing?" Nash breathed in

my ear. "Or are we still asleep?"

I reached over and gave his side a sharp pinch. He flinched and shot me a dirty look. The horse and the woman were still studiously ignoring us, and I took a step backward. Maybe if we just went back to bed, we could act like this wasn't happening. The next morning, we could hitchhike back home and call this whole experience a wash. Unfortunately, the creaky floors chose that moment to groan loudly under my foot and the tiny woman's head jerked up. She froze, and the pamphlet she'd been studying slipped out of her hand to land on the floor, splayed out like an injured bird. The horse must have sensed something because he turned to look at us with baleful brown eyes before ripping off another mouthful of fern.

The woman blinked at us and stood up. "Hello there," she said.

"Hello," we said back.

"Why do you two look like your brains just swallowed a pickle?" she said, cocking her head. She studied our faces, her brow furrowed as though she was searching for something. Finally, she leaned back and placed her hands on her broad polka-dot-covered hips. "Well, I'll be. You're Natalie's boys, aren't you?" The sound of my mother's name in this woman's low, melodic voice sent shivers up my spine. How in the world did she know our mom?

"We might be," Nash said warily. "Who are you?" I thought a better question might be *What are you?*, but that would probably be considered rude. My mom had always told me that people came in all shapes, sizes, and colors, but this lady seemed to be pushing it a bit. I mean, I'd seen Chihuahuas bigger than her.

"Well, paint me orange and call me a pumpkin!" she said, sitting back down in the chair with a thump. "Ace mentioned guests in the house, but of course he wouldn't have mentioned that it was Natalie's boys after all these years. You must be near manhood now, right?"

"Does twelve count as near manhood?" I said. "Because if so, then yes?"

"Is everything he says a question?" she said, turning to Nash.

"Yes," Nash said. "It's obnoxious."

"Thanks a lot," I said, turning back to the woman. "You know us, but we have no idea who you are."

"Where are my manners!" she said, jumping back to her feet. She put both palms on the desk and hoisted herself up with a grunt. She gave the horse a good-natured smack on the rump as she walked by, and he swished his tail in response.

"The name's Flanny," she said, holding out a tiny

hand for us to shake. Nash shook first, using just his thumb and forefinger to grip her minuscule hand. I followed suit.

"Sit," she said with a jerk of her head at the seats we'd occupied earlier that evening.

We sat. Flanny was small, but she had a big presence about her. Maybe it was the hair.

"Where's our grandfather?" I asked.

"Hmmm," she said, considering. "If I had to guess, I'd wager that he's in the lagoon by now." She shook her head. "I do hope he looks out for the crocodiles. Old Buster is really in a mood these days. Liable to take your head off as much as look at ya."

"Lagoon? Crocodile? Buster?" I said.

"There you go with that questioning nonsense," Flanny said. "Say a thing or don't say a thing, but don't make things that don't need to be a question into one! I'd have thought Natalie would have taught her boys that."

"She did," Nash said. "But it stuck better with some than others." I was too flabbergasted by the whole situation to whack Nash for that, but I made a mental note to do it later.

"I'm sorry," I said. "But you just said our grandfather is in a lagoon with crocodiles. The last time I checked, we don't have either of those in Indiana. So forgive me if I have some questions."

"In-Dee-Ann-a," Flanny said, pronouncing each syllable as though she could taste it. "Funny name, that. Don't think I'd much fancy staying here if you don't have lagoons or crocodiles. Where's the adventure in that? I best hope old Ace is faster than Buster. Isn't that right, Fritz?" she said with a glance over at the horse.

"My head hurts," Nash said, dropping his head into his hands.

"I have that effect on people," Flanny said with a wide, gap-toothed smile.

"I feel like I'm reading a book, but someone took out the first five chapters," I said, more to myself than anyone in particular because Nash wasn't alone in his pain. I could feel a dull throb right underneath my temples. Also, it was pretty rich having your state's name insulted by a woman named Flanny of all things. "Maybe you could explain a bit more, I don't know, backstory about the lagoons? And about who Buster is? And why you're here? And how you know our mom?" I thought about asking why she was pocket-sized, but again my mom's admonishments to be polite no matter what stopped me in my tracks.

"Well now, so it's information you're after, is it?" she said. We nodded and her grin got wider. "Then you best be willing to make a trade for it."

I glanced over at Nash and held up my empty hands. "Trade for what?"

"I've got a guinea pig looking for a new home," Nash said with a grimace as he peered under the Band-Aid on his finger.

"What use would I have for a pig?" Flanny said with a disgusted shake of her head. "A pig would get eaten by old Buster before you could spit, that's what. Pigs! Useless creatures, pigs. Now a lagoon goat? One of those might be of some use, assuming it's more interested in climbing than eating your undergarments. No, I deal in information, lads. How else do you think old Jeremy Benson got us to agree to stay here in this wee room?" She gestured around her, and I felt like pointing out that in relation to her size, the room was actually gigantic.

"What information?" I said instead.

"Well, now, I dropped it when you startled me, didn't I?" she said, peering over the edge of the desk. Nash dropped to his knees and fished out the pamphlet she'd been studying when we'd first walked in. He handed it to me, and I flipped it over to read the cover.

The words *Lagoons and Lasses Directions* was printed in a big black font across the top. A quick flip through showed a few illustrations of women dressed in old-fashioned bathing suits just like Flanny, surrounded by crocodiles. I read a line here or there and felt my forehead wrinkle in confusion. These were instructions on how to play a board game, a very weird board game but a board game nonetheless.

"Well, speak up," Flanny said, leaning forward eagerly. "What's it say? How do you win the game? Is it to steal old Buster's jewels? It's to steal his jewels, isn't it? Are they located in the Mountains of Mundane? Or the Cave of Captives? It's the cave, isn't it? I've been saying it's the cave for years, but would the girls listen? No!"

"Who is old Buster?" Nash said.

"The king of the crocodiles!" Flanny said in exasperation before turning back to me. "Read it, boy. Read it."

I was opening my mouth to do just that when I felt Nash's hand on my arm.

"Not yet, Rhett," he said. He gave Flanny a smile I was all too familiar with before leaning back to cross his arms over his chest. "She needs to tell us what's going on first." It was his smug look. The look he got when he knew something that I didn't, or when he knew he had the upper hand in an argument. I really hated that look. Usually, it gave me a very intense urge to tackle him. But tonight, I couldn't have been happier to see it.

"No," Flanny said, leaning back and adopting the same posture. "It's a trade. I tell you something. And he reads me a page. Deal?"

"Deal," Nash said, leaning forward to once again shake her tiny hand.

"Are you . . ." I started, glancing from the black-and-white illustrations in the instruction manual to Flanny and back again. "Were you the inspiration for this game or something?"

"Inspiration?!" she cackled gleefully. "Boy, I'm the princess of that game. That game is nothing without me and old Fritz here. Without Flanny the Fabulous that game's nothing but a swamp of old crocodiles hoarding their treasure and a bunch of half-wits in swimwear stumbling around getting eaten." I stared at her for a second, really wishing that at least part of that had made sense.

"Okay," Nash said. "Maybe I should have been more specific. The stuff you tell us has to make sense. Nonsensical gobbledygook doesn't count as a fair exchange."

Flanny sighed. "So you two know nothing about the Benson family curse, then? Is that right?"

"We have a family curse?!" Nash and I said at the exact same time in two totally different ways. He said it in the same way you might exclaim over winning the lottery. I said it in the same way you'd exclaim over finding a dead frog in your bed.

Nash sat up straighter and leaned in. "We really have a family curse?!" he said. "What is it?!"

Flanny waved her hand at him in annoyance. "Stop flapping those lips about and I'll tell you, won't I?" She waited until Nash and I had both leaned forward in expectation.

She smiled "Why, board games, of course."

CRESS

There is always a way out. That's a rule. No game is unwinnable, although it feels that way about 99 percent of the time. Lucky for me, that elusive 1 percent is where I operated. I won games.

I felt the hairs on my neck stand at attention, and I ducked before my brain could even register why I was ducking. The snick of something slicing over my head a second later made me grateful for the split-second reflex. I glanced up to see a thin, razor-sharp seashell sticking out of a tree five feet away. If I'd hesitated, if I'd decided not to trust my gut just this one time, that seashell would have been lodged in the back of my head. I turned, remaining in my crouch, to see a massive octopus come churning up from bubbling blue water ten feet away. The creature was the green of a ripe lime with knobs and warty bumps all over its massive head. If I had to estimate, which I was excellent at, I'd say it was twenty feet, or at least the part sticking out of the water was. Who knew what was flailing around beneath the surface.

In each of the monster's thrashing tentacles was a seashell, which I knew from painful experience it planned to use as a projectile. We'd been here before. This moment was one I'd lived three times already. The first time I'd made the mistake of attacking from above. I'd lost almost instantly. The second time I'd tried to attack from shore, leveraging spears at the beast. I'd been hit from behind, probably by one of those blasted seashells, and back to the beginning I'd gone. The third time I'd run, thinking that this might be one of those obstacles I was supposed to avoid, not fight. The beast had plucked me from the ground mid-stride, and I'd been done for.

This time was going to be different. This time I was going to advance in the game. This time I wasn't going to be sent back to the start. It wasn't that I couldn't get here again; the beginning of this particular game wasn't super difficult as long as you didn't mind submerging yourself for long periods of time in dark, monster-infested water, but it was the principle of the fact at this point. No game beat me four times.

On the fourth attempt, I always succeeded. I always won. I always found a way out. It was why I was paid so well, I thought with a smirk. The smirk faded as yet another seashell came flying in my direction, forcing me to lunge behind a nearby rock for cover.

I stifled a sigh as I drew the small knife at my belt and dove into the water. To advance to the next part of the game, I was going to have to slay this guy. That part was obvious enough, although I wish I'd managed to find some kind of specialized weapon a few moves back so I could have done this a little more easily. A bow and arrow would have been nice, or even a decent-sized spear. I'd had an opportunity when I'd landed on a Take a Gamble card, but all it had done was send me back four moves.

The tiny dagger would have to do, even if I was going to have to plunge the sucker in up to my armpit and hope to hit a vital organ. I racked my brain trying to remember where an octopus kept its heart, and failed. I held my breath as the icy water closed over my head, and blinked to adjust my eyes. Ahead of me was the swirling underbelly of the creature that would have happily slaughtered me. Unfortunately for it, I was going to be the one doing the slaughtering today, thanks. I dodged a muscular tentacle and was just angling for a good place to strike when I spotted the sharks. Man, I hated games with ocean themes.

SIX

I felt my face twist in confusion as I stared at the woman. "Board games?" I said. "How in the world can board games be a curse?"

"Hmm," Flanny said, putting a hand on her chin. "Maybe *curse* isn't the word I'm looking for. I am much better at my native tongue. Your language doesn't know its ups from its downs or its ins from its outs most of the time. Maybe I should have said unusual ability, or terrible talent? Whatever you want to call it, you Bensons have been mucking about in board games for generations."

"Curse sounds cooler," Nash muttered.

"Mucking about?" I said.

She nodded emphatically. "It all started back with your great-great-somebody or other, I think it was a grandmother, married a Wanderer."

I opened my mouth to speak, but she held up a

finger to stop my question before I could ask it, her bushy red eyebrows drawn together in annoyance. I shut my mouth with an audible click.

"Easy there, Mr. Question," she said. "I know you want to know what a Wanderer is." I nodded as Nash snickered "Mr. Question" under his breath. I sighed, knowing that nickname was going to stick whether I liked it or not.

"A Wanderer," Flanny went on, "is the name your grandfather gave to a board game character that has escaped their game to roam your world. Although," she said with a disapproving wiggle of her nose as she took in our grandfather's cluttered office, "I have no idea what the appeal is. There isn't a single Snogwhiler as far as I can tell, and it smells stale in here. I like my air to smell of salt and brine."

"Wait a second," Nash said with a snort. "So when you say board game character, you mean, like, that guy in the top hat from Monopoly could just pop out of Park Place and start strolling around Indiana?" The image was pretty unbelievable, but a quick glance at Flanny showed that she wasn't the least bit amused.

"I'm not sure about your top hat man," she said, "since I've only met a few Wanderers in my day, but he sounds like he'd get eaten by old Buster faster than you can spit."

"And old Buster is . . ." I asked.

"Biggest crocodile this side of Wayward Swamp," she said proudly. "Thirty feet if he's an inch and teeth as long as your arm. But Wanderers are no laughing matter. They can cause more trouble than they're worth. Thank the lord only one emerges every few centuries. Well, it was just your great-great-whoever's luck to fall in love with one. Because of that, all the Bensons that have come after have been able to flit in and out of whatever board game they please, not taking into consideration the mess they leave behind them."

"So are we Wanderers?" I said.

She huffed in exasperation and shook her head. "Are you from a board game, child?"

"No," Nash said.

"Then you can't be a Wanderer, can you?" Flanny said. "Your family can go into board games because you have Wanderer blood in your veins, but you yourself are not a Wanderer. That's an earned title, not an inherited one. Got it?"

"Maybe?" I said.

"So are *you* a Wanderer?" Nash asked.

"I most certainly am not!" Flanny said. "I was conscripted into this."

"Conscripted?" I said.

"Drafted, lobbied, volun-told," Flanny said. "That's part of the curse. If a Benson goes in, something in the game has to come out. In this case, two somethings," she said with a jerk of her head at the horse that had almost demolished the fern. "Your grandfather always travels with that moose of a dog of his, so that means old Fritz and I had to come here for a bit."

"Why did you agree to it?" I said.

"Mostly because I didn't have a choice, now did I. But I came along nicely enough because of that!" she said, pointing at the pamphlet in my hand. "*That*, my boy, is the one and only instruction manual to Lagoons and Lasses in existence. There used to be a copy in a children's museum in Indianapolis, but then some brat pushed the vintage board game display over and it was ruined by a blue slushy."

"Wow," Nash said. "That's, um, specific."

"So the instruction manual is important because . . ." I said.

"That is how you learn how to win the game," she said.

"So how do you win the game?" I said with a jerk of my chin at the pamphlet.

"If I knew that," Flanny said, "would I be standing here gabbing at you?"

"Weren't you just reading it?" I said. The paper in my hand was yellowed around the edges and brittle feeling. I paged carefully through it.

She sniffed and glanced down to inspect her long red nails, obviously choosing not to answer.

Nash was leaning forward to peer at Flanny's face, and I knew he was reading her expression. I hated when he did it to me, but I loved how uncanny he was at figuring out the inner workings of someone's head.

"No," he said. "She can't read."

"I believe," Flanny said with a sniff, "that this was to be a trade of information. Here I've told you a whole kit and half a caboodle and you've told me diddly-squat."

"Rhett," Nash said. "Read the woman a page." I glanced down and cleared my throat as Flanny and even Fritz leaned forward in anticipation.

"Lagoons and Lasses is a breathtaking adventure through the Lagoons of the Lost, the Caverns of Corruption, and the Mountains of Mundane," I read. "Each player must choose either the blue, green, red, or yellow Lass and place their piece at the start."

"*Blue*," Flanny said as though the word tasted bad. She turned and spit off the side of the desk.

"Once the Lasses are at the start, each player must take turns rolling the dice and progressing down the board. Each Lass must acquire a crocodile companion, a jewel of Abernathy, and four different-shaped seashells." I was about to go on when I felt Nash's hand slap over my mouth. Back in the day, I'd lick his hand when he did that. It was an effective way to get him to pull it off in disgust, but the germs unit in our fifth-grade science class had ruined that maneuver for me for life. I glanced over at him in annoyance, but he wasn't looking at me. He was looking at Flanny.

"Your turn," he said.

She leaned back with a harrumph. "What else do you want to know?" she asked.

"So, our family can enter any of those board games," Nash said, pointing to the stacks upon stacks of boxes behind their locked glass case.

"As far as I know, yes," Flanny said.

"Are there magic words?" Nash asked.

"Do you think Jeremy Benson goes around telling every board game character he swaps places with all the ins and outs and roundabouts of his family's secrets?"

"Darn," I said, snapping the instruction manual shut. "And here I was hoping that you had something else good to trade." I'd been reading ahead during Nash's interrogation, and I knew how to win Flanny's game.

"Oh, I have something good," Flanny said.

"She's bluffing," Nash said.

"She's not," Flanny said. "I happen to know that your grandfather is in my game at this very moment looking for his daughter."

The dots connected in rapid fire.

"Our mom is in your game?" I said.

Flanny shrugged. "Maybe. Maybe not. That's for

Jeremy and that bear dog, Chief, to find out."

"I knew she wasn't in a hospital!" I said.

"Unless that's a board game, then no," Flanny said. "She's not."

"But what is she doing in a board game?" Nash asked. Flanny was just opening her mouth to answer when there was suddenly a faint buzz in the air. It was a staticky feeling, like when your sheets get so dry and crinkly in the winter that they shock you. I felt a tingle go up and down my skin, and my toes and fingers felt cold. Nash and I jumped to our feet, our chairs slamming backward into the wall with a thump. Flanny's eyes went wide, and she turned to me, her face urgent.

"Tell me!" she cried. "How do I win the game!" She started to disappear in front of our eyes, as though someone was taking an eraser to her and rubbing away at her hands and hair in slow smudges. Her horse was experiencing the same thing and stood with his four tiny hooves firmly planted on the desk, his ears pinned back in disapproval. I was so shocked by this sight that it took me a second to realize that two things were reappearing behind them. A half second later, I realized it was Ace and Chief.

"You have to take the seashells all the way up the Mountains of Mundane!" I cried to Flanny just as a loud fizzling sound filled the air and she and Fritz disappeared completely.

CRESS

The moment I entered the game The Labyrinth Lost, I wanted to leave. I had no idea why I suddenly felt a bone-deep urge to run in the opposite direction, but I'd been in the games long enough to know that a gut instinct wasn't something you ignored. So I froze, looking around me at a game that seemed innocent enough. I'd been hired by a tall bony man with an oversize hooked nose, thin arms that hung down by his sides like spaghetti, and one large blue eye set dead center on his forehead. He'd seemed nice enough, and the price was right. It was hard to pass up a gemstone, and the one he'd held in his hand was the size of a chicken egg and the most unusual green I'd ever seen. All I had to do was find my way through the labyrinth and tell him how to get past a bridge that apparently fell apart the moment you set foot on it. Easy.

In front of me was a gray cobblestone path that led

in a curved arc into the woods ahead. I felt the rough wood of a spinner in my hand, and I looked down at it. The small black metal rod in the middle was waiting for me to give it a flick, but I waited. I wasn't ready yet.

Around me birds squawked, and somewhere in the distance something roared, maybe a mountain lion, maybe a bear. In this game, either of those were equally likely. Something about this game was tugging at my memory, nagging me to remember something I'd forgotten. Finally, I gave up and flicked the spinner. It spun wildly around its small card before landing on the number six. It was time to get moving.

My six moves took me into a wood unlike any I'd ever seen before. The farther down the path I moved, the closer the trees became until there was a solid wall of living wood on either side of the path, boxing me in. A moment later the smell hit me. It was a musty, woodsy smell with a strange, spicy undertone, and the memory that had been shuffling around the perimeter of my subconscious stepped forward to reveal itself. I'd been here before, and I hadn't been here alone.

I'd never known the name of this game. I'd just thought of it as the Maze of Madness, which, if you asked me, was a much better name than The Labyrinth Lost. He'd brought me here the first time he'd taken me from my own game. I'd never left my game before. I hadn't had any idea that I could leave it, but he'd held my hand and smiled a challenge that I couldn't resist, and I'd followed him. He'd been so confident that it made me feel confident, and we'd maneuvered our way through jungles and deserts and forests, avoiding different wildlife and dangers as we took turn after turn in the giant, spiralizing maze. I'd been the one to find our way out. It had seemed easy at the time, and I remembered the way he'd looked at me when I'd placed my feet on the very last square of the game. He'd been impressed, and for the first time I'd realized that this was something that I could do. I could win games.

I looked down at the spinner again and raised my other hand to flick it. I'd won once. I could win again. I didn't flick it, though. Instead, I reached into my pocket and pulled out the gemstone and dropped it on the ground. It was nice, but it wasn't worth the memories that were clawing back toward me. Memories I'd purposefully tried to forget, that I'd locked away carefully in a place I thought they couldn't escape. This place, the smell of it, the feel of the uneven cobblestones under my feet, had let them out. They rushed forward, piling on top of one another in their hurry to remind me of the horrible thing I'd done. They ripped at my subconscious like a wild beast desperate to escape, and I gritted my teeth as pain I'd been avoiding hit me like a stampeding rhino. The moment the gemstone hit the cobblestones, I was gone.

SEVEN

A ce and Chief finished materializing from thin air at the same instant, and froze at the sight of us. We stood there for a second staring at one another. Chief got tired of it first and wandered out of the office to lie in front of the large potbellied stove. Our grandfather gave himself a little shake and let the large burlap bag he was holding thump onto his desk. It popped open, and I recoiled as part of a massive, toothy snout poked out.

"Is that a crocodile head?" Nash asked, looking positively green.

"Well, it's not the whole croc, now is it?" Ace said as he plopped down into his chair. He looked gigantic in it after Flanny, and I shook my head and glanced over at the fern. It was half eaten; small bits of munched-on leaves lay scattered here and there. I needed that piece of evidence to convince me that I hadn't just made up the whole encounter. A quick glance at the instruction manual in my hand solidified it. Nope. Not dreaming.

Ace noticed the pamphlet in my hand and narrowed his eyes at us. "Were you talking to the Lass?"

"You mean Flanny?" I said.

"Was that her name?" he said as he flipped the burlap back over the snout of the crocodile. I stared at the lumpy mass on the desk and wrinkled my nose. I'd never really thought about what a dead crocodile head might smell like, but the combination of swamp, iron, and what I thought might be moss seemed pretty spot-on. My stomach rolled, and I tried not to think about the cheeseburgers we'd had for dinner.

"You didn't know her name?" Nash said, cocking his head to the side. "She knew yours."

"They all know my name," Ace said with a grand gesture to the bookcases behind him.

"Flanny told us about the curse," I said. "Is it true? Can our family go into board games?"

"Curse?!" Ace said. "Is that what she called it? What we do is not a curse, boys, it's a gift."

"Whatever," I said, flapping a hand. "Why is Mom in Lagoons and Lasses?"

"She's not," Ace said, shaking his head. "I checked every nook and cranny of that blasted board game, and if it weren't for Chief that guy would have had *my* head." He jerked his chin at the covered crocodile head.

"But the games," Nash pressed. "We can go into games?"

"That Lass must have been a fast talker," Ace said with a shake of his head. "I should have gone with the Blue Lass. She has a lisp, a stutter, and three teeth. She'd barely have been able to tell you hello before I got back."

"But Flanny said—" I started, but Ace held up a hand to stop me.

"Rule one of board game bounding, you don't talk to the characters. You don't tell them any more than they need to know, and you don't tell them any personal details about yourself. You *never* under any circumstances befriend them. You didn't tell Red Lass any details, did you?"

"Um," I said with a worried glance at Nash. Had we told Flanny anything personal? I wasn't sure.

"She wanted to know what her instruction manual said," Nash said. "We wanted to know why there was a tiny horse eating your plant. We traded information." Ace's face went white, and he sat up with a start.

"You didn't read her the instruction manual, did you?" he said. "Rule number two of board game bounding is that you never let a character from a game read their own manual."

"But didn't you give it to her?" I said.

"Well, yes!" Ace said with a harrumph of frustration. "But that was only because I knew that she couldn't read!"

"Why didn't you tell us these rules before we made a mess of things?" I asked.

"Because I wasn't to tell you about the games!" Ace snapped. "I promised your mother."

"Our mother, who is currently in a board game somewhere?" I said, because honestly, I felt like I needed that clarified a couple hundred more times before it was going to sink in.

"Yes," he said sharply. "*That* mother. Last I checked, you only had the one. *That* mother, *my* daughter, Natalie, hated bounding. She didn't want you boys to ever be a part of it. Thought she could keep you away."

"She did," I said. "We've never been allowed near a board game."

"Impressive," Ace said. "But not all that surprising. Natalie has always had a will of iron. Stubborn as a lagoon goat, that one."

"What's a lagoon goat?" I said, remembering that Flanny had mentioned them too.

"Doesn't matter," Ace said with a dismissive wave of his hand. "But their spit *is* poisonous, so make sure you always bring protective eyewear."

"Man," Nash said, shoving his hands into his hair. "I always thought Alice falling through the looking glass sounded like a good time. Now I think it probably just gave her a migraine."

"The Looking Glass is not a game you want to visit," Ace said with a shudder. "Awful creatures in there, not a decent one to swap with in the place. Your mother went in despite my warnings when she was thirteen. Let loose a caterpillar that ate half the couch before she got back."

"Mom's in a game now," I said in an attempt to refocus Ace. "Why?"

Ace threw his hands in the air and his face clouded. "That's the question, isn't it!" he said. "I haven't heard from your mother in years, and then the next thing I know I'm getting a bloody voice mail saying I need to protect you two. As though I hadn't been calling her every month for ten years trying to do just that!"

"What voice mail?" I asked. "Can we hear it?" Ace hesitated for a second before pulling out a battered cell phone. He looked at it, sighed, and fished out a pair of reading glasses from the pocket of his denim shirt. He peered at it for a minute before punching a few buttons and setting it down on his desk. A second later our mother's voice came out of it sounding tinny and far away.

"Dad, I don't have much time," she said, and the hairs along my neck stood on end. I'd only ever heard our mom sound like that one other time, and it was when we'd lost Nash at the mall when he and I were five. He'd wandered off, and it had taken two hours to locate him sleeping under a rack of sweaters in Nordstrom. Mom had been frantic, and I'd sat on the changing-room bench equal parts terrified and furious at Nash for getting himself lost. I didn't remember much about being five, but I remembered how scary it was to have the adult in your life be so utterly terrified that their very voice changed.

"I need you to take care of the boys," came Mom's voice, and my stomach gave a sickening churn. "They're at Harrison Middle School. Go get them. Keep them safe." There was the sound of something crashing and then what sounded like a small explosion in the background. I shut my eyes as our mom's voice rose an octave in panic. "He found me, Dad. Don't let him get the boys." Then the line went dead.

My mouth was bone-dry, and I tried unsuccessfully to swallow. "What happened to her?" I finally managed to rasp.

"A Wander Lost," Ace said through teeth clenched tight. "That's what happened to her."

"A Wanderer is a board game character that escaped

their game, right?" Nash said. "Flanny said that our great-great-somebody or other married a Wanderer and that's why we can go into board games."

Ace shook his head. "Not a Wanderer, a Wander Lost. There's a big difference."

"Okay . . ." I said slowly. It felt a little like Ace was speaking a foreign language.

"A Wanderer is exactly what you said. Someone who figured out how to win their game and therefore escape. They are able to go into and out of any game they wish. They are also able to travel to the real world, which is how we became board game bounders."

"So we aren't Wanderers?" Nash asked.

Ace nodded. "Correct. We are not. We have Wanderer blood running through our veins, which allows us to bound in and out of board games. Although," he said, his brow furrowing, "the bloodline gets weaker with every generation. There may come a day when Bensons can no longer enter the world of the games."

"So what's a Wander Lost? And why did one take our mom?"

"I have a few theories," Ace said darkly.

"Care to share with the class?" Nash asked, not bothering to hide his annoyance.

"Theory one is to get back at me for destroying his game," Ace said.

77

"Well, I don't have to ask why he doesn't like you," Nash said dryly. "I'd hate you too if you destroyed my game. I mean, isn't that like what that Romulan guy did to Spock's planet in *Star Wars*? Or was it *Star Trek*? I can never keep those two straight. Either way, doesn't destroying this Wander Lost's game make *you* that bad guy?"

"History is written by the winners," I murmured. It was something our teacher had said once that had haunted me. I'd never thought about it before, but it cast our history books in a whole new light that I wasn't entirely comfortable with.

"By destroying his game, I destroyed his access back to his own world," Ace snapped. "You shouldn't pass judgment on events you weren't a part of."

"What's theory two?" I asked.

Ace glanced over at me, and then looked away quickly. "You aren't ready for theory two yet," he said. "Suffice it to say that a Benson, any Benson, can be very useful to a Wander Lost, or a Wanderer for that matter."

"I have a question," Nash said.

"Just one?" I asked. I felt like questions were erupting in my brain like popping popcorn.

Nash ignored me and looked at Ace, crossing his arms over his chest. "Why could you pop back out of that board game, but Mom can't come out of whatever game this guy took her into? If she's a bounder too? Why can't she just leave?" He gave his chin a sharp jerk toward the box still sitting innocently on the edge of his desk.

"There are ways to hold someone prisoner inside a game," Ace said without bothering to elaborate.

"So if this Wander Lost didn't take her into *his* game, what game did he take her to?" Nash asked.

"Yeah," I said. "And why would he take her there?"

"That's a question I'm trying to figure out," Ace said with a sweeping gesture to the boxes stacked behind him. "But as you can see, I have a lot of ground to cover, and I'm only one man." He let that phrase hang in the air, waiting. He'd issued an invitation, and he was waiting to see if we'd bite. I suddenly had the sensation of standing at the edge of a cliff, peering down over the edge, waiting for someone to give me a shove, and, just like I knew he would, Nash shoved.

"We can help!" Nash said excitedly. I swallowed a sigh. Our mom was right. I was the look, and Nash was the leap. She usually told us this fact in the middle of a lecture about something dangerous or stupid we'd managed to do. The incident with Mrs. Jacob's koi pond came to mind. It had taken hours to catch the massive goldfish Nash had decided needed a field trip to our neighborhood pool. Mrs. Jacob had given us the stink eye every time she saw us after that. Which was fine. We more than deserved it. Nash swore the grounding was worth it since that particular escapade had made us legends in our subdivision for about two months. We might still be legends back at Poplar Lane, who knew. We'd moved and never gone back to visit Mrs. Jacob or her koi pond. I glared at the side of my oblivious twin's head. Just once I'd like to be the leaper. To make the harebrained decision and then drag Nash through the consequences. Although our mom had pointed out on various occasions that roadkill were the leapers, and look how they ended up. It was too late to point that out now. Nash's words had made our grandfather's face light up like Christmas morning.

Ace leaned forward, pressing his hands together, his smile wide. "I was hoping you'd say that."

EIGHT

B oard game bounding had a lot of rules while simultaneously seeming like a completely unorganized free-for-all gamble of chance. The rule part I liked. Rules made things feel more solid, like if I could just learn them, then I'd be able to do this seemingly impossible thing. The unorganized free-for-all bit was more Nash's ballpark.

Normally this kind of chaos would have sent me running for the hills or quitting whatever endeavor had sent me down this particular path. I was good at quitting. I'd quit the baseball team when the practices had gotten too rough, I'd quit the school musical when they wanted me to sing a solo, and I'd given up honors classes when the tests required too much studying. But this time was different. This time, my mom was at stake. This time quitting wasn't an option.

It turned out that in our one short interaction with Flanny, we'd already broken about half the rules of board game bounding. For one thing, if I *had* managed to tell her how to win her game, I would have basically handed her the ability to become a Wanderer herself. A Wanderer, as Ace was quick to inform us, was only able to escape their game one of two ways. The first was if they won their game, a feat that was apparently nearly impossible. I'd stared at the stacks of boxes behind him while he talked, trying to imagine all those board game characters in a never-ending journey through their games, only to fail and get sent back to the starting line over and over again. The majority of the rules involved how to handle yourself once you entered a game. The list seemed long, with everything from *don't lose the dice* to *don't help a board game character in their pursuit of victory.* There were a few about not eating the food in a game or falling asleep, but compared to *watch out for holes in the ground because there's usually something in there that wants to kill you,* they seemed pretty unimportant.

"And most important," Ace said as the sun started to rise in the window to his right. Nash jerked upright from where he'd been nodding off beside me, almost knocking the pad of paper I'd been taking notes on out of my hand. I stifled my own yawn as Ace leaned in, his eyes narrowed as he waited to make sure he had our full attention. Deciding he did, he waved a stern finger in front of our noses. "If you forget every other rule, don't forget this one. If you get injured in a game, you will have the same injury when you leave the game." He leaned back, waiting for some kind of reaction from us, but Nash and I just sat there and stared at him. This entire thing had felt like trying to get a drink out of a fire hose, and my brain had a strange overstuffed feeling to it.

"Got it," Nash finally said around another wide yawn.

Ace shook his head. "I don't think you do. Board game injuries are a whole different ball game. It's a real bear to explain how you got stung by a giant jellyfish in the middle of Indiana, let me tell you."

I put my hand up and Ace raised an eyebrow at me. "Yes?" he said.

"What if you die in the game?"

"Then you're dead," Ace said flatly.

"That's what I was afraid of," I said.

"So if Mom gets killed in whatever game that Wander-person took her into, then what happens to the thing that came out of the game to replace her?" Nash asked.

"That's the second way a board game character can

83

leave their game," Ace said, leaning back in his chair. "Learned that lesson the hard way."

"So they become a Wanderer?" I asked.

"No. They become a poor imitation of a Wanderer. They become a Wander Lost. A Wander Lost doesn't have the same freedoms as a Wanderer, and unlike us, they can't remove things from a game, which is incredibly lucky or our world would be in a real mess."

"Why?" I asked.

"Imagine someone getting their hands on a sword that can't be beat or a ring that turned the wearer into a monster?" He shuddered and shook his head. "There are things in board games that need to stay in board games."

"What's all that, then?" Nash asked with a jerk of his chin at the bookcase behind Ace.

"That?" Ace said, turning to take in his vast collection of oddities. "That is the collection of a lifetime of board game bounding. Very few dangerous items, with a few exceptions of course."

"What's that one?" I asked, pointing to a huge hunk of rock that sat in the bottom left-hand corner of one of the bookcases. It looked like a normal rock with one exception. At the very top was a perfectly rectangular hole.

Ace turned to look at where I was pointing and

waved a dismissive hand. "That's just a rock."

"Just a rock," I repeated slowly, not really believing him.

Ace nodded. "It used to hold Excalibur, but I left the sword in the game. The rock was just a souvenir."

"That's some souvenir," I said. Ace shrugged.

"Wanderer, Wander Lost," Nash repeated, his face scrunched up in confusion. "Who in the world thought up these names?"

Ace sniffed, looking slightly offended. "That would be me."

"Oh," Nash said lamely. "Um, good job."

"What's his name?" I asked. "This evil Wanderer, I mean Wander Lost, that grabbed Mom?"

"Ogden," Ace said with a grimace as though the very word tasted bad in his mouth. We sat in silence for a moment, letting that name hang in the air between us before Nash abruptly turned to me.

"Have you ever noticed," he said, "that bad guys always seem to have bad guy names? Darth Vader, Magneto, Doctor Doom, Bane. I mean, wouldn't it be nice to meet an evil villain named Bob or Joe or Ben sometime?"

"I don't know. I think it's kind of nice that their names alert you a bit. I mean, I don't think anyone thought someone who called himself Darth Vader would make an excellent babysitter, right? Ogden," I said just to see what the word felt like in my mouth. It felt oddly ominous, and I did a quick, involuntary shiver.

"Are you two done?" Ace said, his voice strained.

"Sure," Nash said, leaning back in his chair again. "Go on about this Ogden. He sounds like he'd be large and hairy with warts on his nose, possibly one eye, and a little troll-like, yes?"

Ace sat back in surprise, eyebrows raised. "Well," he said. "That's almost correct. He's also exceptionally tall."

Nash waved a dismissive hand. "Tall and menacing is a given for a bad guy. Go on." I could tell from Nash's tone that he was just giving him a hard time to give him a hard time. Nash did that sometimes, hassled people just to see how far he could push them before they cracked. It was a sport for him, and Nash was good at sports. I was not good at sports, the psychological or the physical, so I cracked after about five minutes. Two, if I was being really honest. Our mom? Now she was made of tougher stuff and could make it through a solid hour of Nash's incessant pestering before she lost it on him and sent him to his room. The thought of Mom brought my wandering thoughts back into focus, and I glanced over at Ace's brooding expression. Suddenly Nash's commentary didn't seem quite so funny.

"What did you mean that lesson was learned the hard way?" I asked, recalling what Ace had said earlier. "Who died?"

"Your mother never told you about Sam?" Ace said, and he suddenly looked so hurt I was worried he might cry. "I knew she kept a lot from you two, but I never thought that she'd keep Sam from you."

"Who was Sam?" I said, even as I remembered the family portrait hanging in the living room. Mom had been standing next to a boy her own age. A boy who had the same bright green eyes and dimples that she had.

"Your uncle," Ace said, his face tight. "It's why your mom didn't want anything to do with board game bounding. After losing her twin, she was done."

This made Nash and me both sit bolt upright in our chairs. "Mom was a twin!" Nash said at the same exact moment that I did. Our mom used to smile whenever stuff like that happened, but her smile had always held just a hint of sadness. Now, for the first time, I knew why.

NINE

It felt weird to go back to bed after having just eaten breakfast, but I was exhausted enough that I didn't really care. After our crash course on board game bounding, Ace had made us a fast breakfast of scrambled eggs on toast and sent us to bed. Nash had wanted to try his hand at board game bounding right that very second, but Ace had shut that idea down. Apparently going into a game as exhausted and sleep-deprived as we were was a recipe for disaster. Nash had started snoring the second his head hit the pillow, but I lay awake staring at the too-bright room. Why did Nash seem so unfazed by all of this while I felt like I'd had my insides tied into knots? He'd seemed equally baffled by me before we'd turned out our light.

"It's super simple," he'd said with a barely stifled eye roll. "This Ogden guy has Mom stashed somewhere in a board game. Ace needs our help finding her, so we learn how to do it. What is there to think about or ponder or stress about or whatever it is that you're so fond of doing? Seriously, you'd overthink about where to store ice cream."

"The freezer," I muttered, even though I knew the point he was trying to make. "You aren't completely blown away by the fact that Mom was a twin or that she never told us about Sam?"

"Sure." Nash shrugged. "But she also kept the whole board game bounding thing a secret too, didn't she? That's the headline, not Sam." I shook my head. I wasn't so sure. Sam felt like the headline to me. Something horrible had happened to him, that was obvious, but our grandfather hadn't been willing to go into details about what exactly had happened. I'd noticed the pinched look of pain he'd gotten when we'd asked about Sam, but Nash had been oblivious, chattering on about the logistics of getting into a board game. I'd opened my mouth to argue back, but snapped it shut again. I was exhausted, and the only thing arguing would do was make me more exhausted. It wasn't simple, though; it was complicated and confusing, and more than that, it was making me rethink my entire childhood. Sam. The name seemed so unfamiliar for someone who'd apparently been as close to my mom as I was to Nash. I tried to picture a life where I never said Nash's name, where I pretended like he didn't exist and never had, and failed. It would be like pretending I didn't have a left arm.

Sleep was starting to win out, and I felt my eyelids droop. Was Sam the adventurous to Mom's cautious? The leap to her look? Or had she taken on the cautious twin role after losing her more adventurous half? It was easy to understand why she'd never told us about him. It would have opened up an entire can of worms that she'd have then had to explain. I felt a surge of anger at my mom for that. Why had she kept so much from us? If this was our family's legacy or curse or whatever, she should have been preparing us for it, not hiding it from us. Now we were a day late and a dollar short for this entire thing. Worse yet, she wasn't the one who was going to teach us; that job had fallen to Ace.

I thought about Ace then and tried fitting the role of grandfather over his no-nonsense, cowboy-boot-wearing persona and failed. Maybe it was because I'd never experienced a grandfather in any capacity, but I thought they were supposed to be jollier somehow. I lay there wondering if everyone felt slightly nauseous right before they started a new adventure. My eyelids won, and I fell asleep in the top bunk of a strange cabin in the middle of nowhere Indiana.

I woke up around three in the afternoon and shook Nash awake.

"What are you doing?" he grumbled as he rolled over.

"Waking you up," I said flatly. "If you think I'm going to go stumbling around in a board game all by myself you've got another thing coming."

Nash lay there for a second, his eyes closed, and then he sat bolt upright so fast that his forehead slammed into mine with a resounding whack.

"Wow," I said, leaning back as my vision filled with black polka dots. "That's a great start."

"Sorry," Nash said, rubbing his own head. "It took me a second to remember where we were." He let his hand drop to his lap and glanced around the small room. "Um," he said. "Do we actually know where we are? Other than the backwoods of Indiana?"

"Nope," I said. "If Ace decided to murder us, they'd never find our bodies."

"Super reassuring," Nash said. "Love the way your brain works."

"You wouldn't love it if you were inside it," I muttered.

"I know," Nash agreed as he climbed out of bed to stand beside me, "that was sarcasm." I was about to ask him what we should do next, go find Ace or make a run for it, when suddenly a deep baritone bark split the silence of the cabin. Nash exited the room with me at his heels to discover Chief standing at the door of the cabin, his nose pressed to the glass as a very angry Geronimo Jones the Third squeaked at him from the other side. Chief let out a loud woof again, and then turned to look at us, his head cocked.

"Is it just me or is he asking for permission to eat Geronimo?" Nash said.

"He is," Ace said from behind us, and we both jumped in surprise. "Chief is incredibly intelligent. He's one of the reasons I've made it out alive on more than one occasion." Ace turned his attention from Chief back to us. "Good morning," he said. "Or should I say good afternoon? Would you like another round of breakfast or some peanut butter and banana sandwiches?"

"Sandwiches," Nash and I said in unison. Chief gave one more hopeful bark before turning to follow Ace into the kitchen. Nash quickly opened the door and scooped up his indignant guinea pig. He deposited him in our room and shut the door behind him.

"He's a pain, but he's not lunch, got it?" Nash instructed Chief.

"Um, Nash?" I said. "Are you forgetting something?"

Nash looked over at me, eyebrow cocked. "Probably?"

"Don't you think you should, I don't know, feed Geronimo?" Nash slapped his forehead and scrounged around in Ace's fridge until he found some celery and disappeared back into our room.

"Stick him in a box or something!" I called, imagining the mess our room would be in if Nash let Geronimo roam free. It didn't take much imagination, since he'd had a habit of doing that at home. Nothing made our mother angrier than guinea pig poop on the carpet, and I thought about reminding Nash of that but didn't. He grunted a response, and a moment later he was back. He sat down at the kitchen counter and grabbed his sandwich.

I took a bite of my own sandwich and chewed thoughtfully. It was the same sandwich my mom had been making us for as long as I could remember, and now I knew why. I thought about my analogy last night of feeling like I was reading a book with missing chapters. Maybe that wasn't quite right. Maybe I was just reading the first chapter of a book I'd thought I understood but didn't.

"So where do we start?" Nash asked. "Which game do we get to cannonball or swan dive or jump into first? How do we get in them exactly? I don't think you covered that part. I saw one with dragons on it that looked pretty awesome, and that one with Flanny in it looked cool. I mean, I've never seen a giant crocodile before. Or what about the one with the bugs on the box?" When Nash finally paused to take a breath, Ace held up a hand to stop any further questioning. Nash shut his mouth with an audible click, and I glanced back at Ace, waiting for him to launch into a big explanation, but instead he just took another large bite of his sandwich. We watched as he chewed his sandwich before washing it down with a glass of milk. His Adam's apple bobbed as he swallowed, and I looked away out the window. Stuff like that really creeped me out sometimes.

"Eat," he commanded. "You don't want to go into a board game hungry, you might be tempted to eat something."

"And that would be bad because . . ." I said.

"Because I said so," Ace said. "I told you that was a rule yesterday, weren't you paying attention?"

"I mean, I thought I was," I said as I swallowed a bite of sandwich not quite big enough to fully choke me but big enough that it hurt all the way down.

Ace looked from me to Nash and back again, sizing us up.

"That's why we start with the easy stuff first," he said. "Training wheels."

"Training wheels?" I said, liking the sound of that.

Nash might think dragons sounded like a good time, but I didn't. Ace walked over to the door of his office, Chief at his heels. The dog sat down expectantly as Ace bent over to fish around under Chief's furry neck. A second later he produced a key on some kind of retractable string that he used to unlock the office door. He carefully lowered the key back down to Chief's neck, where it disappeared in his fur. I felt the hairs on the back of my neck prickle as I watched. That door hadn't been locked since we got here. In fact, it had been standing open the night before. Why? And why lock it now that we knew the secret about the board games?

"If you're trying to keep us out of there, you're doing a lousy job of hiding that key," Nash said, taking the words right out of my mouth.

Ace looked at us. "You're not the ones I'm trying to keep out." My mind flashed back to my mom's voice mail. She'd said that someone had found her. Ace thought it was Ogden the Wander Lost. Did he think there was a possibility that he'd find us here? Was that the reason for his overreaction when we'd first arrived and I'd yelled over getting bitten by Geronimo Jones?

"Don't just sit there like two lumps, get in here!" he called as he headed to the office, and Nash and I hurried to follow. As we entered, I saw Ace remove a battered box from a bookcase and tuck it under his arm. He relocked the bookcase door using a different key that also apparently resided around his dog's neck. I craned my neck to read the large bubble font across the front of the box.

"Training Wheels?" I said. "The game is actually called Training Wheels?"

"He was being literal," Nash mused. "Interesting." More interesting than the box, though, was the ring of keys that Ace had casually slipped back around Chief's neck after locking the case. It had to have at least ten keys on it, and I wondered what the others were for.

"This game was produced in the 1950s," Ace said, thumping the box on his desk. "It was created by two brothers who were obsessed with the invention of the bicycle."

"How do you win the game?" I asked, leaning forward to peer at the illustrations of winding roads etched across the box's lid.

"You need to read this to find that out," Ace said, carefully opening the lid of the box and sliding out a small paper manual. "You have to find the fastest path from the start to the finish by bicycle," he said with a smirk. "There are, of course, obstacles in your way."

"Are those obstacles crocodiles?" I said as my stomach churned nervously around the partially digested sandwich I was starting to regret eating.

"No crocodiles," he said.

"Darn," Nash said, and even though he sounded like he was joking, I knew he wasn't really. Nash would love nothing more than to come toe to toe with a giant crocodile.

"So how do we get in there?" Nash said. "Are there magic words? Or some kind of cool antique compass? I've always wanted to use an antique compass."

"Hush," Ace said. "You talk too much."

"Amen," I said under my breath, which earned me an elbow in the ribs from my twin.

"First, we need to prepare," Ace said. "Training Wheels is one of the less dangerous games, but even so, we can never predict what will come out of a game when we go in."

"Hold on," Nash said, holding up a hand. "Flanny made it sound like you two had made a deal. Like you had some say in who came out."

"I do," Ace said superiorly. "Of course, I can't control what animal swaps places with Chief, and that can get a bit hairy at times. But odds are good that you two don't get to choose your swap. Your mother and uncle couldn't, that's for sure." I saw something dark flash across his face when he said that, but it disappeared almost immediately.

"That's not fair," Nash said.

"Life's not fair," Ace said. "Board game bounding cares nothing about fairness. As far as I can hypothesize, the Wanderer blood weakens with each generation. I wonder . . ." he said, putting his hand on his chin as he surveyed us. Whatever he was wondering stayed in his head, and he gave himself a little shake and went on. "This time there will be four things, people, or creatures coming out, and we are responsible for the havoc they wreak while we are gone."

"Four?" I said.

"Chief," Ace said with a jerk of his head at his dog, who had settled himself into a furry puddle at his master's feet. "He's number four. Nash, shut that door and throw the bolts. Rhett, go secure that window," Ace instructed. Nash stood up and shut the office door, and to my surprise I saw the complicated set of metal braces and bolts set across its thick wood interior. I hadn't noticed them the night before, but that door had been wide open then. As Nash slid bolt after bolt into place, I realized that our grandfather leaving the office door open the night before had been no accident. He'd *wanted* us to stumble inside. He'd said that he could choose who he swapped places with, and I had a feeling that despite what he'd said earlier, he'd purposefully chosen the talkative Flanny. He'd wanted us to talk to her. He'd wanted us to know the family secret without

98

betraying the promise he'd made our mother.

"Don't just sit there, move," Ace snapped, and I jumped to my feet and headed over to the small square window and then froze. Unlike the door, there were no obvious latches or bolts to throw. It was just a window. I glanced over at Ace for guidance, and he sighed in exasperation.

"Open it, grab the exterior shutters, and bolt them," he said, as though this should have been obvious. I opened the window and leaned out to find two heavy metal shutters perched on either side. I grabbed them and pulled them shut before securing a similar system of bolts and latches that had been on the door.

"This seems like a fire hazard," Nash muttered from behind me, and I had to agree. The small office felt even smaller now that the only sources of natural light had been eliminated.

"What about the case?" Nash said with a jerk of his chin at the shelves of board games behind Ace. "It's glass. That seems kind of dumb if you ask me."

"No one asked you, now did they?" Ace said. "And it's not dumb. It's two inches thick and bulletproof, not that I've ever had anything that came out of a game test that theory. As a whole, the things that come out of a game are concerned only with their own game. With very few exceptions, quids are extremely self-centered and don't spend much time trying to destroy book-cases."

"Quids?" I said.

"Quids," Ace repeated. "Short for quid pro quo. They are a swap. A trade of one thing of value for another inside the game. Quids are any creature that comes out of a board game once we go in," Ace said, as though this should have been obvious.

"You made up that name for them, right?" Nash said.

"What's your point?" Ace asked, crossing his arms over his chest.

"Nothing," Nash said, throwing up his hands in surrender.

"What would you have named a board game character that traded places with you?" Ace challenged.

"Trade trade lemonade?" Nash said, and I snorted. It was a phrase our mom used to use when we couldn't agree on who got to play with a certain toy.

"Quid," Ace said firmly. "If you wanted to name things, you should have been born a few generations ago."

Nash shrugged. "Fair, I guess." He leaned forward impatiently to inspect the game. "How do we get in here?" He balled his hand into a fist and tapped on the cover of the game as though he were knocking on a door. "Knock knock!" he sang out. "Anyone home?" Nothing happened, which I was expecting. We'd touched a board game here and there, and I'd remember if I'd accidentally been sucked into one.

"Hmmm," Ace said, his hand on his chin, watching us. "I wonder."

"That's your second unexplained *I wonder*," Nash said. "Someone, not me of course, could point out that it's extremely obnoxious." Ace didn't seem to hear him, which was probably a good thing. Nash's sarcasm tended to drift across the line to downright rude, and I had a feeling that Ace wasn't the guy to appreciate a twelve-year-old talking back to him like that. Ace turned away from the game to walk down the length of his bookcases. He paused at the far end and let out a sharp whistle, and Chief lunged to his feet and trotted over to provide his service as a dog key chain.

"You will need a little help to get started, just like your mom and uncle did. Bloodline isn't what it used to be, not that that's your fault, of course." He unlocked the case and reached up to grab a glass jar near the top that I hadn't noticed before. Inside appeared to be a jumble of game pieces of every shape and color, all thrown together like tiny bits of metal and plastic confetti. Ace opened it and started digging around, pushing pieces aside as he searched for something.

Nash glanced over at me questioningly, but something had caught my eye on the shelf behind Ace's head. It was a glass cloche, like one of those old-fashioned ones I'd seen people put plants under, and inside it, suspended on a small metal stick, was a large black beetle. I swallowed, remembering how Ace had picked up a beetle just like that one the last time we'd visited this house. Or, I squinted, taking in its slightly mangled appearance with its broken antennae and bent legs, was it the same one?

"Got it," Ace said as he clanged the lid on before shoving the glass jar back up onto the shelf. The bookcase door was relocked, and he was back, his hand outstretched.

Nash and I leaned forward to study the two small wooden game pieces he held in his hand. They were short and squatty, curved in a way that reminded me a bit of a snowman. One was a light green and the other was a faded orange.

"What are these?" Nash asked, reaching out a finger to poke one experimentally.

"These, boys, are two of the pieces from the original game. The game your great-great-grandfather won to become a Wanderer."

"Cool," I said. "But why are you showing them to us now?"

"I used the blue and red pieces when I first started training your mother and Sam. It helped them get the knack of getting into a game, and it may help you too."

"Do we just hold them?" I asked.

Ace shook his head. "No, you need your hands free. Besides, if you lose it and it falls into the wrong hands . . ." He shuddered in horror, and I didn't need him to finish the thought. Ace opened the desk drawer and dug around until he came out with an old shoelace and a wad of string. A few moments later he'd managed to do a complicated knot around the pieces and looped them over our necks. I'd gotten the shoelace version, and I stared down at the green knobby board game piece.

"Well," Nash said. "Think it works?" He leaned over and rapped his knuckles on the Training Wheels box for a second time. "Knock knock?! Anybody home?"

And then he disappeared.

CRESS

Payment was almost always a problem. For one thing, it wasn't like there was a standard board game currency. Some characters had access to more traditional payment options, like a large hunk of gold, or uncut gemstones, but most didn't. I still remembered one memorable game entitled Farmyard Frenzy where I'd been paid with two chickens and a goat. The chickens had been straightforward enough, and I'd enjoyed having eggs when I wanted them. The goat had been a curse. It had eaten holes into everything from my coat to my gear. I hated that goat. I'd made a new rule for myself on the spot, no live animal payments. So far it had saved me from acquiring a tank of piranhas, a woolly mammoth, a crocodile egg, a dragon hatchling, four live rabbits, and an oversize toad that supposedly could grant three wishes. The toad may have been a mistake to pass up.

This was my first mission where I was employed by a ghost, which was proving to make payment extra tricky. The graveyard itself wasn't so great either. I glanced behind myself, catching another glimpse of the two-headed ghost that had been following me ever since I'd entered the game. He wasn't the one that had hired me, but he'd taken an interest in me that made me edgy. I'd have to deal with him at some point, but I wasn't willing to waste time, energy, or brain space on him yet. At least he was a ghost I could avoid. The one that lived inside my head was harder these days. Entering The Labyrinth Lost had flung open a door to my memories that I'd worked really hard to close, and images I'd tried to forget kept flashing into my mind when I least expected them. The boy with the sparkling green eyes who'd given me a key to freedom even as I sealed his fate. The boy who had had confidence in me before I had confidence in me. I shook my head hard and glared over at the two-headed ghost that was now hovering in a nearby tree. Today was not the day to mess with me. This job had put me in a foul mood, at least that's what I told myself.

My payment was supposed to be delivered up front, and originally I'd thought that ten pounds of gold chain sounded like a good deal for figuring out how to get past the gruesome graveyard's skeleton bridge, but I hadn't accounted for the fact that the chain was underground. The dice in my hand had an unnatural chill to them, and I shifted them carefully from hand to hand, careful not to accidentally roll them. I wasn't going to figure out squat for this ghost if he couldn't pay up, and the fact that he wasn't able to hold anything in his translucent hands was proving to be a real pain.

"Listen," I said, trying hard to keep the frustration from my voice. "I can come back. You figure out how to get that chain up from the grave of Gershwin the Gruesome, or whatever his name was, and I'll figure out how to get past the bridge. Deal?" I wasn't sure what the ghost said back, since I wasn't great at ghost languages, but he seemed to get the point. I nodded, dropped the massive bag of candlesticks I'd been preparing to use, and left the game. I'd be back. But not until payment was procured. I didn't work for free.

TEN

I stood there with my mouth hanging open for a few
seconds, staring at the spot Nash had been standing
in just moments before. Had that really happened?

"Well," Ace said with a smirk. "That worked better
than I expected." A loud, fizzling noise came from my
right a second later, and I jumped sideways in surprise
as a large man dressed head to toe in a black jumpsuit
stood up, glancing around. His face was obscured by a
pair of oversize black racing goggles that magnified his
eyes in a way that made him look rather like a large
black bug. He blinked at us in surprise.

"Hello," Ace said with a nod. "Good to see you."

"Always a pleasure, Jeremy," the biker said in a
surprisingly high-pitched voice before plopping himself
down in an armchair. I looked over at the spot where
Nash had been standing only moments before and

tried to ignore the dizzy, off-balance sensation that was threatening to overwhelm me.

"That's all you have to do to get into a game?" I asked, glancing back at Ace. Chief had made his way over to sit with his shoulder pressed hard against Ace's side. Ace rested his right hand on the dog's massive head; the other he placed flat on the lid of the box. His long, bony fingers splayed out wide, almost obscuring the words Training Wheels.

"There are a few ways," he said. He had a knowing smile on his face that I didn't like, and he made eye contact with me as he leaned forward. "Open sesame," he said, and he and Chief disappeared. For the second time, I felt my jaw drop open in shock.

A resounding pop came from my right, and a second later a large brown bear appeared next to a woman. The woman was crouched low, her hands held up in front of her as though she'd been gripping the handles of a bike only moments before. She wore a gray puff-sleeved jacket that buttoned up the front over a full skirt. The woman looked confused. The bear looked angry.

"Janet," the jumpsuited man said in a bored voice. "Still trying to win the race in a skirt, I see?"

"Mel," Janet said, straightening up from her crouch to adjust her jacket. "Still hanging about without a brain in that noggin of yours. It's a bloomin' miracle!" Neither of them was paying any attention to the bear, whose bulk seemed to take up half of Ace's small office. He busied himself sniffing the shelf to his left, his large black nose leaving a damp fog on the glass, and then he turned to look at me. I froze as a heady combination of fear and adrenaline zipped down my spine, freezing me in place.

"Open sesame!" I cried before squeezing my eyes shut and bracing myself for impact. Nothing happened. I stayed like that, frozen, holding my breath as I waited. The only thing that happened was that something breathed a wet, musty puff of air into my face. I opened my eyes and found myself inches away from the giant black nose of the bear.

"Well, that didn't work, now, did it?" the woman, Janet, said.

"The other bloke put his hand on the box, I believe," Mel said. "Better not make any sudden movements, though. That looks like one of the males, and they can be a might testy this time of year. Liable to take your head clean off as easy as look at you." I swallowed hard, and so slowly I wasn't even sure if I was actually doing it, I inched my hand toward the lid of the box.

"This is incredibly entertaining when it isn't you, isn't it, Janet?" Mel said in obvious appreciation.

"Oh, stuff it, Mel," Janet said. "This jaunt is going to ruin my chances at the win, I'd wager."

"My dear Janet," Mel said condescendingly. "You were never going to win. Just give it up. Go knit or something."

My fingertips bumped the edge of the box, and I felt my heart leap into my throat. I was almost there. The bear snuffled, and I was so close to him that I saw his nose twitch a half second before he sneezed. I winced as bear snot coated my entire face, and then I went for it. I slammed my hand forward onto the lid of the box and croaked, "Open sesame."

This time, I didn't even have time to brace for impact. I felt something yank hard at what felt like my spine, and a second later, I was standing in the middle of a dusty dirt road. Empty farm fields surrounded me on all sides, and I still had bear snot running down my face. It dripped from my cheek, and I reached up to wipe it off with my sleeve.

"Watch it!" someone yelled, and I glanced up to see a pack of bikers speeding toward me over the hill. There had to be at least fifteen of them, all wearing the same round biking goggles Mel had been sporting, hunched over the handlebars of old-fashioned bicycles. I dove off the road and into the underbrush seconds before they would have collided with me. Dirt flew up in a giant cloud as they whizzed by. I coughed, sitting up gingerly. I'd landed hard on some unforgiving rocks, and if I wasn't covered in bruises after this, I'd be shocked. I stood up and stared after the disappearing bikers. Was I supposed to follow them? Where were Nash and Ace? Where was Chief, for that matter?

I glanced back at the road and blinked in surprise. There, sitting in the middle of the road like it had been there all along, was a bike. I approached it cautiously and gave it a poke with a finger. It was solid enough, but there was something off about it. I glanced up and down the road in case another pack of rogue bikers was headed my way, and decided I should probably investigate this thing elsewhere. I grabbed the bike and attempted to lift it, only to discover when my arms gave a painful pop that the thing weighed a metric ton. Well, at least a solid fifty pounds. So I got smart and wheeled the thing off the road. It wasn't until my arms stopped throbbing that I noticed the small wood box affixed to the handlebars. Sitting neatly on top, as though it were the most normal thing in the world, was a set of dice. I picked them up and dropped them carefully onto the wooden box. They clattered around a bit, but to my surprise they stayed neatly on their small platform. Two single dots stared up at me.

"Snake eyes," I murmured. My legs suddenly moved,

as if I was no longer in charge of them, and a second later I was on the bike. I glanced back down at the dice. I had gotten a two. Two what, though? The balls of my feet tingled painfully, and I jerked them up and onto the pedals. The feeling immediately disappeared. Apparently, I was supposed to ride the bike, so I pushed off. It felt heavy under my hands and a bit clunky to pedal, but a bike was a bike, and I headed down the road.

I rounded a corner, lost in thought about my missing twin and what in the world rolling a two meant, and stopped short. The path split into four different directions, each of them nearly identical. I looked this way and that, decided that when you're lost, it doesn't really matter which way you went, and tried to head down the first path. My bike had other ideas. Despite my attempt to turn the handle, the bike took me down the second path. Well, I thought. That's one mystery solved. You roll a two, you take the second path.

I pedaled for what felt like an hour but was probably only ten minutes before I rounded a bend in the road and came face-to-face with a ten-foot-high pile of rocks that completely blocked the path. I slammed on the brakes, only to discover that there apparently weren't any. A second later my wheel made contact with a boulder the size of a hippopotamus, and I pitched forward over the handlebars. My head hit first with a thunk that I felt all the way down to my toenails. I lay sprawled on the rocks in a daze staring up at the blue sky above me. There was something wet underneath the back of my head, and I knew it was blood without checking. I hated blood. Blood was almost a guarantee that I was going to either pass out or puke. This time it was puke, and I rolled to my side and vomited spectacularly all over the rocks to my right. That done, I lay back and shut my eyes, willing the black spots dotting my vision to go away. I had no idea what would happen if I passed out inside a strange board game, but I didn't want to find out.

I'm not sure how long I lay there before I finally got myself together enough to sit up, but when I opened my eyes, I discovered that I'd gained a visitor. A huge bird was perched on the rock above me, staring down with interest. It was black with a fleshy red head that made it look like someone had run over it with a car. I scooted backward with a start as I realized that it was a vulture, and it was currently trying to decide if I was dead.

"Go away!" I yelled, flapping a hand at the bird. It just cocked its head to the side and clacked its beak threateningly. I scrambled to my feet and swung my leg back onto my bike. I was out of here. Except, when I put my foot on the pedal and pushed, it didn't move.

For a second I thought the crash had busted something. With one eye on the giant bird, I gave the bike a quick once-over. Nothing was broken. Desperate, I hopped off and grabbed the handlebars. I'd walk it out of here if I needed to, but the wheels refused to budge. It was like someone had dipped the entire bike in cement. It was then that I remembered the dice. I grabbed them, only to discover that they too were stuck fast in their little box. It wasn't my turn, I realized. The vulture squawked and hopped down a few rocks to inspect the small puddle of blood I'd left on the rock, and my stomach roiled. If I hadn't already hurled everything I'd eaten, I'd have thrown up again.

"There you are!" Ace cried, and I glanced up from my defunct bike to see my grandfather climb over the crest of a pile of rocks, a unicycle slung over his shoulder as casually as you'd carry a tennis racket.

"Where have you been?!" I yelled, all my fear turned into anger in an instant. "I could have been killed! You just disappeared without me! We never read the manual! You said we were supposed to read the manual! You said you were going to train us! This is not training! This is abandonment! Do you even know what came out of this game after you left? A bear! A bear came out of it! And I'm bleeding. I probably have a concussion, and there was this giant vulture-looking thing that I'm pretty sure was considering having me for lunch!"

"Is that all?" Ace asked, eyebrow raised.

"No!" I thundered back. "Where is Nash?"

"I believe he's currently tied up in a race with some early 1900s cyclists. Those were the ones that had one giant front wheel and one tiny back wheel, if memory serves. He was heading toward a Spare Tire card spot, though, so odds are good he'll get held up by something."

I watched my grandfather's lips move, trying desperately to follow what he was telling me. The vulture, undeterred by the appearance of Ace, suddenly landed with outstretched wings to my right and let out a raspy caw that made me jump.

"Hm," Ace said. "Looks like he's not given up on you dying yet." He put his fingers in his mouth and let out a shrill whistle. A second later Chief came bounding up over the rocks to stand beside him, his tongue out and lolling to the side. I'm not sure if dogs can smile, but whatever Chief was doing looked pretty close.

"Good boy," Ace said as he patted the massive creature's head. "Now go catch that oversize chicken before he starts munching on the boy." Chief didn't need any other encouragement. The vulture took one look at the massive dog careening toward him and decided I wasn't worth it.

"Can we leave now?" I whined as I watched it flap away.

"Not quite yet," Ace said. "I think you need to get a couple of more turns under your belt since it looks like your first turn was a bit of a bust. Come over here and let me get a look at that noggin." I obliged. "You're fine. Head wounds just bleed like a stuck pig," he pronounced after a two-second inspection of my skull. "Now, move." He clambered down the rocks before plunking his unicycle down. Then with more grace than I'd have thought possible, he hopped on it, balancing on the single wheel like he'd been doing it his whole life.

"I can't," I said, giving my own bike a tug to demonstrate what I was talking about. Just like before, it stayed stuck to the dirt.

"Oh!" Ace said, slapping his forehead. "That's because it's my turn." He pulled out a small box almost identical to the one affixed to my handlebars. He popped it open and grabbed the dice. He was about to roll them when he froze mid–dice shake and glanced over at me. "Once I roll this," he said, "I'm going to have to move. Be prepared to roll your dice and follow me."

"How do I get out?" I said. "If something happens to you or I can't find you or whatever. How do I get out of this game?" I felt like this should have probably been lesson one.

"Right," Ace said, cocking his head to the side in consideration. "I probably should have gone over that before you two entered the game."

"Ya think?" I muttered. Chief looked over at me and whined, but Ace just considered me a moment, weighing me with his eyes. "Don't you know?" I finally asked. My head hurt, and I was sick of wasting time. Besides, the fact that Ace was only vaguely aware of the whereabouts of my twin had me on edge.

"Sorry," Ace said. "It's like this. How would you explain to someone how to breathe?"

"Um, I don't think anyone has ever *actually* explained that to someone," I said. "It's just something you automatically know how to do."

"Right," Ace said. "Well, this is the same way. As far as I can figure it, I *think* my way out. I imagine myself back in my office, I pull that image up from my toes through my veins, past my stomach and lungs, and embed it in my head. And once it's good and stuck, I open my eyes, and then I'm back."

I blinked at him in astonishment. "Seriously?" I said. "All that to get out, but the way in is open sesame?"

"I never said that board game bounding made a whole lot of sense," Ace said. "If that doesn't work, just give that game piece around your neck a good twirl—that should do the trick too. Now let's go." He rolled the dice in his hand before dropping them into a small box that matched the one on my own bicycle, and before I could ask any more questions he was pedaling away on the unicycle, Chief trotting along at his side as though this was just a regular Tuesday. I made a mental note to ask Ace why the dog didn't need to roll dice to make a move and glanced down at my own set of dice. This time when I grabbed for them, they came free easily, and with a deep breath, I rolled them for a second time. "Lucky number seven," I muttered as I glanced from the little black dots to the road ahead. The uncomfortable tingle in my feet started immediately, and I put my feet on the pedals and took off after Ace and Chief. I was so focused on keeping my ancient bike upright while simultaneously keeping an eye on my quickly disappearing grandfather that I almost didn't notice the sound coming from behind me until it was too late.

ELEVEN

"That was amazing," Nash said as he thumped down into the threadbare chair across from Ace and his intimidating desk. His eyes were shining, and he had a dopey grin on his face that seemed to stretch from ear to ear. My palms tingled, and I flexed them before shoving them deep into my pockets. Smacking that look off my brother's face would feel good. Fantastic actually, but it wouldn't really be helpful, or even fair for that matter. It wasn't his fault that his first time in a board game had been, what had he said, amazing? My head throbbed, and I shifted the bag of frozen peas Ace had handed me onto a tender spot on my head. They were thawing faster than seemed fair and ice-cold water was dripping down my neck and making the back of my shirt wet. Still, it was an improvement over being in Training Wheels.

"Incredible," Nash went on, oblivious to the fact that I was finding new levels of misery to enter as he sat there waxing poetic about a board game. "I had no idea that's what it was going to be like. I mean, I've never felt more alive!"

"Probably because you didn't almost get killed," I muttered. "Twice."

"Oh!" he said, sitting up so fast his bottle of water went flying, further drenching me. "I did! Three times actually. Did you make that stampeding herd of buffalo mad? They do NOT like bikes, let me tell you. I thought I was a goner for sure. That was before I almost fell off that cliff! I knew I'd drawn a dead-end card, but I didn't realize how literal a dead end could be!"

This play on words made our grandfather chuckle as he watched Nash. His eyes were shining too, although I had a feeling that his were shining for an entirely different reason.

"Don't look so glum!" Ace said, noticing the sour expression that I was making no effort to hide. "You didn't die either!"

"It could have gone better," I said.

"True," Ace said.

"When do we go again?" Nash said. "Are we ready to start looking for our mom now?"

Ace shook his head. "Not yet," he said. "The games

Ogden would have hidden your mother in make Training Wheels look like, well, training wheels," he finished with a shrug. "Besides, your first lesson didn't exactly go as planned." Nash sagged in disappointment, and I wondered just how many games we were going to have to go into before Ace deemed us "ready."

"Can we go in another one today?" Nash said. "I think Rhett needs to get right back on that horse!"

"Horse?" Ace said. "We can do a horse." With a quick spin of his chair, he was on his feet and facing the bookcases. He walked down the line of boxes, murmuring to himself as he tapped at his chin. "Horses, hm," he murmured. "Mustangs, perhaps? Rodeo? No, no, they aren't ready for the bulls yet. Miniature ponies? No, too easy. Perhaps, hm, yes, I think this will do."

He whistled for Chief, who trotted over, happy to fulfill his purpose as a furry key chain, and Ace unlocked a bookcase. He reached up and drew out a box with lettering made to look like a rope twirling across the cover, and sat it down on his desk before carefully relocking the case and returning the key to Chief's neck. I made a mental note to check out Chief's neck at the first opportunity as Nash jumped to his feet. I slowly got to mine to see what new horror was awaiting us.

"Winning the West?" I said as I squinted at the faded image pressed into the cardboard. It looked like the silhouettes of cowboys.

"Well, this looks awesome," Nash said as he tapped his finger on the cover. And then, for the second time that afternoon, he was gone.

"Seriously?" I said. "Why is getting in *so* easy? And getting out so hard?" It had taken me five tries to think my way out of Training Wheels, and I'd eventually given up and used the game piece tied around my neck. There was a now-familiar fizzle to our right, and a woman appeared wearing a floor-length calico dress with a dirty apron tied around her waist. She seemed too thin, the bones on her face too prominent, and she was holding what I was pretty sure was a potato. She seemed shocked to find herself standing in an office instead of a garden, until she saw the box on the table.

"So the game does have a rope on the cover," she murmured, sinking down into the chair Nash had just left. "I always thought that was just a legend."

"Sorry, ma'am," Ace said, tipping an imaginary hat in her direction. "No time to chat. I have a young'un that just took your place in the game. Any chance you know if it's your turn soon?" I raised an eyebrow at Ace. He'd adjusted his speech ever so slightly to match the woman's. I wondered if it was a conscious decision or an unconscious one.

"No, sir," she said. "I just pulled a Tornado card."

Ace muttered something under his breath I was pretty sure you weren't supposed to say in front of a lady, and before I could say a word, he'd grabbed my arm. A second later he was knocking on the cover of the box, and I felt something yank on my spine for the second time that day. It was time to enter the game.

And so our training had begun. Not how Ace had planned it, or how I expected it, but it went. It turned out that the only way to learn how to board game bound was to actually board game bound. A lot. That first day we went in and out of five different games. My least favorite one was Lava Land, which wasn't a huge surprise since volcanos were usually not a ton of fun as a general rule. I walked into our small room at the end of the day on legs that felt like jelly. Along the way I'd collected another head wound, bringing my grand total of noggin knocks up to two. Thankfully the second hadn't resulted in any blood. I'd also skinned my left knee, jammed the big toe on my right foot, sliced my hand open, and contracted what I was pretty sure was poison ivy. Nash hobbled in beside me, grimacing. The golden boy hadn't bounded unscathed, a fact that shouldn't have made me happy but did. He'd gotten a black eye from a grumpy gorilla and an arrow in the shoulder from a warrior of the Woebegone Tribe.

"What about Mom?" I said as I flopped down onto

my bunk, my head heavy. I heard Nash flop down and then jump to his feet with a surprised yelp.

"What!" I said, sitting up.

"Sorry," he said. "Just lay down on a guinea pig."

"That's probably the tamest thing you've done all day," I said.

"Compared to that gorilla, anything would be tame," Nash said as he dug around in the sheets to extract a grumpy Geronimo Jones. He'd obviously chosen to ignore my advice to put the stinky animal into a box. "But you're right," Nash continued. "How long before Ace lets us start looking for her? I mean, we did pretty good today, all things considered."

"Does poison ivy blister?" I asked as I inspected my wrist. "Asking for a friend."

"I think so," Nash said, and then sighed. "Mom would know."

"Do you think it's weird that Ace is Mom's dad?" I asked as I propped myself up on my arm.

"What do you mean?" Nash said. "She had to have a dad. That's how biology works."

"Not that, dummy," I said. I'd have chucked a pillow at him if I'd had even a shred of energy left, but I didn't. So instead I stared up at the ceiling, counting the knots in the wood.

"It's just that they aren't really that alike," I said.

"With the exception of the peanut butter and banana sandwiches."

"I don't know," Nash said. "I was thinking about that today while I was lost in that dust storm in Winning the West, and I think maybe she *used* to be like Ace. But she had to change, because of us. Because of what happened to Sam."

"Maybe," I said. There was a long pause, and I wondered for a second if Nash had fallen asleep.

"I'd never be the same if something happened to you," Nash said, and I nodded, swallowing hard. I wasn't going to imagine life without Nash.

"We need to be careful," I said. "It's all a game, but it's not, ya know? If we die in there, that's it."

"Do you think Mom's okay?" Nash said.

"I do," I said. "I think I'd feel it if something had happened to her. Like, the universe would shift or something." I blinked at tears that were suddenly in my eyes and forced myself to refocus on the ceiling. I think it was because I was trying so hard not to think about my mom that I suddenly saw it. Her name, Natalie, was carved ever so lightly into the soft pine wood of the ceiling. I reached up a finger and ran my hand over it. It looked like she had taken a pencil or a toothpick and ever so carefully left her mark.

"This was Mom's room," I whispered.

"Duh," Nash said, yawning. "Where else would she and Sam have slept?"

"Oh," I said, feeling dumb, then shook off the feeling. "I think you're right," I said. "We need to make Ace let us start looking soon. He can train us at the same time. Lord knows we need it."

"Speak for yourself, I'm a natural," Nash said, but the words dripped with his signature sarcasm, and I smiled.

"Right," I said. "That gorilla thought the same thing."

"Didn't a vulture try to carry you away?" Nash said. "I mean, that's a fantastically dumb way to die."

"Yeah," I said. "Good point. Let's get some sleep, though. If we have to do that all again tomorrow, we're going to need it."

"Right," Nash said. A moment later his soft snores filled our small room, and I let my eyes shut. I'd survived day one. I was almost certain that I'd survive day two.

CRESS

Now this game was more like it. I smiled down at my newest job offering. The Orange Bug Catcher had employed me on more than one occasion, and he always paid up. Of course, his payments came very close to breaking my no live animal rule, but sugar bugs stopped being bugs and turned into solid sugar as soon as you got them out of the game. Orange Bug Catcher was an expert at catching the elusive butter-scotch butterflies, and he knew they were my weakness. Besides, Sugar Bugs was a game I didn't mind lingering in—no ghosts, no vicious octopuses, no mazes full of memories. There were the bugs, of course, but those didn't bother me. I'd never tell Orange Bug Catcher this, but sometimes I visited Sugar Bugs just for fun. If he knew that, he'd think he could get away with paying me less.

The job seemed pretty straightforward. Get through the first few turns of Sugar Bugs and figure out how to get past the River of Rainbow Gelatin. I agreed to the job but made sure I let him know that I wasn't going to be able to get there for a bit. I had to beat this blasted game first. I heard a click behind me and ducked as someone fired a shot at my head and missed. Whirling, I spotted a man wearing a masquerade mask holding a smoking gun. Mystery games were a particular favorite of mine, and I was fairly positive that I had the gunman right this time. If I didn't, and I called out the wrong name, I'd have to go back to the start and that horrendous ballroom.

"Herbert Humphrey!" I called out. The man in the mask froze, and as though his arm had a mind of its own, he pulled off his mask. I smiled, my lips curling upward. "Gotcha," I said.

TWELVE

"**I** told you yesterday, you're not ready yet," Ace said the next morning. "Not even close."

"We know that," I said. "Trust me. If yesterday showed us anything, it was that we aren't exactly great at this. But we still have to try."

"Yeah," Nash agreed. "What if something happens to our mom while we're taking joyrides through the easy games?"

"That's a risk we're going to have to take," Ace said, but he averted his eyes when he said it. I leaned forward to scrutinize his face, noticing the prominent dark circles under his eyes as he reached for what had to be his third cup of coffee. I wasn't positive, but I'd bet Geronimo Jones that he'd been busy after we went to bed. We might not be ready to find our mom, but he was.

"Your games," I said, deciding to change the subject for a moment. "Why don't I recognize any of them?"

"Why would we?" Nash said. "We've never been allowed to play any." He paused, cocking his head as he turned to grin at me. "You know, how weird Mom was about that makes a whole lot of sense after yesterday. Remind me to apologize for giving her such a hard time about it."

"I'm not apologizing," I grumbled. "She should have warned us or prepared us. Not lied to us." Thinking of all the bizarre ways our mother had kept us from board games over the years refocused me, and I turned back to Ace, not ready to drop my question just yet.

"Mom didn't let us play games, but we weren't raised without any access to the outside world. I mean, I've watched a commercial or two, so where are all those games?" I asked. I held up a hand and started rattling off the names of a few of the more popular board games I'd heard about. I looked up at Ace. "Why are all of your board games so, um, old?"

"Because they *are* old," Ace said. "They are all over fifty years old. That one," he said, pointing to a box positioned on a top shelf next to a jar of moss, "is over a hundred years old if it's a day. The older the game, the easier the bounding. Newer games don't hold the same level of imagination that the older generation does. In fact, some of these games are the last copy in existence." Ace took a sip of coffee. "Those games you were prattling on about," he said, "they're tough. Too new. The board game characters haven't figured out up from down yet. I don't mess with them as a general rule. Besides, Ogden would never enter a new game, not if his life depended on it."

"This Ogden character," I said. "What can you tell us about him besides the fact that he became a Wander Lost? What game is he from?"

"The Pirate's Wrath," Ace said with a shudder. "Worst game to ever be created, if you ask me. I only ever entered it once, and once was more than enough." Nash and I leaned forward simultaneously, and then as though we'd planned it, we propped one hand under our chins and waited expectantly. Ace watched this performance with an eyebrow raised in amusement. "I take it you boys want me to elaborate?" he said. We nodded and he stifled a grimace as he considered us. Reading our faces as though trying to weigh how badly we wanted this information.

"It's not my favorite subject," he finally said, pouring himself yet another cup of coffee. Chief whined at his side, and Ace slipped him a bite of cinnamon roll.

"Where did the game come from?" I asked, hoping to get things started.

"Sam," Ace said. "He liked to poke around old antique stores and flea markets in search of rare board games. He bought it off a man at a flea market that he was convinced was an actual pirate." Nash's hand shot in the air, and Ace paused.

"Yes?" he said.

"How in the world do you know if someone's a pirate?" he asked. "I mean, I didn't think people walked around with a peg leg and a hook for a hand anymore. We have prosthetics and stuff now, right?" He looked to me for confirmation, like I was now an expert on prosthetics. I shrugged an affirmative. After all, I hadn't ever seen someone walk around with a hook.

"Apparently the man had an eye patch and parrot and the whole nine yards. I figured it was just a story, a persona put on by a clever salesman. Anyway, Sam brought it home and hid it in his room. Unknown to me, he started going in and out of the game on a regular basis. Your mother found out and insisted that he take her along. That's when it all went south. On that last trip into the game, Ogden came out. That was an unpleasant surprise to discover, let me tell you. The mermaid was no picnic either. Ghastly beasts, mermaids."

"So Ogden's a pirate too," I said.

"He's a monster," Ace snapped, and I jumped. "But yes," Ace went on, "he's also a pirate. Or he was before he became a Wander Lost."

"So he came out when our mom and Sam went in," Nash prompted. "Was he in your office?"

"He was," Ace said. "He is one of the first board game characters I've ever met who wasn't completely focused on returning to his own game. He was intrigued by our world. By the other games in my bookcases. Your mother and Sam left it unlocked. Foolish. Stupid. Careless." Chief let out a low woof, and Ace glanced down at him.

"Correct," he told the dog. "They also didn't take you with them. Which was equally foolish."

"Did you go in after them?" I asked.

Ace's face turned an unnatural gray, and his entire demeanor changed. He shook his head. "Not then. I should have. But I was too concerned about the damage Ogden was inflicting on my office. He was poking around the games. Damaging some of them. Destroying others. The bookcases were regular glass back then, and he'd shattered two of them by the time I got there. Of course, the second I opened the office door, he made a run for it. So I didn't go in after my kids. And it's a decision I'll regret every second of every day for the rest of my life."

Nash caught on faster than I did. "Sam never came back out, did he?" he said, his voice so quiet he was practically whispering.

Ace shook his head ruefully. "Your mother came back. Hysterical. Absolutely beside herself, and so worked up that I couldn't even understand what she was trying to tell me. Through all the tears and the screaming I gathered that something horrible had happened to my Sam. I gave up on containing Ogden then, and he immediately took off. I let him go. I knew that as soon as I got Sam out of the game, Ogden would have to go back into the game. I entered The Pirate's Wrath, but I was too late." He let that statement hang in the air, and I had to bite my lip to keep from asking how exactly he'd been too late. I wanted to know details that were obviously too painful for him to discuss. Still, questions ran in a furious loop through my brain. Had he recovered Sam's body? Was there a body to recover? Was that why Ogden didn't get pulled back into his game?

"Is that why you destroyed Ogden's game?" Nash asked, snapping me from my own spiral of unanswered questions. "Because of what happened to Sam inside it?"

Ace huffed an impatient sigh, as though he wished he could just get on with it and wrap up the entire conversation. "Partially. Part of me wanted to destroy the thing that had destroyed my son, but a bigger part of me wanted to keep my family safe. I knew that as soon as Ogden figured out that he could bring his cronies or anything else he fancied out of his game by shoving a Benson into it, we'd never be safe. It was on his orders that Sam was killed. He'd been watching Sam flit in and out of his game, and he'd bribed one of his crew for information on the strange boy who kept showing up. He figured out that in order to leave The Pirate's Wrath and gain the freedom that Sam had, he needed to eliminate Sam. So he put a plan into place for his crew to carry out should he ever disappear and the strange boy appear in his place."

"What happened to Ogden after you destroyed his game?" I asked. "You said he got away from you. Did you ever find him again?"

"I didn't have to," Ace said. "He found me. And he would have found your mother, but thankfully she was gone the night he found me."

"I take it that didn't go well?" Nash said.

Instead of responding Ace just turned his head to the side and slid down the collar of his shirt to reveal a long white scar that encircled half his neck. Nash let out a whistle of appreciation.

"How do you know that Ogden became a Wander Lost, and not a Wanderer?" I asked. "Because Sam died in the game and couldn't come back?"

Ace nodded as he looked down at Chief. "You have

to know how to win your game to become a Wanderer. It's earned, and it's rare. Other than your great-great-grandfather, I've only heard of one other Wanderer in all my years of bounding." He shook his head. "No, Ogden became something different. Had he become a true Wanderer with the ability to carry things out of games, our world wouldn't be safe. Not for a minute." His lips pressed together in a line, and I got the distinct feeling that he was hiding something.

"There's another Wanderer?" Nash said, leaning forward. "Who?"

"A girl, probably a hair older than you two," Ace said. "Although a true Wanderer doesn't age, as far as I can figure. She's thirteen, but she's been thirteen ever since I met her."

"Do we get to meet her?" Nash said.

"Not if I can help it," Ace said. I decided not to push the subject. There was something about the set of his mouth that made it clear that we weren't going to win this battle.

"Is it time to start training now?" Nash said. Ace nodded. My stomach churned, but I pushed the nerves aside. The story of Ogden and The Pirate's Wrath was one that would stick with me as long as I lived. I knew that. I didn't have to witness my mother's hysterics to be able to picture it in vivid, heart-wrenching detail.

Losing your twin would feel like losing a part of yourself. A part you couldn't ever get back, no matter how hard you tried. It would make you want to run, to hide, to avoid any mention of the thing that had ripped that gigantic hole in your heart. The tight feeling of anger in my chest loosened ever so slightly as I felt myself forgive my mom a little bit. I was starting to understand now why she left and never looked back. Except, I remembered, she *had* looked back.

I leaned against the wall as Ace locked the bolts on the office door behind us, thinking. Our mom *had* come back. She'd hauled Nash and me to this cabin years ago when we were nothing but a couple of drooling toddlers. Why?

I had to push the memory aside, though. It was time to train.

Ten minutes later Nash and I were staring at the board game in front of us with similar expressions of confusion.

"Seriously?" Nash said. "Sugar Bugs? This looks like a toddler's game or something." I had to agree. The cover sported lollipops the size of trees set in front of mountains of what looked like giant gumdrops. Cotton candy clouds flew overhead, and on a candy-paved path were four smiling men holding oversize bug nets.

Ace huffed out a sigh. "Look closer," he instructed.

We did, leaning in so we could get a better look at the detailed illustration. It took me a second, but I saw it. "Are those bugs?" I said, sitting back.

"That looks like a candy bar," Nash said, pointing, "but it's actually some kind of giant centipede. Isn't it?"

"I thought sugar bugs were cavities," I said, glancing over at Ace. "Mom always said we needed to brush our teeth at night to get rid of the sugar bugs."

"Well, these sugar bugs are real," Ace said. "It's about time you two learn that you can't judge a game by its box." He gingerly opened the box, using the same cautious movements I'd seen actors use to defuse bombs in movies. He slipped out a yellowed instruction booklet and passed it to me.

"Read this. When you're done, holler, and we can go in together."

"Wait, where are you going?" I said.

"The woods. Firewood's running low," Ace said, as though this was all the explanation we should need. He left, banging the office door shut behind him, and I glanced over at Nash.

"Now what?" he said.

"I guess we read about candy bugs?" I said. Nash grunted his agreement, and we hunched over the ancient-looking booklet. It seemed straightforward enough. The candy-coated path had a start and a finish. To get to the end, you had to make your way through Gumdrop Mountain, Lollipop Landing, Syrup Swamp, and the Cinnamon Caves, all while trapping, avoiding, or catching different sugar bugs. Just like in Training Wheels, there were cards that would either really screw things up for you or catapult you farther down the board.

"What's it mean about spinning a red?" Nash asked, shouldering me to the side so he could squint at the tiny print.

"You need glasses," I muttered, not for the first time.

"Do not," Nash said. "This is just written in mouse-sized handwriting. People must have had better eyesight back when this thing was made. When *was* this thing made?" he said, flipping the box over to inspect the back. The contents inside rattled, and I found myself holding my breath as he casually handled the box.

"Careful!" I said. "You shouldn't touch that until Ace gets back. Remember yesterday?" I instinctively reached for the game piece still hanging around my neck and wondered if we should take them off whenever we were handling a game. They obviously amplified our Wanderer blood, or whatever it was that let us bound into games.

"Right," Nash said, setting the box back down.

"If you get stuck, you have to spin a red to get unstuck," I read.

"This seems like a baby game," Nash whined.

"We thought that about Training Wheels too," I pointed out. "And I ended up with a head wound and a vulture problem."

"Right," Nash said, folding his arms across his chest, considering. "Who do you think the other Wanderer is? The one Ace mentioned. She apparently knows how to beat games." He thrust his chin out toward the box. "That's not that impressive. I bet we could beat this one with our eyes shut."

"Speak for yourself," I muttered.

"Where is Ace?" Nash said, shifting impatiently from foot to foot. "What's so important in the woods?"

"Firewood?" I said.

"Boring." Nash sighed and then glanced over at me. "Think he'd be mad if we went in without him? I mean, the game seems pretty straightforward."

"Yes," I said. "Furious."

"Darn," Nash huffed. "That's kind of what I thought." He thumped back into one of the office chairs to wait, but I walked down the long glass bookcases behind Ace's desk, reading the names on boxes.

"You know," I said. "Some of these games actually sound familiar."

"No way," Nash said. "That's impossible. Ace said they're all old and crusty."

"I don't think he used the word *crusty*," I said.

"Whatever," Nash said. "Old as dirt."

"Phantom's Parade," I said, tapping the glass as I peered in at one of the boxes. "I know I've heard of that."

"Wait, what?" Nash said, hopping to his feet. "No way that's in there. That's a video game, isn't it? I think it just came out, like, a month or two ago."

I nodded. Now that Nash said it, I was almost positive that I'd heard some guys in one of my classes talking about it.

"It must be a coincidence," Nash said. He stood beside me and inspected the boxes behind the glass. "Wait a minute," he said, leaning forward. "There's another one. Giant Games. I know for a fact that's a video game."

"It's not that uncommon to take something and make it into something else. Look at how many books have been turned into movies. Maybe that's a new thing, turning old board games into video games." Before Nash could answer we heard footsteps, and Ace came stomping back into his office in mud-covered boots. He looked grouchy as he plunked himself down behind his desk.

"Read it?" he asked.

"Yes, sir," I said. Nash glanced over at me with a

raised eyebrow and I shrugged. I'd never used the word *sir* in my life, but now seemed like as good a time as any to start.

"Then let's go," he said gruffly, and he put a hand down on the top of the lid and waited. Nash and I followed suit, and I was proud of myself for not hesitating this time.

"All together now," he said.

"Open sesame!" we said, and I shut my eyes as I dropped out of my own world and into the world of Sugar Bugs.

THIRTEEN

There are probably a lot stupider ways to die than death by gumdrop, but I was having a hard time thinking of any. Granted, this was no ordinary gumdrop. For starters, it was purple. Which doesn't make it any scarier, but I doubted I was the only one who didn't want to get squished by something that probably tasted like grape Tylenol. For another thing, when it unrolled, it was actually a Gumdrop Glowworm, complete with a gaping mouth that made the most awful sucking noise I'd ever heard. I made a mental note to tell Nash that if I did in fact die in a board game, which at the moment seemed pretty darn likely, he was allowed to lie through his teeth about what actually killed me. Unless it was a lion or a dinosaur or something, in which case he could advertise that far and wide.

"Rhett! Catch!" Nash's voice called to my left, and

I took my eyes off the giant rolling purple lump long enough to glance over at my brother. If *anyone* else had said *anything* else, I wouldn't have looked. But I'd learned the hard way that when Nash yelled "catch" it meant that whatever he was throwing was already launched. I'd been brained by everything from a log to a piggy bank shaped like Yoda in the learning of that particular lesson. So I looked, my hand going up instinctively to catch whatever it was before it made contact with my skull. My fingers closed around something flat and flimsy, and I glanced down to see that he'd thrown me the spinner. How he'd managed to get the spinner, I didn't know, but when you're about to get smashed by a bug disguised as a giant gumdrop, you don't really question how your butt is about to be saved, you just save your butt. At least, that was my motto.

I flicked the spinner and watched as it whirled around the flimsy cardboard square. The rolling glowworm was making a horrible squelching, squishing noise that reminded me of someone plunging a toilet, and I glanced down at my feet, wishing with all that I was worth for the spinner to land on red. If it landed on red, my feet would be released from the brown sugar sludge. Any other color? I'd get smashed.

I braced for impact just as the spinner finally

stopped on red. My feet popped free of the sticky brown muck, and I catapulted end over end down the candy-encrusted path. I landed with a thump that knocked the wind out of me and I lay staring up at the sky, wheezing painfully as air tried to force its way back into my deflated lungs. A second later I saw Nash's concerned face over mine, followed a second later by the less concerned face of Ace.

"Anything broken?" Ace said.

"I don't think so?" I said, peering up. "Do you have a way to check?" Ace snorted in amusement and stood up, his face disappearing from view. I sat up gingerly. My clothes were liberally coated in something crusty and white, and I brushed at it.

"Powdered sugar," Ace said without looking at me. He was scanning the horizon, his nose wrinkled in concentration. I got some of the white stuff on my finger and was about to taste it when Ace knocked my hand away from my mouth. "You don't eat in a game," he thundered. "I told you that." I froze, looking down at my sugar-covered clothes. I'd forgotten.

"Amateur move," Nash joked. "It's almost like we've only been doing this for a day."

"The rules are the rules," Ace said. "You need to engrave them in your brain."

"Sounds painful," I said as I stood up with a wince.

145

"We better be getting back," Ace said. "You two need another lesson on the rules. That's obvious. Besides, there's no telling what mess is awaiting us in my office."

"Is there a way to know what comes out of a game when we go in?" I asked.

"Yeah," Nash said. "Like, is there a giant ice cream cone cicada dripping in your office right now? Or one of those Syrup Swamp Spiders that almost got us three moves ago?"

"I swapped places with a Butterscotch Butterfly," Ace said.

"That seems pretty tame," Nash said.

"It is," Ace agreed. "Tamest critter in this game. Of course, it's made out of actual butterscotch, so there is usually a mess to clean up. I have no idea who swapped places with you two, though. That should be a fun surprise to go back to. Follow me, boys." He shut his eyes, and a moment later he was gone.

I let out a sigh and glanced around at the candy-coated world. To our right a line of ladybugs sporting hard jawbreaker shells marched in a line while a grasshopper made completely from spun sugar hopped lazily from here to there and back again. The game had been harder than we'd thought.

"Do you think it's weird that we never saw those

bug catcher men from the box?" I said, glancing around.

"Rhett," Nash said. "Everything about this is weird. In fact, weird doesn't even begin to cover it."

"Good point," I said as I glanced around at the brightly colored world full of sweets and swarming insects. I inhaled the overpowering sent of cotton candy and sneezed. Wiping my nose, I turned back to Nash. "We better follow Ace," I said, shutting my eyes as I grabbed my game piece and prepared to attempt the uncomfortable mental flip that would bring me back to my own world.

"Wait," Nash said, his hand on my arm. I opened my eyes to look at him.

"What?" I said.

"Let's do a couple of turns by ourselves," Nash said. "Without Ace. How are we ever going to prove that we're ready to look for Mom unless we start doing some of this on our own?"

"Do I need to remind you that I almost just got smashed by a Gumdrop Glowworm? A glowworm so massive that I thought it was a mountain?"

"*Almost* is the key word there. Right?" Nash said, and then laughed. "You should have seen your face when you started climbing that thing and realized it was actually a worm."

"Thanks," I said dryly.

Nash flashed one of his wide smiles that always seemed to win people over. "Come on," he cajoled. "We're bound to do better on our next spin." I stared at him for a second and then huffed.

"Fine," I said, "but just one turn. We can tell Ace that we had a hard time thinking ourselves back out of the game or something."

Before I could second-guess this decision, he had the spinner out of my hand and was inspecting it cautiously. Ahead of us stretched the candy-coated path that reminded me a lot of Dorothy's yellow brick road in Oz. Only this one was paved in round, brightly colored candies the size of sewer grates. My stomach rumbled, and I huffed at the irony of hanging out in a world made of candy, but not being allowed to taste any. A lump of rock candy by my foot chose that moment to stand up and scurry away, and I changed my mind. I wouldn't eat a thing in this game, even if it was an option.

"You're up," I said. "My last spin got me out of that sugar trap, or whatever it was."

"Right," Nash said, taking a breath. He held up the spinner and gave it a decisive flick. It didn't budge, and Nash squawked and flapped his hand. "Ouch! That hurt!" he said, inspecting his nail.

"Why didn't that work?" I asked.

"No clue," Nash muttered, sucking on his sore finger. "You try."

I gave the spinner a more cautious flick, but it didn't move for me either. Suddenly there was a loud crack to our right, and I ducked instinctively, throwing my hands over my head. A second later I felt something small and hard raining down on us. My first thought was hail, and I winced as whatever it was hit my bare arms and neck. Glancing down, I saw that it wasn't hail at all, it was sprinkles.

They were no ordinary sprinkles, though, just like the gumdrop that almost crushed me hadn't been an ordinary gumdrop. They were huge, each one roughly the size of a pencil. Still getting pelted, I bent down to inspect the pile at my feet and blinked in surprise. The sprinkles were moving, or at least it looked like they were. Flashes of green, yellow, blue, and hot pink quivered at my feet.

"Rhett?" Nash said, "are these sprinkles? Or snakes?" That was when I noticed their eyes. A blue one reared back and struck my hand faster than lightning, leaving two perfect puncture marks in my forearm.

"Both!" I yelped, taking off at a run. All around us Sprinkle Snakes were falling from the sky only to land at our feet in squirming piles. I had no idea if Nash was following me, but I headed off the path toward what looked like a bunch of trees made out of twisted black licorice. As soon as I got underneath their shelter the battering of Sprinkle Snakes dropping from the sky stopped, and I whirled to see if Nash was behind me only to have him collide with me at full speed. We both went sprawling backward into the underbrush. We didn't stay down long, though. Nash got to his feet first and launched himself onto the branch of the closest tree. I followed suit. It was only then that I stopped panicking long enough to attempt to catch my breath. Below us hundreds of Sprinkle Snakes climbed all over themselves like tiny pastel nightmares.

"Can we go now?" I finally managed to gasp.

"Gladly," Nash said. "Where in the world did they come from?"

"Sugar Suggestion card," came a female voice directly over our heads, and we both yelped as we craned our necks back to look up. The tree twisted skyward into thick, gnarled branches that wound over one another in dizzying licorice loops. Above us was a shadowed figure perched on a branch like some kind of strange bird. She moved, climbing down gracefully as she swung from branch to branch with an almost unnerving grace. Not like a bird, I thought as I watched, like a lion. The hair on the back of my neck stood on end, and I felt Nash shift nervously beside me. We'd been in a handful of games, but we'd never actually talked to anyone *inside* a game. It had always just been us and Ace. Even in Training Wheels, where other bikers were racing around us almost constantly, not one of them had ever noticed us or paused to talk. It was like every single one of them had some kind of odd tunnel vision that made us invisible. I'd liked being invisible.

The figure stopped on a branch a few feet above us and lowered the ruby-red cloak from her head. To my surprise I found myself staring at a girl roughly our own age. Her eyes were bright green, set wide and barely visible behind a massive tangle of black curls. She had half the curls pulled back with a thick leather strap, but a fringe of wayward coils had sprung free around her face. Her brown skin had a thick smattering of freckles across the bridge of her nose, and she wore one gold earring shaped like a key. Her legs were covered in thick black leggings, and a leather belt around her waist held a variety of small pouches and sheaths for what I assumed were knives.

"You're not the Orange Bug Catcher," she said, sounding disappointed.

"No," Nash said slowly. "Are you?"

The girl snorted in surprise and shook her head. Her curls jumped happily around her face, and for the second time I got the impression of a lion shaking out its mane. There was something feline in the way she moved, as though her muscles were more liquid than ours. She made me uneasy, as though it *were* a lion perched on the branch above us, and not a girl our own age.

"No," she said. "Definitely not. But if you're not a bug catcher, then who are you? I thought all characters in this game were candy themed." She looked us up and down and raised an eyebrow. I opened my mouth to answer and then closed it with a snap. Wasn't there a rule about not revealing ourselves to be—What had Ace called us? Interlopers? Intruders? Trespassers? I couldn't remember the exact word, but I knew it meant that we didn't belong here. I wished fervently that Ace hadn't headed back before us, or that we hadn't been dumb enough to think that we could do a turn by ourselves.

"I'm Nash and this is Rhett," Nash said. I let out a sigh of relief. Leave it to Nash to figure out how to answer the girl's question without actually answering it. She narrowed her eyes at us.

"Are you from the Chocolate Swamp? Or Lemon Drop Lake? I heard some of the merpeople sometimes shake their tails and wander about the game. Not that I blame them; terrible place, Lemon Drop Lake. So sour it will make your tongue bleed. I wouldn't want to stay there either."

"Really?" Nash said dryly. "Is it snake infested?

152

Because right now anywhere sounds better than here."

"Sorry about the Sprinkle Snakes," she said, wrinkling her nose.

"You did that?" I said, unable to keep the accusation out of my voice. "That was disgusting."

"*Creepy* is the word I'd use," Nash said with a shudder.

"Not my best first move," the girl said a bit ruefully. "But I didn't get sent back to start, or maimed, so that's always something." She glanced down to the foot of the tree, where the snakes were still swarming around like multicolored spaghetti. "They should get absorbed by the game after the next player spins," she said with a dismissive wave of her hand. She gave the spinner in her hand an experimental flick and huffed in exasperation when it didn't move.

"This is the worst part," she said. "Waiting for some player on the other side of a game to finally get around to making their move." We were both staring at her, a bit bewildered, and she gave us a sympathetic look. "Sorry," she said. "I always forget that supporting cast never has a clue what I'm talking about. Most don't even realize they're in a game, bless their clueless little hearts." She glanced over at us again. "No offense."

"None taken." I shrugged.

She sniffed, gave the spinner another useless flick, and then leaned back against her branch. Obviously settling in to wait it out. I glanced over at Nash, who had a look on his face that I wasn't sure I liked.

He pulled our spinner out of his pocket and gave it a hard flick. Instantly the sound of slithering snakes below us disappeared, and I looked down to see the Sprinkle Snakes dissolving. The girl sat bolt upright and stared down at us with wide eyes.

"How did you get a spinner?" she snapped. "Who are you?!" Nash was making his way quickly out of the tree, and I shot the girl an apologetic glance before hurrying after him. I landed in the mercifully snake-free dirt a moment after Nash, and we both waited as though bracing for impact. No impact came.

"What did you spin?" I said.

"A four," he said. "A green four." The path in front of us wound deeper into the woods, and I glanced back longingly at the open, sunlit field behind us. Granted, I'd almost died out there from a moving Gumdrop Glowworm, but still, it hadn't been nearly so dark and gloomy as what lay ahead of us.

"You know," Nash said, swallowing hard. "You'd think a forest made out of candy would be, I don't know, cheerful?"

"I don't know who you two are," the girl called down to us. "But if you were hoping for cheerful then you're in the wrong place." She narrowed her eyes at us, studying us more closely. Nash was shifting back and forth uncomfortably, and I remembered the horrible tingling sensation I'd felt the last time I'd spun. After your move was made, the game wanted you to move and move quickly. Nash must have reached his limit, because suddenly he was off and running, the path ahead of him lighting up as his feet hit the colored candies.

"Mistake," the girl above me said in a bored voice as she swung down to land beside me. "He's going to end up stung by a Bubble Gum Bee and back at the start faster than you can say goodbye."

I ignored her and reached around for the spinner in my own pocket. The spinner I'd managed to drop at the exact wrong moment during my last turn. If Nash hadn't gotten it back in my hand, I wouldn't be here. I reached out to flick it, but the girl's hand shot out and grabbed my wrist.

"Wait a second," she said, leaning in so close that I could count the freckles on her nose. She squinted at my face. "There's something familiar about you I can't put my finger on. Who are you?"

"Nobody important," I said, and gave my spinner a hard flick. It was time to move.

FOURTEEN

"I'm telling you, that was her," Nash hissed at me across the dinner table. Ace had his back to us and the snap and sizzle of chicken was so loud I doubted that he could hear himself think, let alone hear us. Still, I really wished that Nash would shut his mouth.

"The other Wanderer," Nash insisted. "I'd bet anything that was her."

"We should have asked for her name," I said.

"What good would that have done?" Nash asked. "Ace didn't tell us her name!" We were interrupted by Ace slamming down two bowls of what looked like chicken and rice. He'd chopped up the chicken and mixed the chunks into the cheesy rice. I immediately hated it. I wasn't a big fan of my food touching. It gave me the creeps, but a quick glance at Ace's no-nonsense face made it clear that it was eat this or starve. My stomach gave an impatient gurgle, and I picked out a piece of rice that wasn't touching any of the surrounding chicken. I would eat it, but I wouldn't be happy about it.

"So, boys," Ace said, sitting down with his own heaping plate. "Should we talk punishments now? Or later?"

"What punishments?" I asked.

"Later," Nash said around a mouthful. "The answer to that question is always later."

"For staying in the game an extra turn," Ace said. "For deliberately disobeying. For forcing me to show up to save both of your scrawny backsides."

"We were totally going to handle those Bubble Gum Bees," Nash protested.

"Right," I agreed. "I forgot for a second that it was a game when they all started swarming." I rubbed at my arm that sported not only two tiny puncture holes from a Sprinkle Snake, but a large lump where a Bubble Gum Bee had managed to sting me.

"You can *never* forget that it's a game," Ace thundered, and Nash and I both jumped. Ace sighed and rubbed his eyes. "I'm too old to be raising two knucklehead boys," he muttered. He dropped his hands and opened his eyes to glare at us. "Where were we? Oh yes, your punishment."

"I vote for a stern reprimand and sending us to bed to think about our actions," Nash said, straight-faced.

Ace snorted. "I was thinking manual labor was a much better option. There's something about working your muscles until they scream that really makes you think about your life choices," he said as he slipped a piece of chicken to Chief.

"I don't think I like the sound of that," I said.

"I *know* I don't like the sound of that," Nash echoed.

"The cow pasture needs mucked," Ace said as though he were carrying on this conversation with Chief instead of us. "I also need those logs split. But that would mean using an axe, and I don't trust these two with a butter knife."

"Hey!" Nash said indignantly, but Ace ignored him, staring at his dog as though the animal were giving him sound advice about what our punishment should be.

"Shouldn't we be practicing board game bounding so we can help save Mom?" I asked. "Not picking up cow poop?"

"You can learn a lot from picking up cow poop," Ace said. "Finish up. I'll get you started."

"Wait, we have to do this tonight?!" Nash said. Ace just nodded, and we fell into a silent dinner, each of us wrapped up in our own thoughts. I was also wrapped up in eating only the rice that hadn't touched the chicken.

We cleaned up dinner and put on our shoes to follow Ace out of the cabin and into the woods. I realized that we hadn't left the cabin since we'd arrived two days ago. Well, I thought, I guess we'd left it if you counted leaving to enter a board game.

I inhaled, taking in the familiar Indiana scents of pine and mud and approaching night as Ace opened a nearby shed and removed two pitchforks and a rust-eaten wheelbarrow. A jerk of his head let us know that the wheelbarrow was our job. I grabbed the two dirt-encrusted wooden handles while Nash took charge of the pitchforks, and we followed Ace. I wondered what our mother would think if she could see us now. Nash and I were notorious for moaning, groaning, and complaining about any sort of chore, but here we were dutifully marching after our grandfather to scoop poop. Chief trotted along beside us, happily sniffing a log here or a rock there, his tongue lolling out to the side in a doggy smile.

"Can I ask a question?" I finally said, breaking the silence that had settled over us like a blanket.

"You can ask," Ace said. "Doesn't mean I'll answer."

"You mentioned there was another Wanderer besides us. A girl. You've met her, right?"

"Sure have," Ace said.

"What's her name?" Nash said. "What's she like?

How did she become a Wanderer like us?"

"She's not like you," Ace said. "You two aren't Wanderers. You're bounders, I told you that. It's your Wanderer blood that allows you in and out of games, but it doesn't make you part of the games. If you get hurt, you get hurt. If you get killed, you don't go back to the start to try again."

"That doesn't seem fair," Nash said.

"Fair," Ace said, and then spit. "That's a word only the young and naive think matters two figs. It doesn't. The girl is a Wanderer because she earned it. You're a board game bounder because you had the fortune, or misfortune, to be born a Benson."

"I'm going to need you to elaborate," I said.

"She won her game," Ace said simply. "No board game character ever wins their game. But she did. And she got out. Ever since, she's been able to go in and out of other board games. She gets hired by some of the board game players to help them advance them-selves in their games, and she's paid well for it. I don't approve of her line of work. The last thing we need is to allow other board game pieces to roam in and out of whatever board game strikes their fancy."

"What's her name?" Nash said.

"Cress," Ace said. We let that sit for a second, and I tried to picture that name with the girl we'd met in

Sugar Bugs. It fit like a glove. I replayed our brief conversation with her, trying to make sense of some of the things she'd said.

"Here we are," Ace said. Nash and I peered around him at a large, fenced-in clearing in the woods, where two sleepy-looking cows were grazing.

"Clean it," he said simply. "Dump the manure over there and put the wheelbarrow away when you're done." He glanced over at Chief and held up his hand, palm up. "Stay," he commanded. Chief whined in protest, cocking his head as though asking a question.

"Keep them safe," he said. "I'll be fine without you this once." I watched this performance with interest. Chief seemed to actually understand our grandfather, and I wondered if it was because of the board game bounding. Had going in and out of games changed the fundamental makeup of the dog somehow? Would it change mine?

"Keep us safe from what?" Nash said, interrupting my thoughts. "The scariest thing we have around here is a possum. And they aren't even scary, they just look like giant rats."

"You two need protection from yourselves," Ace said flippantly, turning to head back into the woods. "Better get to work!" he called over his shoulder. "It'll be dark in an hour or two. Real hard to find poop in the dark."

"Now that's a bumper sticker," Nash said. Chief watched Ace leave, only lying down with a huff when Ace was completely out of sight.

"Sorry," Nash said to Chief. "I guess you're stuck with us."

"Might as well get it over with," I said. Nash nodded his agreement, and we unlatched the gate and headed in. The cows paid no attention to us, and we started working our way around the pasture, shoveling the mounds of cow poop into the wheelbarrow as we went. It wasn't as bad as I thought it would be. Ace had been right. The manual labor gave my brain space to think. To my surprise Nash was quiet too, and I wondered if he was replaying our last move in Sugar Bugs. The licorice forest, or whatever that place was, had held more surprises than Sprinkle Snakes. While Nash's move had landed him safe and sound in a green square, my move had resulted in a very unfortunate encounter with the now infamous Bubble Gum Bees. They'd been furry pink monstrosities that might have actually been cute if they hadn't had stingers as big as my hand. The memory of that sting was going to last the rest of my life, and I paused in my shoveling to rub my still sore arm. I guess I was lucky I'd only gotten stung once. Three more were zooming my way when a furious Ace had shown up and hauled Nash and me back to his office.

The night noises of the woods were starting to amp up as we worked, and my arm muscles burned. It turned out that cow poop was a lot heavier than it looked. I could hear the rumble of an approaching storm in the distance, and a quick look at the sky showed a dark row of clouds heading our way. It didn't matter, though, since we were almost done. I'd just glanced up to inspect the approaching storm when Chief sat bolt upright and let out an earsplitting bark that made me jump. It spooked the cows too, who skittered nervously to the far corner of the pen to look at us with wary eyes. Chief barked again, jumping to his feet, his body stiff as he looked back at the house. A second later there was a loud bang followed by the sound of breaking glass. Chief abandoned his post and bolted for the cabin. I dropped the handles of the wheelbarrow and took off after him, Nash at my heels. There was another earsplitting crash, and someone screamed.

"What do you think it is?" Nash called as we sprinted back down the path through the woods.

"I think Ace decided to look for Mom while we were busy scooping cow poop, and something went wrong." Chief was faster than us and was already throwing himself at the locked office door by the time we made it inside. Nash fumbled for Chief's collar before producing the ring of keys. Chief whined, moving from foot to foot as he waited anxiously for Nash to find the right key. It took three tries and a lot of fumbling, but Nash finally jammed it into the lock and threw the bolt. I grabbed the nearest object that I could use as a weapon. It turned out that was the toaster. I stood there, toaster cocked over my shoulder, waiting for whatever it was to come out of the office.

Chief was no longer throwing himself at the door and instead was hunched low, the fur on his neck standing on end as he growled. Nash glanced over at me, his finger on the last bolt that would open the door, and I swallowed hard before nodding. Nash nodded back. He took a deep breath and put his hand on the doorknob, then with a quick sidestep, he grabbed a nearby brass lamp, ripping the cord from the wall so he could hold his makeshift weapon at the ready. What a pair, I thought dryly. I hoped whatever was behind that door was intimidated by a toaster and a lamp.

Nash yanked open the door and Chief bolted inside in front of us. Nash followed, with me and my toaster bringing up the rear. The office was a mess. One of the bookcases had been ripped off the wall and lay propped against Ace's desk, all the board games inside open and in disarray among the dislodged jars and bric-a-brac pressed against the unbroken glass of the case. The steel-covered window was no longer covered, and the night sounds were pouring inside. It looked like someone had ripped it open violently from the outside. The metal panels were bent back like the pried-open lid of a tin can, and pieces of glass lay in shards all over the floor. That wasn't the only thing on the floor. I held out a hand to stop Nash before he stepped on the girl.

For a half second, I thought it was Cress, but then my brain caught up to what I was seeing and I knew it wasn't. For one thing, while Cress's black hair had been curly and wild, this girl's was so sleek and straight it looked like polished onyx. Cress's skin had been freckled and brown, but this girl's skin glowed an almost unnatural white. Her lips stood out in sharp contrast on her face and were the unsettling color of fresh blood.

"Is that a vampire?" Nash said, taking a step back.

"Man, I hope not," I said.

Nash shoved his hands into his hair and looked at me, eyes wide. "What happened to Ace?"

Chief ignored the girl, actually stepping on and over her as he busied himself with searching the room. The girl didn't move.

"More important," I said, "is she alive?"

"I mean, it looks like she's breathing," Nash said. "Do vampires breathe?" He reached down tentatively and put two fingers on the girl's neck. He snatched them back almost immediately and nodded.

"She's alive," he confirmed. "What game is she from?"

"I don't see a game anywhere," I said, glancing around. Usually, Ace put the game box on his desk, and we crowded around and put our hands on it. This time, there was no box. The girl chose that moment to wake up.

FIFTEEN

She sat up with a gasp, and I realized that she was older than I'd first thought. Her cheeks were perfect circular spots of pink as she pressed her manicured fingertips to them in an overdone pose of surprise.

"Where am I?" she trilled in a voice that reminded me of a very high-pitched bell.

"Um, Indiana?" Nash said.

"Are you a dwarf?" she asked, tilting her head to the side. Her motions seemed practiced somehow. Like she'd studied how to be a person, but she'd only read the CliffsNotes.

"What?" I said. "No."

"Oh," the woman said with a sigh. "That's a shame. Dwarves are wonderful."

"Not a vampire," Nash said, his hand on his chin. He studied the girl through narrowed eyes. Suddenly his eyebrows shot up in recognition, and he laughed.

"What?" I said, not finding anything about this particular moment funny in the least.

"No way!" Nash crowed. "You're Snow White! Please tell me you're Snow White."

"How do you know my name?" said Snow White, and Nash started laughing again. I just stared at the girl as the pieces fell into place. This *was* Snow White. It fit. The hair, the bloodred lips, the snow-white skin, all of it made sense once you realized who she was. Although I had to admit that Nash's guess of vampire could have also been spot-on. No normal human looked like that.

"What game are you from?" Nash said. "No, no, let me guess. It's got to be something like Fairy Tales and Fables. Or Once Upon a Game. Or Dwarf Dilemma."

Snow White sat up completely and dusted off her gown while Nash talked.

"Lost Lore," she said.

"Drat," Nash said, snapping his fingers. "I wasn't even close."

Snow White ignored him and went on, her eyes unfocused and dreamy, her pretty hands clasped under her pretty pointed chin. "The object is to find all the missing lore from fairy tales and fables. It's full of magic and myths and wonder!" When we continued to stare at her in confusion, she huffed indignantly and lost the dreamy look. "You know," she said, her voice suddenly not quite so bell-ish, "like Cinderella's slipper, Sleeping Beauty's spindle, Hansel and Gretel's house, Jack's candlestick."

"Let me guess, you're missing a dwarf?" Nash said.

"Don't be silly," Snow White said with a dismissive flip of her hand. "You can't lose a dwarf. They have an excellent sense of direction. Guess again."

"I don't want to," I snapped.

"Fine," she said with a pout. "It's the poisonous apple."

Nash slapped his forehead and grinned. "Of course! The apple! Does it have a bite out of it?"

"What's your game look like?" I said, ignoring my brother as I peered under the tipped-over bookcase on the off chance that the game had been knocked to the floor.

"I have no idea," Snow White warbled, and I winced. Her voice made my brain hurt. The sooner we could get her back in her game the better. While this was all going on, Chief had continued his investigation of the office, smelling everything as though he were reading secret messages. He paused by the window and whined. I went over to investigate and found what looked like muddy boot prints.

"Who did this?" I asked.

"I can't be positive," Snow White said. "But my guess would be the pirate." My heart slammed to a surprised stop before jump-starting itself in double time.

"Pirate?" Nash and I said in unison.

"Yes," Snow White sighed with a practiced flip of her hair. "Although I fell asleep as soon as he ripped open that window, so I can't be sure."

"Fell asleep?" I said. I could think of a lot of reactions I'd have if a pirate ripped open my window, but falling asleep wasn't one of them.

Snow White nodded. "I have a severe case of narcolepsy. Stress makes it worse. Pirates are very stressful, you know."

I turned to Nash. "Do you think it was Ogden?"

"Know any other pirates with a vendetta against our grandfather?" Nash said dryly. "Yeah, I'm pretty sure it was Ogden."

I nodded, walking over to inspect the damage done to the window, my feet crunching over broken glass. The muddy boot prints went this way and that, as though Ogden had been pacing the room. I took my foot and pushed some of the glass aside, pausing as I saw something shiny and gold among the fragments. Bending down, I carefully picked the larger shards of glass out of the way, revealing a gold skeleton key. For a second I thought Chief had somehow lost one of the keys Ace kept tucked around his neck, but as I picked it up I saw that someone had tied it onto a leather strap. Behind me Nash had started a full-blown interrogation of Snow White, and I slipped the key into my pocket as I turned to face him. It was a mystery that could be dealt with later; we had bigger problems to solve at the moment.

"Did the pirate do something to Ace?" Nash asked for a third time. Snow White ignored him. She'd caught her own reflection in the glass of the fallen bookcase, and she was carefully inspecting the bow perched on top of her jet-black hair. Nash gritted his teeth in annoyance and threw his hands up in exasperation. I watched her, my brain churning. She was only the second quid that I'd had an opportunity to talk with for longer than five seconds. All in all, I'd preferred Flanny, but Snow White was definitely an improvement over the bear. I turned to look at Nash as understanding dawned on me.

"Ace wasn't here," I said. "He couldn't have been here, or Snow White *wouldn't* be here!"

"Oh man," Nash said, plunking himself down into a chair just to jump back up again when he discovered that it too was covered in shards of glass from the broken window.

"Ace was in Snow White's game," I went on, turning back to Snow White. "What did you say it was called?"

"Lost Lore," Snow White said proudly, turning to us. "Fairy tale fun for everyone!"

"If she's here," I said, "that means Ace is *still* in her game."

"And if the game isn't here," Nash said, continuing my sentence, "then somebody took it."

"Not somebody," I said. "Ogden." I turned to Snow White for confirmation, but she was busy inspecting her nails.

"Did you see the pirate take anything?" I said.

Snow White glanced up from her nails. "How should I know?" she said, pouting out her bottom lip. "I was asleep, remember?"

"Right," I huffed in exasperation.

"Why?" Nash said. "Why take the game? Can't Ace just think his way out of it and back here?"

"He probably didn't realize he needed to until it was too late," I said. "Remember how he told us that there was a way to trap someone in a game? Ogden trapped Mom somewhere, and now he's got Ace too." The thought crossed my mind that Ogden could have destroyed the game, just like Ace had destroyed The Pirate's Wrath, but I shoved that idea aside.

"At least we know which game he's trapped in,"

Nash said. "That's more than we know about Mom."

"I guess it was lucky that we were scooping cow manure or we'd probably be in that game too," I said, deciding that if Nash could find a way to see the silver lining, then I could too.

"Doubly lucky," Nash said. "Chief was with us. If he'd been here, Ogden would have had the keys to the bookcase." We both turned to look at the wall of bookcases, part of which was still standing, their display of artifacts and oddities still intact. The one that had been ripped off the wall was the center unit that sat directly behind Ace's desk, its contents a horrible jumble. Ace had mentioned that as bounders we could remove things from a game, which he obviously had been doing for years to amass the collection he had, but he'd said that a Wander Lost like Ogden couldn't. What had Ogden wanted out of Ace's bookcases?

"Not necessarily," I said, my brain still churning. "Chief would have been in the game. Ace always bounds with Chief, but he left him with us. For protection."

"Do you think he knew Ogden was going to show up here?" Nash said.

"Maybe," I said, thinking about Ace's overreaction to my squeal of pain from Geronimo's bite. He'd practically tackled us from his truck in his hurry to get us out of harm's way. Had he done the same thing by leaving us in a cow pasture with Chief?

"What are we going to do now?" Nash said, looking around the room. The place was an absolute mess, and the thunder from outside the window was getting louder by the minute. We'd only been board game bounding for a couple of days. Now Ace was gone, the office was trashed, and we were apparently stuck with a narcoleptic princess. I felt a sense of hopelessness settle over me like a weight, and I sat down in one of the office chairs despite the fact that it was covered in potting soil and the shreds of the fern that had lived on Ace's desk. I leaned my head back and shut my eyes.

"What's he doing?" I heard Snow White say. "Does he fall asleep when he's stressed too?"

"He's thinking," I snapped.

"Think later," Nash said. "We need to get this window closed up or this office is going to be trashed and soaked." I opened my eyes and stood up. Nash was right. Take care of the easy stuff first, like the broken window. Together we managed to bend the shutters so that they somewhat closed. Nash found a metal coat hanger and did a rough job of wiring the two shut enough that when the rain did come, pounding down on the tin roof in a torrent, the office would stay dry. The next job was the upended bookcase full of games and Ace's odd assortment of treasures. Together we managed to get it upright, but the mess of game pieces, opened boxes, upended jars, and broken pottery jumbled behind the glass made me feel ill. It would take hours to straighten the mess out. Snow White helped, bustling about the office, straightening this and that, brushing up potting soil and shredded fern, all the while humming almost manically. She eventually discovered the open office door and busied herself with cleaning up the rest of the cabin. I watched her joyfully scrubbing the counters and sighed. I guess if you had to be stuck with a board game character, having one that liked cleaning wasn't a bad way to go.

"Now what?" Nash said, coming to stand beside me.

I bit my lip and shook my head. "I wish I knew," I said. "We need to get Ace back, but I have no idea how to get into a board game without the actual board game."

Nash was watching Snow White scrubbing the sink, his forehead furrowed. "If only there was someone we could ask."

I nodded. Ace would know the answers to our questions, but of course Ace wasn't here. I thought back to earlier that evening when I'd asked him about the girl we'd met in Sugar Bugs, and the idea hit me so hard I gasped out loud.

"What now?" Nash said.

"Cress," I said, turning to him. "She'd know. She's an expert at games. Ace told us that."

"Interesting but not exactly helpful," Nash said, "seeing as Cress isn't here."

"Yet," I said with a smile. "She isn't here *yet*."

"Oh," Nash said as understanding dawned on his face. "Do you think we can find her again?"

"Assuming she hasn't completed the job in Sugar Bugs, we should be able to," I said with way more confidence than I actually felt.

"Only one way to find out," Nash said, "but what do we do about Snow White?" We both looked over at the kitchen, but Snow White was no longer there. She'd stretched out on the couch and was fast asleep, her arms crossed over her chest and her body perfectly straight. She looked like she should be lying in a coffin instead of on a threadbare La-Z-Boy.

"That's creepy, right?" Nash said.

"Super creepy," I agreed. "But I think she's safe to leave for the time being. If she wakes up, she'll probably just clean the bathroom or something." Together we turned and entered the office, careful to lock the door behind us. It took some time to locate Sugar Bugs in the bookcases, and another few minutes to convince Chief to let us have the keys that were dangling off his collar, but finally we were in business. The box sat on the desk, waiting. Chief whined, and I glanced down at him. He clearly wanted to come with us, but I hesitated.

"You need to stay here and keep whatever comes out in line," I told him. I had no idea if he understood what I was telling him, but he whined again and lay down, his brown eyes watching us dolefully.

"Ready?" Nash said, glancing over at me, his hand poised above the box.

"No," I said. "But we don't really have a choice, do we?"

"Not if we want to help Ace or Mom," Nash said.

"Right," I agreed. "But we make this fast. We get in. We find Cress. We ask her some questions about what could have happened to Ace, and we get out." Nash nodded and together we knocked on the cover. "Open sesame."

SIXTEEN

There was something comforting about entering a game for a second time. I landed on the now-familiar candy-coated path and stood up cautiously. The licorice forest was to our left, and behind us loomed the gigantic, but not as stationary as you'd hope, Gumdrop Mountain. The spinners from the game were sitting on the path in front of us, and together we picked them up and tucked them into our pockets.

"How do we find her?" Nash asked.

"I have no idea," I said.

"How do we even know if she's still here?" Nash said.

"We don't," I said. "But we can't move until we spin." Nash nodded and held up his spinner, but before he had a chance to flick it, there was an eruption to our right. We both turned to look as something red and thick burst from the ground like a geyser. A second later the spot beside it erupted with a steaming blue substance that fell to the ground with a gelatinous splat. We stood mesmerized as a yellow, then an orange, goo erupted next. We were still standing in stunned silence when an orange man carrying an oversize bug net appeared, running for all his little stubby legs were worth.

"Run, run, run!" the man cried. "As fast as I can!" He looked back over his shoulder and tripped, pitching forward. Moments later the oozing river of multicolored slime overtook him. I wasn't sure what happened next, if the slime dissolved him on the spot or just swallowed him whole. All I knew for sure was that one second he was there, and the next second he was gone. The oozing river was still on the go, and it was heading right for us.

"Spin!" Nash yelled. "We need to move." I spun and felt a rush of relief as it landed on yellow. Ahead I could see the yellow square looking completely and utterly uninhabited and harmless. Better yet, it was out of the way of the oncoming goo. I didn't need the tingle in my feet to tell me to run. I hit the yellow square and turned just as Nash flicked his spinner. The goo was still a good ten feet away from him, and I let out a sigh of relief. It looked like he was going to be fine too. That's when his spinner landed on green.

I glanced to my left, where the green square lay, only to spot the telltale Sugar Suggestion card popping up. I'd learned to hate game cards. Almost every game seemed to have them, and they had usually a cutesy name that rhymed or used obnoxious alliteration. I squinted at the card as Nash ran for his square. It didn't matter what the cards were called, they were dangerous. They could do anything from catapult you forward to drag you backward, to any number of horrible scenarios in between. I remembered Cress's Sprinkle Snakes and shivered. What was next? Chocolate cockroaches? Nash was almost to his spot, and I glanced away from his progress to see that the goo had covered up the spot we'd been standing in moments before. It appeared to be carving out its own rainbow-colored river as it made its way across the game.

I glanced back at Nash just in time to see him reach up to grab the Sugar Suggestion card out of the air.

"Stop!" someone yelled, and we both spun to see Cress. She was standing on the other side of the newly formed Rainbow River, and she was watching Nash with wide eyes.

Nash took her advice and froze, his fingertips a mere inch from the card suspended in midair. Once Cress was satisfied that he'd listened, she turned her attention to the churning river of goo in front of her.

"Don't touch it!" I called.

She looked up at me and raised an eyebrow in exasperation. "I know," she said dryly. "The guy that was supposed to pay me just got taken out by it."

Cress took a few steps back and looked around. She yanked a large lollipop out of the ground and cracked it over her knee. The lollipop separated from the stick, and she nodded in approval. She approached the river and carefully tossed the lollipop head out like a Frisbee. It landed on the surface and floated like a small pink-striped island. Cress took a few calculated steps backward, the long lollipop stick still held firmly in her hand. She reminded me of a pole vaulter sizing up a jump, her makeshift pole held up vertically in front of her. A second later she took off at a dead sprint for the river of goo. For a heart-wrenching second, I thought she wasn't going to make it. Her initial jump looked way too short, but she landed neatly on the floating lollipop head just long enough to catapult herself back into the air. She used the lollipop stick to seamlessly vault herself over the rest of the goo and landed effortlessly on the other side.

"Whoa," I heard Nash say. I took it a step further and applauded. Cress tossed the lollipop stick into the river before brushing off her hands on her pants. She was still wearing the dark red cloak she'd been in before, but the hood was pulled back from her face, leaving her hair free to spring out in every direction. She tucked her spinner into one of the leather pouches looped onto her waist by the oversize leather belt before making her way over to where Nash and I were standing a few squares apart.

"We meet again," she said.

"We were looking for you," Nash said.

"Why?" Cress said warily.

"We wanted to talk to you," I said with a glance over at Nash.

"Talk?" Cress said, raising an eyebrow. "Maybe you haven't noticed, but there's not a whole lot of room for chitchat in a game like this."

"It's some game, all right," I agreed, glancing around.

"You can have it," Cress said, sounding disgusted. "I'm going to move along. My reason for being here just got sucked up by the Rainbow River and sent back to the start without paying up. The ninny probably won't remember he hired me, and I'm not wasting my time convincing him."

"The Orange Bug Catcher?" I said. "What did he hire you for?"

"He wanted to know how to get past the Rainbow River," she said with a roll of her eyes. "I should have made him pay up front. What a giant waste of time."

"Um, not to interrupt," Nash said through gritted teeth. "But can I grab this card now? My arm feels like it's on fire." I could see that his arm was trembling, and I looked back at Cress.

"Sure," Cress said, "but only if you want to get sent back to start."

"What do you mean?" I said. "How can you possibly know what's on that Sugar Suggestion card?"

"Oh," Cress said. "I don't. But about every other card makes you go backward. Do you really want to go backward into that?" She jerked her head at the Rainbow River of goo. She glanced down at her wrist, where a clunky pocket watch had been strapped with a piece of the same thick leather belt that she had wrapped around her waist. "Thirty more seconds," she said. We waited, Nash's arm trembling more violently by the second as her watch clicked down the time. "Twenty-seven, twenty-eight, twenty-nine," Cress counted. "Thirty." She looked up just as the Rainbow River got sucked back into the ground with a loud squelch. Nash yanked the card out of the air and let out a gasp of relief. He looked down at it.

"Hip hop, turn about, go back to the color you just left out," he read aloud. The spot we'd just left lit up, and Nash sheepishly walked back to the square that had been under the goo just moments before.

"How did you know that?" I asked.

"This isn't my first game," Cress said flippantly. "But you answer first. Who are you, and why are you looking for me? Are you hiring?"

"We need help," I said.

"That's obvious," Cress said as she dug around in one of her hip bags for something.

"Hey!" Nash called indignantly from his spot. Cress glanced up at him, eyebrow raised. Nash scowled. "I mean, you're not wrong, but that's still kind of rude."

"That's my personality," Cress said. "Kind of rude. And I don't *help*. I get hired. There's a big difference."

"Okay," I said. "Can we *hire* you to help us?"

"Maybe," Cress said. "If the price is right. What do you need help with?"

"Something bad happened to our grandfather," I said.

Cress nodded. "Something bad always happens in board games. Otherwise, no one would ever play them."

I shot Nash a "what now" look, and he shrugged. This wasn't going at all the way I'd hoped. I was going to have to play this exactly right if I wanted her help.

"You're a Wanderer, right?" I said.

"I've been called that," Cress said warily. "Are you? I haven't seen you two around before."

I glanced over at Nash, who gave me an almost imperceptible nod. Calling ourselves Wanderers was as good of an explanation as any. Ace had warned us not to reveal ourselves to board game characters, and there was something about Cress that made me feel uneasy.

"New Wanderers," Nash said.

I nodded, liking where his head was. "Really new," I said.

"What game are you from?" she asked, sounding suspicious.

"That doesn't matter," I said. "What matters is that we need help."

"What kind of help?" Cress said skeptically, her eyebrow raised.

"We need to know how to get into a certain game," I said.

"So you need information," Cress said. I nodded again. She propped her hand under her sharply pointed chin and eyed us consideringly. "And what will you give me for this information?" she finally said.

"What do you want?" Nash countered.

"What do you have?" she said, cocking her head. I glanced over at Nash. What did we have?

"Any chance you'd take a guinea pig?" Nash said.

Cress shook her head. "I have a very strict no live animal rule."

"Money?" I said, not that I really had any to offer. It just seemed like a logical choice.

Cress shook her head again. "You two *are* new.

Currency between games is useless. I deal in precious metals, gemstones, unique artifacts, magical objects, or cursed objects."

"Cursed objects?" I said, interested despite myself.

Cress nodded. "Downright useful when you're in a pinch. Plus, they trade fairly well." I saw Nash's hand flick toward the game piece at his neck, and I shook my head. Not that. He bit his lip, thinking, and then his face lit up with sudden inspiration.

"What about a rock," Nash said.

"You're kidding, right?" Cress said. "A rock?"

"Not just any rock," Nash said. "The rock that Excalibur used to be stuck inside. You know, King Arthur and all that."

Cress crossed her arms over her chest. "Keep talking," she said.

"If you tell us how to get into a game, we give you the rock. Is it a deal?" Nash said.

"I'd prefer the sword, but the rock's got to be worth something. Deal," she said with a smirk that made me uneasy. Nash held out a hand and Cress shook it. "Easiest payday I've had in a while," she said. "Clearly you don't know about Tunnels."

"We know what tunnels are," I snapped, wondering if we'd just made a mistake.

Cress rolled her eyes in exasperation. "Good night," she said. "If I didn't know any better, I'd say that you

186

two were from that game Village Idiot."

Nash snorted. "There's a game called Village Idiot? What's that like?"

"Obnoxious," Cress said. "The entire point of the game is to find the missing village idiot and return him to his village. And idiots are very hard to work with." Nash snorted again.

"What tunnels?" I asked, not nearly as amused as my twin.

"The game Tunnels," Cress said. She must have noticed our blank expressions because she went on. "Think of it like a train station. It's the hub, the center, and all the games connect to it. Some are easier to find than others, but once you're in Tunnels, you can get to any game you'd like."

"Okay," I said. "How do we get into Tunnels?"

"The same way you got here," she said slowly, as though I'd just asked the world's stupidest question. "Through a tunnel."

"But," Nash said, but I slapped a hand over his mouth before he could go any further. He licked it, and I pulled it away in disgust. Clearly the fifth-grade germs unit hadn't had the same impact on him that it had had on me. I grimaced and wiped my hand on my pants. Cress couldn't know that we got here through the board game's box. If she realized that, she might just realize that we weren't the lost Wanderers we were making ourselves out to be.

"So how do we find the tunnel that leads to the game we want to go to?" I asked.

Cress eyed us suspiciously. "All the tunnels lead to Tunnels," she said. "Of course, you can't use them unless you really are a Wanderer."

"Which we are," Nash said a hair too quickly.

"Do any of these tunnels take you anywhere else?" I asked.

"What do you mean?" Cress said.

"Do any of them take you out to the real world?" I said, thinking that maybe Ace could use one of those to escape the game he was stuck inside.

Cress shook her head. "You can only get out of the game world through the game you beat. Which game was that exactly?"

"What do you know about a game called Lost Lore?" Nash said quickly, probably hoping to distract her. It worked.

"Lost Lore?" Cress said, turning to him. "That game is a piece of work. Secret passages. Castles. Dragon infestations. Trolls, ogres, dwarves, and don't even get me started on the princesses." She shuddered. I thought about Snow White and her irritating bell voice and had to agree. From my limited experience they weren't as delightful as Disney made them out to be. "I've had some of my best paydays there, though," Cress said.

"Cinderella bartered me her glass slipper for information about how to get past the ballroom."

"*The* glass slipper?" Nash said, impressed. "The one the prince found at midnight?"

Cress flapped a dismissive hand. "Not that one. The one she kept. Everyone always seems to forget about that one." She turned back to me and narrowed her eyes. "Is that the game your grandfather is in?"

I nodded. "But he's been a Wanderer longer than us, so he knows all about Tunnels." I said that with way more confidence than I felt. It was entirely possible that Ace didn't know anything about this mysterious game that could be accessed through actual tunnels in board games. She'd said only a Wanderer could use them, and as Ace had told us on more than one occasion, we weren't technically Wanderers.

"He knows about Tunnels, but he's still stuck in the game?" Cress asked, and we nodded. "Hmmm," she said, considering. "There are ways to keep a player trapped inside a game. A cat's game prison cell comes to mind. I've seen those before."

"A cat's game?" I said.

Cress huffed in exasperation. "Don't you know what a cat's game is?" When we just stared at her, she shook her head and went on. "A cat's game is a game that no one wins. There's a cat's game spot in every game, a spot where no one can win the game. That's how you trap a Wanderer, in one of those spots."

"That makes sense," I said.

"How do you save someone from a cat's game spot?" Nash said.

Cress rolled her eyes. "How do you save anyone from anything? You get them out of it, of course."

"Right," I said. "Um, could you show us the tunnel out of this game? And once we use it, how do we find the entrance to Lost Lore?"

"Here," Cress said, pulling a piece of paper out of her pocket. She quickly scribbled something down on it before handing it to us.

"What's this?" I asked.

"Directions," she said. "Even if you follow me through the tunnel, there's a good chance you'll end up in a different section of the game. Tunnels is kind of wonky like that. Never kicks you out at the same place twice. I wrote down how to get to Lost Lore. I'll meet you there to collect my payment. Okay?"

"Okay," Nash and I said in unison. Cress smirked. "Then let the games begin." Before I could respond she turned and walked over to the candy-paved path, lifted up a large purple disk the size of a sewer grate, and disappeared inside.

SEVENTEEN

My brain hurt, but not nearly as bad as my eyes. Those felt like someone had taken them out and rolled them around in sand before popping them back into my head. The image made me queasy, and I wondered how long it had been since we'd eaten that chicken and rice with Ace. If my stomach was any clue, it had been a long time. The titles on the game boxes in front of me blurred, and I rubbed my eyes with the palms of my hands.

"Do you think she was messing with us?" Nash asked. "Is there even a game called Tunnels? It was called Tunnels, right?" This was not the first time he'd said that exact phrase. If I had to guess, I'd say it was probably the twentieth. Although occasionally he'd throw some variation into the mix and say something like, "I knew we shouldn't have trusted her." Or, "If she

191

could get into Tunnels without holding the physical box, then why couldn't she have taken us along?"

"I have no idea." I sighed. After Cress has disappeared down her conveniently placed tunnel, we'd tried to follow, only to discover that we couldn't. It shouldn't have been a surprise since she'd as good as told us that it could only be used by a Wanderer. The hole was there, but it was like someone had built an invisible brick wall across the opening. Nash had tried to jump in after Cress only to hit the oddly solid air and have his knees buckle underneath him. The sight would have been funny in any other circumstance. We'd tried everything to follow, only to eventually give up when some oversize praying mantises made out of what looked like marzipan sugar noticed us and decided to investigate.

"All I know is she said Tunnels was a game, which means that there's a solid chance that Ace owns it. If we can just find it, we can use it to get into Lost Lore and save him."

"Maybe she was just trying to get rid of us. Oh, yuck!" Nash suddenly yelped, and I jumped in surprise and looked over at him. He was holding up a hand dripping in something brown.

"Relax," I said, turning back to the jumble of boxes. "It's just fudge." My own clothes were liberally coated in the stuff. We weren't quite sure what had been hanging out in Ace's office while we chatted with Cress in Sugar Bugs, but we'd returned to an office covered in slimy chocolate. Chief had been so coated he didn't even look like the same dog, and he'd given us a reproachful look that made it clear who he blamed for the mess. We hadn't bothered to clean much of it up since Snow White was still bustling around the house and would probably get to it eventually. Besides, we had bigger problems, like finding Tunnels.

The first place we'd looked was the bookcase that Ogden hadn't touched, and it had been a matter of minutes to scan the names on the neatly stacked boxes. I'd spotted a game called Fee-Fie-Foe-Fum, but nothing called Tunnels. Then we'd turned our attention to the bookcase that Ogden had upended. While he hadn't been able to get the case open, as evidenced by the partially mangled lock and the deep gouges and scratches on the glass, he *had* managed to make a giant mess. All the boxes inside the case had fallen off their respective shelves, their lids popping open and pieces scattering into a mixed-up mess that had come flooding out onto the floor as soon as we'd opened the lock. So despite the hour, and despite our exhaustion, and despite the fudge covering almost every surface, we'd sat down and started sorting.

Some of the games were simple to put back together.

The board game matched the box and the pieces made sense. For example, the game Nature Mania had a board covered in leaves with tiny brass animals as the game pieces. The cards were shaped like little paw prints, and the dice were kelly green. Easy. Others were more complicated, and it took me almost a half hour to figure out that the board game pieces in Dragons at Dawn were not dragons, they were tiny tin knights with different-colored flags, and the cards were shaped like swords. Slowly the pile in front of us got smaller as we sorted out each game piece by piece and board by board. Some of Ace's treasures had come tumbling out of the bookcase as well; these we set off to the side or threw in the trash depending on how broken they happened to be. I made a mental note to ask Ace to explain what some of this stuff was later. Nash located the rock that had held Excalibur on the off chance that we ever actually made it into Lost Lore and had to pay up. I found the pieces to a game called Bigfoot Begone, and what I was pretty sure was a piece of a meteorite, but still, no Tunnels. Geronimo Jones had moseyed in at some point and took it upon himself to eat what was left of Ace's fern.

I leaned against the office chair behind me and tipped my head back onto the cushion. My hair stuck in the fudge that covered the seat, but I didn't care. I was just going to shut my eyes for a second. Then I'd go back to searching for the elusive board game that may or may not have been a prank by Cress. If it was a prank, I thought, my eyes shut, it was a good one. She'd escape to who knew what game, and we were right back where we started. Missing mom. Kidnapped grandfather. Chocolate everywhere. I had no idea that I'd fallen asleep until I was woken up by the sound of breaking glass.

For a heart-wrenching second of panic, I thought that Ogden was back. My sleep-muddled brain reasoned that he'd decided to come crashing in through the windows this time instead of prying the metal shutters off the windows. I sat up and attempted to jump to my feet only to hit a patch of fudge sauce and go flying. I skidded across the floor, arms pinwheeling like the propellers on a helicopter.

I hit one of the game-filled bookcases at full speed and grabbed on to the front door latch with both hands to steady myself. Unfortunately, we'd never gotten around to relocking the case the night before, and the giant glass doors of the case popped open and swung in toward me, knocking me off-balance for the second time. I pitched backward, but I didn't let the handle go. That's where I made my mistake. Maybe it was because Ogden had already ripped a bookcase off the wall, or maybe it was just physics and bad luck, but the entire bookcase came crashing toward me. I had the image of a giant wall of boxes, jars, and taxidermied owls tipping in my direction, and I yelped and finally let go of the handles. Dropping to the floor, I covered my head with my hands as I braced for impact.

Somewhere Nash was yelling, and I wondered if I was going to get him smashed too. Forget finding our mom or Ace, we were going to be human pancakes. The impact I was expecting never came. Instead, the bookcase caught on Ace's desk for the second time, and the boxes we'd painstakingly reassembled once again pitched off their shelves to clatter down on top of my head. I winced as the edges of boxes, small metal board game pieces, geodes, the owl, and dice rained down on top of me. The downpour slowed to the occasional small crash as a few straggler boxes gave it up and fell off the shelf.

"Smooth," Nash said, and I uncovered my head to peer up. Above me the shelf was propped against Ace's desk, exactly how we'd found it after coming in from mucking out the cow pasture. Only this time, the glass case was open, spilling the contents of the bookcase across the office floor. Nash was peering at me through the crack between the desk and the floor, a look of supreme annoyance on his face.

"Am I alive?" I said.

"Yes," Nash said. "But I'm debating whether or not I'm going to let you stay that way. What was that?!"

"Something crashed and woke me up. Breaking glass or something. I thought maybe Ogden . . ." I let the sentence trail off as Nash held up one of the glass cups from the kitchen. It was broken and cracked with a large shard missing on the right-hand side.

"Geronimo knocked my water glass off the desk," he said dryly.

"Oh," I said, feeling dumb. I glanced above my head at the empty shelves before looking down at the absolute mess surrounding me. I blinked hard at the tears I felt pressing against the back of my eyes. All our hard work putting the games back together had been undone in a matter of a second, and all because I overreacted to a guinea pig pushing a glass off the desk. I dropped my head and took a deep shuddering breath, trying without much luck to calm myself down.

"Come on," Nash said, sounding only slightly less annoyed as he offered me a hand. I took it, scattering board game pieces as I clambered to my feet. Together we surveyed the damage. The bookcase had left big gouges in Ace's desk, and I noted again the heavy bracket that had been attached to the wall with screws as thick as my thumb. The fact that Ogden had been able to rip the thing off the wall the first time was equal parts impressive and frightening.

"This thing is no joke," Nash said as he braced his shoulder against the side of it and waited for me to do the same.

"Déjà vu or whatever," I grumbled as I assumed an almost identical position to the one I'd taken a few hours before. The last time had been easier, since the doors had been shut and locked. This time they were wedged open, and I placed a palm flat against the back wall of the bookcase to give myself some leverage.

"One, two, buckle my shoe," Nash counted. He'd never counted to three like a normal person in his life, and I rolled my eyes as I shoved. Last time it had taken some serious muscle and grunting to get the thing upright. This time, it didn't budge. Instead, I felt something buckle under my hand as the wood in the back of the bookcase gave way with a sharp crack. My hand went from pushing hard at the back of the bookcase one second to being through the wood of the bookcase in the next. I yelped as shards of wood sliced into my wrist.

"What did you do now?" Nash cried, stepping away from his corner of the bookcase to inspect the damage.

"I have no idea!" I snapped as I gingerly attempted to pull my hand back out of the bookcase. It didn't work.

"That looks like it hurts," Nash said as he leaned down to inspect my trapped hand, and I stopped struggling long enough to glare at him.

"Right," Nash said. "Hold on, I'll help you maneuver your hand back through." He left my side to walk around the back of the bookcase. I waited, breathing through my nose as my wrist gave another painful throb. I had no idea if it was bleeding, and I wasn't going to look. The last thing we needed was for me to start vomiting all over the mess on the floor. To my annoyance, Nash was back at my side a moment later, looking puzzled.

"Where exactly *is* your hand?" he said.

"Seriously?" I snapped. "You can't figure that out?!"

Nash shook his head and disappeared behind the tipped-over bookcase again. A second later he was back looking even more baffled.

"Your hand's not through the back," he explained. "The back of the bookcase is completely intact."

"I beg to differ," I growled through gritted teeth.

"I don't get it," Nash said, disappearing for a third time. I shut my eyes, reminding myself that murdering him was a bad life choice in the long run. When he finally came back, he stopped at the side of the bookcase and bent over, squinting one eye. "What do you feel with that hand?" he finally asked. I swallowed my sarcastic retort and gingerly unclenched my hand from the tight protective fist it was currently in. If this was some kind of joke, then Nash really needed to work on his timing. I wiggled my fingers, but instead of feeling open air, I felt solid wood. I also felt something else.

"No way," I murmured as my fingers explored the familiar object.

"I think it's got a false back," Nash said, returning to the side of the bookcase to squint down its length with one eye. "There's a hidden compartment or something in there."

"Just big enough to hide a board game?" I asked.

Nash's eyes lit up. "Do you think?" he said.

"I don't think. I know," I said. "I can feel the corner of a box."

EIGHTEEN

Getting the bookcase upright was a trick, but we finally managed to heave it back onto the wall despite the fact that I was still stuck to it. Freeing my hand was harder, but thanks to the pliers an awake and helpful Snow White found in the kitchen, we finally managed it. She proved to be an adept hand at bandaging and, singing nonsense the entire time, wrapped my throbbing wrist neatly in a kitchen towel.

We waited until she'd left to inspect the hidden compartment concealed in the false back of the bookcase. Chief let out a low woof, his eyes nervous. He knew we'd stumbled across something that his master wanted hidden. Together we ran our hands over the shelves and back wall of the bookcase, feeling along inch by inch, our fingertips searching for a hairline crack that concealed the hidden compartment. I stopped when I got to the far left side of the bookcase and gave my throbbing hand a shake. Between that, the Sprinkle Snake bite, the bee stings, and the head wound I'd gotten in Training Wheels, I was turning into a bit of a mess. I glanced down at the bottom of the bookcase and blinked. The shelves were completely empty, their contents lying in a jumbled pile at my feet, with one exception. There, standing perfectly upright all by itself on the shelf, was a small black pawn. I glanced around at my feet, where the pile of upended board games, pieces, knickknacks, cards, taxidermied animals, broken jars, piles of marbles, and game boards lay strewn about like confetti. How in the world had the little pawn survived the shelf being upended? Had Ace glued the piece to the shelf? And if so, why? I crouched down and wrapped my fingers around the piece and gave it a tug. It tilted forward as though on hinges. Above me I heard a small pop, followed by Nash's triumphant laugh.

"I got it!" he said. "I must have pressed the right spot or something. Rhett, quit being a lazy bum and get over here and look." I opened my mouth to correct him but shut it again. It didn't really matter. I got to my feet, careful to leave the little pawn in its spot, and walked over to where Nash was standing. The back of the bookcase now showcased the outline of a rectangular panel, a panel that I'd accidentally put my hand through. Nash reached in and carefully pulled the square back to reveal the hidden chamber. The first thing I saw was the word *Tunnels*, and my heart lurched excitedly inside my chest. A second later my feeling of triumph evaporated. The bookcase had been hiding something else. Lying on its side, its paper yellowed and brittle around the edges, was an instruction booklet.

"*The Pirate's Wrath*," Nash breathed as he read the title on the front of the booklet.

"I thought Ace said he destroyed the game," I breathed, ignoring the shiver of fear that raced down my spine.

"He did," Nash said. "He just didn't destroy the directions." He glanced over at me, and I could see the same question in his eyes that must be in mine. If he didn't destroy the directions, how did we know for sure that he destroyed the game?

"But why keep the directions?" I asked.

"How in the world would I know?" Nash snapped, reaching a tentative finger out to touch the booklet as though it might burn him. I snatched his hand back before he made contact and glared at him. Why did he always feel the need to play with fire? I leaned forward to get a better look at it. It wasn't a rectangle like other instruction booklets I'd seen, but octagonal in shape.

Its thick yellowed paper was illustrated to look like it had metal clasps on the corners like the latches on a treasure chest, and in the center was a skull-and-crossbones Jolly Roger. Threaded through the empty eye socket of the skull was a heavy-looking golden chain, studded with oversize jewels.

"Too bad it's not the actual game. That would be something to see," Nash murmured wistfully, and I took my eyes off the booklet to glare at him.

"You're joking, right? You'd actually want to go joy-riding in a pirate game? A pirate game that killed our uncle, might I add. What's wrong with you?"

"No clue," Nash said, and then held up his hands in surrender as I narrowed my eyes at him. "It was a joke," he said. I turned back to the booklet as he muttered "sort of" under his breath. I reached in gingerly and picked up the booklet. The paper felt stiff and brittle under my hands, its edges crinkled and wavy as though someone had dropped it in water once.

"It's not a snake," Nash pointed out. "It's not going to bite you."

"Sure feels like a snake," I breathed as I carefully paged through the booklet, scanning the text. The goal was to get your trading vessel around the world, picking up precious cargo and goods as you went along, all the while avoiding the dread pirate Ogden and his evil crew. I scanned the small map inside, noting the Island of Hidden Caves, the Bay of Blood, and the Strait of Skulls. I got to the back of the booklet and paused.

"Where's the last page?" Nash asked, looking over my shoulder.

"It's gone," I said. "It looks like someone tore it out." I ran my finger over the torn edge of the paper.

"That stinks," Nash grumbled. "That's the page that tells you how to win the game."

"I guess it doesn't matter," I said, closing the booklet. "The game doesn't exist anymore." I turned to Nash. "I can understand why he'd hide the Pirate's Wrath directions, but why would he hide Tunnels?"

Nash shrugged. "Cress said it was a gateway game or whatever. Didn't she compare it to the subway or something?"

"Train station," I corrected him. "She said it was like a train station where Wanderers could travel to and from games that were not their own."

"Maybe Ace didn't want Ogden to get it?" Nash said. "Maybe you can still get into The Pirate's Wrath through there? Even though the game has been destroyed."

"I hope not," I said with a shudder. "That's one game I never want to experience."

"Is it possible that he was hiding it from us?" Nash asked.

"Maybe," I said, biting my lip.

"Do you still have the directions or whatever Cress gave us?" Nash asked, interrupting my thoughts. I nodded and reached into my pocket to pull out the small scrap of paper that Cress had scribbled her instructions on. To my surprise, my fingers brushed up against something metallic. I pulled it out and held it up.

"What's that key for?" Nash said.

"I don't know," I said as I turned it over slowly in my hand. "It was on the floor by the window. I totally forgot I picked it up. Do you think Ogden dropped it?"

"No clue," Nash said.

"Oh, I love clues!" said a female voice so close to my ear that I jumped and almost dropped the key. Snow White had glided into the room to peer over my shoulder. She smelled like the overly pungent lilies people always had at a funeral, and I sneezed.

"Bless you," she trilled, offering me a heavily embroidered handkerchief. I thanked her but didn't actually use it. It felt wrong to blow snot into something like that.

"Fat lot of good that key does us," Nash grouched. He turned to me impatiently. "Do you still have that paper from Cress or not? Although with our luck, she just wrote down her grocery list on it or something." I stuffed the key back into my pocket and dug around in the other one for a second before finally producing the slip of paper. I unfolded it quickly and scanned her small, neat handwriting, thankful that it was not, in fact, a grocery list. I cleared my throat and read out loud the directions she'd written down.

Enter the game.
Don't forget a flashlight.
Don't get distracted by anything bright and shiny.
Watch out for the badger. He's mean.
Follow the signs to Lost Lore.
Try to avoid the Miner cards. But if you get one,
be prepared to duck. They almost always involve
something sharp swinging for your head.
I'll meet you at the entrance to Lost Lore. You'll
know it's the right one by the symbols etched
around the door.
If you hear a canary sing, hold your breath.
Don't forget my payment.

"Oh good, super simple and straightforward," Nash said in my ear, and I snorted.

"I adore canaries," Snow White said before picking up the dust rag she'd abandoned on the desk and fluttering out of the room. Nash turned and thumped Tunnels onto Ace's desk.

"Ready?" he said as he stretched his neck from side to side and bounced on his feet.

"No!" I said. "Are you serious right now? We're covered in chocolate fudge, Ace's office is trashed, I'm starving, and I think we've had about two hours of sleep in the last twenty-four hours."

"Hm," Nash said, looking around as though seeing the office for the first time. "You may have a point."

"Hey!" I called through the open door. "Snow White!" She popped her head back through the door so fast that we both jumped. "Um, do you know how to cook?" I asked.

"Of course!" she trilled happily. "I'll whip something up!"

"This is a waste of time," Nash protested. "We need to get to Ace. He's our only hope of finding Mom."

"I agree," I said. "But remember what Ace told us? You never go into a game hungry? I feel like we are a recipe for disaster right now." Nash hesitated; his arms crossed over his filthy chocolate-covered chest before he finally nodded.

"Fine," he said. "But let's hurry. Something tells me that she's the kind of girl who won't wait around for us. We eat something, we take a quick shower, and we go. Deal?" I nodded, and we both turned as Snow White started singing something about pancakes.

A half hour later we were fed, showered, and somewhat more prepared for what we were about to do. I'd managed to snatch the instruction manual to Tunnels out of the box and studied it between mouthfuls of pancakes. The object of the game was simple enough: be the first to find your way through the labyrinth of tunnels made by miners. The catch was that the miners were moles. The instruction manual showed small ratlike creatures complete with goggles, hard hats, and large paddle-like feet sporting some not-so-cute claws. There was also a marauding badger that you wanted to avoid, since a run-in with her could send you back to start. It was a dice game with a few tricky spots that involved picking up one of the cards that Cress had mentioned in her note. I glanced around at the office, which we'd left in complete disarray. Board game pieces covered almost every inch of the floor, among the trashed treasures that had so neatly adorned the now empty bookcase. Its glass-fronted doors were still swung wide to reveal the gaping hole where my hand had gone through. The entire place had an overwhelming chocolate smell, and there were smears of the stuff all over the walls and furniture.

"How mad do you think Ace is going to be when he sees this?" I asked.

"Not as mad as if we left him in a game full of

princesses for the rest of his life," Nash said. "Ready?" He moved his hand so that it hovered over the cover of the Tunnels box.

"Wait a second," I said. "What do we do about that?" I pointed a finger to where the Pirate's Wrath directions sat ominously on the corner of Ace's desk.

"Um, I think he's going to know we found it when he sees the bookcase, don't you think?" Nash said.

"But should we leave it here? Unprotected?" I asked. "It feels wrong somehow. Don't ask me why."

"Chief will be here to watch it," Nash said. Chief let out a woof and moved into position next to Nash, his head pressed firmly into Nash's hand.

"I think he just said 'Forget that, I'm coming with you' in dog," I said.

"So what do you suggest we do?" Nash asked impatiently. I studied the booklet for a second, weighing our options.

"Think we should take it with us?" I asked.

Nash shrugged. "Sure."

I gingerly picked it up and tucked it into my pocket next to the mysterious key and the directions from Cress. The feel of the directions against my fingertips jogged my memory, and I turned to Nash.

"Flashlights and Cress's payment," I said.

Nash slapped his forehead. "I'll get the flashlights.

You grab the rock." With that he disappeared from the office, reappearing a moment later with two large lantern-style flashlights. I grabbed the rock that had once held Excalibur, and immediately wished that we'd offered up something lighter as payment. The thing weighed a solid twenty pounds at least, and wasn't going to be easy to transport. I glanced back at the bookshelf, impressed that it had been able to support the heavy treasure. I looked up as Nash shut the office door behind himself, careful to throw all the bolts and locks.

"Um," I said, jerking my head at the rock. "We may have made a bad choice on payments."

Nash walked over and hefted the rock into his hands with a grunt, his face turning red. He dropped it onto Ace's desk with a clunk. A second later there was a splintering sound and the right side of the desk collapsed, sending the giant rock careening to the floor. We both jumped back, narrowly avoiding our feet getting smashed on impact.

"Right," Nash said as we both inspected the rather impressive dent in the floor. "Well, she'll just have to accept something else." He glanced around at the jumble on the floor and dug around a bit before holding up an elongated skull. It appeared at first glance to be the skull of a horse, although that was just a guess since I didn't routinely study horse skulls. A large curled horn stuck out of the front of the skull and ended in a lethal-looking point.

"She's a girl. Girls like unicorns, right?" Nash said, turning the skull this way and that.

"Somehow she doesn't strike me as that type of girl," I said, picturing the no-nonsense Cress.

"Right," Nash said, discarding the skull. He dug around a bit more and came up with a Ziploc bag with what looked like a fist-sized chunk of gold. He held it up for approval.

"What's it say?" I asked, squinting at the small label affixed to the front of the bag. Nash turned the bag around to peer at the label.

"It says, 'Gold. Don't touch'!" he read, and then looked at me.

"That should do the trick," I said. Nash tossed it to me and I shoved it into my pocket, and I picked up the flashlights.

Nash placed one hand firmly on Chief's head as we reached out together and gave the lid of the box three hard raps. "Open sesame!"

CRESS

Ghosts. I was just seeing ghosts. Those two boys didn't look like Sam, they didn't. They were just boys. Maybe that was why I thought they looked like him. They were almost the exact age Sam was the first time I met him. That was it. That was all.

The boys hadn't followed me through the tunnel, which wasn't a complete surprise. The tunnels out of games acted the way they wanted to, sometimes dumping you in the middle of the board game Tunnels, sometimes depositing you near the start. They rarely dumped you in the same place twice. I'd told them how to find Lost Lore, though, so that was where I'd meet them. What had they said their names were? Nash and Rhett? They'd never told me what game they were from, an oversight I'd make sure to correct as soon as possible. They looked a little odd with their strange baggy shorts, and shirts with pictures drawn on the front, so maybe their game was something futuristic, possibly something about outer space. If that was the case it would make sense that I'd never run into them before now. I hated outer space games. Aliens were a big no for me, thanks.

I sighed and pulled my headlamp from its pocket on my belt and flicked it on. The yellow light illuminated a narrow tunnel, the ceiling a mere inch or so from my head, and I looked left and right, trying to get my bearings. I wrinkled my nose at the smell of stale urine and bones. This part of the game was called the Badger's Den, and I usually managed to avoid it. Not that the badger scared me; in fact he tended to give me a wide berth. Still, if he found me poking around, he wouldn't be pleased. It was a short walk to a tunnel intersection, and I stopped to shine my headlamp on the signs I'd posted on the corner. Those signs had been the work of years, but they'd been more than worth the effort. I turned left to head toward Lost Lore just as my stomach let out an unhappy gurgle, and I decided that a quick detour for some food was in order. I turned around and headed in the opposite direction. The tunnel opened up, the ceiling above me getting higher and higher by the minute until it hit a good twenty feet. I heard a scurrying sound to my left and held up a hand in greeting as four different mole men bustled by me with their overflowing wheelbarrows. They were one of the reasons why this particular game was so complex. They just kept digging new tunnels to accommodate new board games. I took two more lefts and a right and felt myself relax involuntarily when I spotted the door to my house. Well, house might be a bit grand, it was a door in the side of the tunnel, but it was my door, and that's what mattered.

Reaching up, I unhooked my earring and slid the key into the lock. The door creaked as it opened, and I ducked inside. I was home. This too had taken years to create, but I'd managed to barter the services of a few of the mole men in exchange for some tips about getting past the badger. They'd helped me dig out three small rooms, and they were my favorite places to be. I had a kitchen, a small living room, and a bedroom, and they were all mine. I'd furnished them with bits and pieces I'd pilfered from board games I'd visited, and the result was a colorful jumble of furniture and artwork. I foraged around until I found some bread and jam, and sat down to make myself a sandwich. The bread was almost the exact color of Rhett's and Nash's hair. The same color that Sam's hair had been. The memory came flooding back, and this time I let it. I shut my eyes, and I remembered.

It had been a cold morning on board The Royal Run, *and my knees had been raw from kneeling on the cold, wet deck. It was my job to scrub the bloodstains off the battered boards, despite the fact that they never really came clean. My back stung, the result of a lashing I'd received that I didn't deserve, and my hair hung in lank chunks down my back for want of a brushing. I hadn't had a decent meal in over two days since I refused to eat the weevil-infested bread that cook had offered up. The sea around us was calm and still, and* The Royal Run *bobbed along like so much driftwood. We hadn't spotted a game player in days, a fact that was making Captain O irritable, and he paced back and forth along the deck, his boots heavy as he scanned the horizon for his next victim.*

The boy had appeared out of nowhere. One moment, Gorf, the second mate, was standing over me sneering and spitting out insults, and the next, there was the boy. I'd peered up at him, wondering if hunger had finally made me lose my grip on reality. He'd ducked behind the masthead, his finger to his lips as Captain O stomped past, oblivious to the intruder aboard his ship. I'd stayed quiet, even as Captain O stepped on my calf, not bothering to step over the deckhand who might as well have been a pile of lobster traps for all he was concerned. I wasn't a main player in this game. I was scenery.

"Hey," the boy whispered. "What's your name?"

"Cressida," I whispered back, deciding that I might as well go along with this hallucination. It was more interesting than swabbing the deck anyway.

"Hey, Cress," the boy said with a grin. "Want to get out of here?"

I did. He'd held out a hand, and I'd slipped mine into it, and we'd left The Royal Run behind. My life had never been the same. I'd never known a world existed outside of my game, or that I could visit other games, better games, than the one I belonged to. That first day we went to a game, had food—good food—and I'd eaten until I felt sick. Then on to a game full of nothing but treehouses and then one with cool, quiet forests. When Sam had finally taken me back to my own game, I felt like I'd opened my eyes for the first time in my life. I didn't want to shut them ever again. I was awake, and I refused to go back to sleep. But that didn't justify what I did next. Not at all.

NINETEEN

The first thing I noticed when I opened my eyes was the smell of the game. Sugar Bugs had smelled overpoweringly sweet, like one of those overly pungent cotton-candy-scented markers, but this game smelled like someone's moldy old basement. It was also pitch-black.

"Well," Nash's voice said beside me, "I guess I know why Cress told us to bring a flashlight." Chief let out a low growl that made my hair stand on end, and I fumbled with my flashlight, kicking myself for not turning it on before we left. Nash managed to flick his flashlight on, illuminating the underground chamber. I yelped in surprise as I saw what Chief had been growling at. Standing less than five feet away from us was a badger roughly the size of a small pony. Her fur was a dirty grayish brown, and long buck teeth protruded from the front of her oversize jaws. Her cloudy brown eyes were magnified by large circular goggles, and her massive feet sported foot-long claws. She studied us a second, clicking her front teeth together as though wondering how we tasted.

I froze, unsure of what our next move was. I could feel the dice for this game in my pocket, but rolling them would require moving, which didn't seem wise at the moment. Chief stalked forward, slinking along in a crouched position until he stood inches away from the thing. The hair on his ruff stood on edge as he let out another furious growl. The badger studied the dog for a moment, as though she were weighing her options. Finally, she huffed, sending a fine mist of saliva over us, and scuttled down one of the tunnels to our right.

"Thanks," Nash said, stooping to rub Chief's head. "I apologize for suggesting that we leave you home." Now that the badger was gone, we had a chance to look around ourselves. We were standing in the center of a large underground chamber with tunnels shooting out from every direction like the spokes of a wheel. The ceiling was domed and made of dirt with a complicated web of roots crisscrossing across its surface to provide some support.

"I know Cress mentioned not letting the badger get

us," I said with a shudder. "But she could have mentioned that it was the size of Ace's pickup."

"Turn on your flashlight," Nash said with a jerk of his chin at the flashlight I still held in my hand. "A little extra illumination in here would be a good thing." I turned the knob on my flashlight, but all it did was click; no light came on.

"Don't tell me that you forgot to check the batteries before we left," I said to Nash.

"Okay," Nash said with a wince. "I won't tell you, then." I groaned in exasperation, chucking my useless flashlight to the side.

"Grab your dice," I snapped. "We need to get a move on." Nash did a quick pat down of himself and found a set of muddy-looking brown dice in his back pocket. A quick rummage in my pocket and I had a similar set in hand.

"Remember," I said, pulling out Cress's instructions. "We can't get distracted by anything shiny, and we need to look for signs pointing to Lost Lore."

"Signs like that one?" Nash asked. To our right was a tall signpost with different-sized boards nailed all up and down its length. Each board had a game's name written on it, and I spotted Pillage, Gone Gnoming, Dragon Disasters, Ghastly Graveyard, Castle Chaos, and more written in handwriting that seemed familiar. I looked down at Cress's directions and then back up at the signs. The handwriting was the exact same, down to the little loop she put at the end of the letter e.

"Hey, Nash," I said, and he looked over at me, eyebrow raised. "Look," I said, holding out Cress's directions.

Nash let out a whistle of appreciation. "She did all that? Wow. She must have had some time on her hands."

"Remember what Ace said? She's been thirteen for as long as he can remember. She's also the only Wanderer he's ever heard of besides our great-great-whoever they were."

"But," Nash said, cocking his head, "didn't Ace say that a Wanderer could go to our world? So why is she spending all her time in games? Why doesn't she get out?"

"If we ever manage to find Lost Lore, we'll ask her, but we aren't going to do that if we don't get a move on. Look," I said, pointing at Cress's signs. "That one says Lost Lore. It's pointing down that tunnel on the left. Do you want to roll first? Or should I?"

Instead of responding, Nash jangled the dice in his hand, the sound oddly muffled in the dirt chamber. Then he rolled. We both leaned forward to see what number he'd gotten.

"Double sixes," Nash said, scooping the dice back up. "That has to be good, right?" He turned to head down the tunnel, but I shot out a hand to stop him.

"Wait," I said. "You have the only light. You can't just leave."

"Um, I kind of have to," Nash said. "Just follow my light after you roll." I stood there a second, trying to think of an argument that wouldn't leave me standing in the dark, rodent-infested tunnel, and came up short.

"Chief stays with me, then," I said, reaching out to grab the dog's collar. He sat down by my side and whined. "You want to find Ace too, don't you?" I said, rubbing the soft fur between his ears. Nash was shifting uncomfortably from foot to foot, and I knew he was experiencing that painful tingle that escalated the longer you failed to move. With one last glance at us, Nash headed off down the far-left tunnel. The light in his hand illuminated the dirt ceiling arching overhead. As soon as he entered the tunnel his light faded and got dimmer. Suddenly him rolling double sixes didn't seem so great after all.

I held on tight to Chief's collar and dug out my own dice, rolling them carefully into the palm of my other hand, afraid to roll them on the ground and lose them in the dark. The light from Nash's flashlight was almost gone, but I could just make out the numbers. I'd rolled a seven. Nash must have rounded a bend in his tunnel then, because I was thrown into complete darkness for the second time in a matter of minutes. The tingle in my feet started immediately. With one hand on Chief's collar and the other held out in front of me to avoid running into a wall, I headed in the direction of the tunnel Nash had disappeared down, my eyes straining to find the light. Chief must have better night vision than I did, though, and I felt him tug me hard toward the left. I followed. I felt the air around me shift, and I had a sense of the walls being closer. A moment later I knew that following Chief's lead had been the right choice as I saw a faint patch of light shining ahead. I hurried then, anxious to be back with Nash and the flashlight. We rounded a corner, and I caught sight of my brother up ahead. He was standing beside what looked like a giant pile of gemstones, his eyes as round as saucers as he stared at them in wonder. I took a step forward and hit an invisible wall of air. My turn was up.

"Roll again!" I called to Nash, but he didn't respond. He was completely enthralled, and I remembered Cress's second warning. "Don't get distracted by anything bright and shiny," I murmured. It was too late for Nash, though. He'd been sucked into some kind of spell, and even though I was yelling his name so loudly that it bounced back off the dirt walls of the tunnel in disconcerting echoes, he was oblivious. Thankfully Chief wasn't constrained by the same rules of the game that I was, and he trotted forward and, without any hesitation or fuss, bit Nash's leg. Nash jumped, snapping out of his trance as he yelped in pain and whirled to face Chief. He was about to turn back to the pile of jewels, and I cupped my hand around my mouth and yelled, "Don't get distracted by anything bright and shiny!"

For a second I thought Nash wasn't going to listen, but then he turned his back on the gems and faced me, the flashlight shining directly into my eyes.

"Whoa," he said.

"How's your leg?" I asked.

"Sore," Nash said, rubbing it as he gave Chief a half smile. "Next time just bark at me or something, okay, man? That bite's going to leave a mark."

"Roll," I said with a quick glance over my shoulder. "I want to get out of this creepy game." Nash rolled, and once again headed off down the path, his light getting alarmingly smaller by the second. I followed, and we slowly made our way down the labyrinth of tunnels, periodically stopping to inspect Cress's hand-lettered signs. The only mishap happened when I landed on a Miner card. Thankfully I remembered Cress's instructions to duck, and narrowly missed experiencing death by shovel.

Finally, we made it to the right tunnel, or at least, what we hoped was the right tunnel. I'd managed to roll higher than Nash the last few turns, and I was in the lead by a few steps. This tunnel was different from the one we'd just left. For one thing, the ground under our feet had transitioned at some point from dirt to cobblestones, and the ceiling was now held up with thick stone arches instead of roots. I rolled a nine and rounded a corner to find a door blocking the path. I shined the flashlight I'd been all too happy to take from Nash up at it and sighed in relief. Etched in the thick wood were symbols from fairy tales. I immediately spotted Cinderella's glass slipper and Snow White's apple, and I ran my hand over the thick carvings as I identified Red Riding Hood's cape, Hansel and Gretel's cottage, and a long, lethal-looking spinning wheel. I leaned in to peer at Red Riding Hood's cape and smiled. I'd seen it before, on Cress. She and Ace apparently both had the same hobby. My hand continued its journey as I waited for Nash and Chief to catch up, and I realized that there were quite a few symbols that I couldn't place with a specific fairy tale. A large, hairy-looking gorilla for one, and a misshapen giant holding a massive mallet for another. I could have looked at the door for hours, but Nash rolled a ten and finally caught up.

"Well, that looks pretty spot-on," Nash said. "How do we get this door open?"

"I have no idea," I said, glancing back down at the note from Cress. "She just said she'd meet us here."

Our flashlight chose that moment to die.

TWENTY

"Awesome," Nash said. "Just amazing."

"Yeah," I grumbled. "It's almost like someone should have checked the batteries."

"Whatever," Nash said. "At least we found the door."

"True," I said. "It could be worse."

"Yeah," Nash said. "There could be a giant vicious badger wandering around in here with us. Oh wait . . ."

"Just help me figure out how to get this door open," I said. "Maybe it's not so dark on the other side."

"It's wild," Nash mused as he took his position beside me. "It's so dark in here that I can't tell if my eyes are open or shut." I ignored him, running my fingers over the etchings I'd just been studying. There had to be a way to open the door. There just had to be. I felt the darkness pressing in on us from all sides, and I shoved aside the panic that was threatening to crush me like an empty soda can.

"You know what would be awesome?" Nash said, still on his sarcastic bender. "If Cress had told us how to actually open this door. Or, better yet, if it had a handle like a normal door."

I pressed my hand flat against it and shut my eyes to concentrate, although Nash was right, it was kind of a pointless gesture. My palm tingled slightly, just like it had tingled the first time I'd placed my hand on Training Wheels. I opened my eyes and stood back.

"It's a game," I said.

"Duh," Nash groaned. "Seriously? That's all you got?"

"Think about it," I said. "Behind this door is a game, right?"

"It'd better be Lost Lore," Nash agreed.

"Right, so how do we get into games?" I prompted. I couldn't see Nash's face, but I heard his sharp inhale, which let me know that he'd finally caught on.

"On the count of three?" I said.

"Do you have a hand on Chief?" Nash asked.

"Got him," I confirmed.

"One, two, buckle my shoe," Nash counted. Together we knocked on the wooden door, the sound echoing back down the empty tunnel behind us.

"Open sesame," we said in unison. The door groaned and swung inward, the light on the other side so bright that I felt momentarily blinded.

"It took you two long enough," someone said, and I blinked hard through eyes that were streaming with tears from the sudden onslaught of light.

"Cress? Is that you?" I said. "Man, it's bright. Is this game on the surface of the sun or what?"

"It's me," Cress said. "Just blink a lot until your eyes stop watering. Transitioning from the tunnel is rough, especially your first time. I was about to give up on you two. What took you so long? Do you have my payment?"

"We had a hard time finding the game," I said. I left it at that, deciding on the spot not to reveal the hidden chamber our grandfather had constructed to hide the game.

"Enough chitchatting," Nash said. "Let's get going."

I glanced back, noting that the door to Tunnels had shut behind us, camouflaged as an oversize rock set against the side of a small grassy hill.

"Payment?" Cress said, holding out a hand expectantly. Nash and I exchanged a nervous glance.

"We had to make a slight change to that," Nash said. "The original offer, the rock that held Excalibur, turned out to weigh a lot."

"A lot?" Cress said, sounding unimpressed.

"Like, it broke a desk and almost broke our feet,

a lot," Nash said to clarify. "So we made a swap." I reached into my pocket and pulled out the hunk of gold encased in its Ziploc bag. Cress's face drained of color as Nash took it from my hand and proceeded to open the top of the bag so he could pull out the gold for her to inspect.

"Stop!" she said. "If that's what I think it is, you can't touch it."

"Um," Nash said, glancing from the bag to Cress and back again. "I kind of already am."

Cress shook her head. "You can't touch it with your bare hand. That's Midas stone. Anything it touches will turn to gold."

"Oh!" Nash said, jerking his hand back out and quickly resealing the bag. "That seems dangerous. You'd think somebody could have a written a warning on it or something." Cress stomped over to him and turned the bag over in his hand to point at the small white label affixed to the bottom corner of the bag, which clearly read *Gold. Don't Touch.*

"Oh," Nash said. "Right."

"It's not what we agreed to," Cress said. "But I'll accept the trade." Nash held it out, but before he could pass it to her I jerked it out of his hand.

"Wait," I said. "The deal was that you help us find our grandfather."

"No," Cress said, shaking her head. "The deal was that I help you get into this game. I did. Hand it over."

"This is worth more than your average rock that used to hold a sword," I went on, talking fast and thinking faster. "So I think you're going to need to help us find him if you want it." Cress gritted her teeth, considering. I'd seen the way her eyes lit up when we mentioned that rock, though, and I knew we had her.

"Fine," she snapped. "But double-cross me again and you'll live to regret it." I blinked at her in surprise. For a second there her voice had changed, taking on the swarthy twang of a seasoned sailor. Nash slipped the Ziploc-covered piece of gold into his pocket gingerly, a look on his face that made it clear that he wasn't really thrilled about the arrangement.

"So where should we start looking?" I asked.

Cress rolled her eyes toward the sky and sighed. "We don't just start looking. You're in a game. You have to play to move. Are you two completely clueless about all of this?"

I said yes at the exact moment that Nash said no. Cress looked from one of us to the other and back again before shaking her head in exasperation. Her curls bounced around her face merrily, completely at odds with her serious expression.

"Okay, how do we play?" Nash said. "Spinner? Dice? Cards?"

"Cards," Cress said, wrinkling her nose in disgust. "You're not going to like most of them. They will send you to different parts of the game, where you have to perform some feat of bravery or chivalry in order to get information. The goal is to locate as many lost items of lore as possible before the game ends. There are easier items like Snow White's apple and harder ones like Merlin's cloak."

"Merlin's cloak?" I said, impressed.

Cress nodded. "Yeah, that one's stupid hard. I've been hired to find it twice and failed. I have a feeling it's invisible, and invisible stuff is almost impossible to find. I had to give back the payment and everything."

"What was the payment?" I asked.

"Talking chipmunk," Cress said. "This was back when I still accepted live animals as payment. I was actually kind of sad to give him back. He was pretty funny for a rodent."

"Wait, how many times have you played this game?" I asked.

She stopped to consider that question, her fingers out as she silently counted on them.

"Seven?" she said, not sounding completely sure.

"Seven?!" I repeated.

"Five times were for jobs," she said. "I've been hired to figure out a few different tricky parts of this game. Twice I played it for my own reasons."

"Reasons like a snazzy new cape?" I asked, eyebrow raised.

Cress shot me a sharp look and rolled her shoulders under the thick red fabric of her cape. "If you could find a coat that made your scent impossible to track, you wouldn't pass it up either."

"That's probably true," I agreed. I made a mental note to ask Ace for a thorough tour of his bookshelves. If he was casually storing a Midas stone in there, what else had he pilfered from board games over the years?

"Where are the cards?" Nash asked, interrupting my thoughts.

"Better check your pockets," Cress said. We did. I shouldn't have been surprised to find a card there—this wasn't my first game, after all—but I still was. Some things about board game bounding were harder to get used to than others. I pulled the card out and held it up for Nash and Cress to see. It was a light green with thick vines in a darker green winding around the outside.

"Wait," Cress said. She moved over to stand beside me, placing a hand on my shoulder. She looked pointedly at Nash until he did the same.

"Um, what are we doing?" Nash said.

"We're acting as one player," Cress said as though this should have been obvious. "If we're touching, we

232

move together. Unless you'd like to wander all over this game by yourself."

I glanced over at Nash, eyebrow raised. "Did we know we could do that?"

Nash shrugged. "Nope, but I guess it makes sense. I mean, that's how we got Chief here." Nash whistled for Chief, who was busy inspecting a nearby bush. He came trotting over to us, taking a seat beside Nash. Nash put one hand on the big dog's collar and looked over at me.

"Ready or not," he said.

I took a deep breath and read aloud. "Proceed to a castle where dragons await, ready to protect a sleeping princess's fate." My feet started to tingle and itch, and I looked up. In the distance a large black castle loomed, its surface covered in a thick tangle of thorns and vines.

"Man, I hate Sleeping Beauty's castle," Cress said. "It's the worst."

"Do you think our grandfather is in there?" I asked.

"Only one way to find out," Nash said. And making sure to stay close enough for contact, we started off into the woods.

TWENTY-ONE

The walk through the woods was interesting to say the least. Cress explained that we needed to stay in physical contact with one another for the entire turn, or we'd be considered a new player in the game. This made sense, but I couldn't help but think that we looked a lot like Dorothy and her buddies walking down the yellow brick road in *The Wizard of Oz*. We moved as quickly as possible down the dirt path through the woods, careful to keep the castle in sight. As we walked, I found myself glancing over at Cress. She was at ease in this game, just like she'd been at ease in Sugar Bugs. I wondered if Nash and I would ever feel like that. Although, I reasoned, it's probably a lot easier to be relaxed when you know that the worst thing that can happen to you is getting sent back to the start of a game. Around us, squirrels, brightly colored birds, and chipmunks scampered from branch to branch, chittering and chirping to one another happily.

"Just don't start singing," Cress warned. "Those fluff balls can be a real nuisance."

"I know Wanderers don't age," Nash said. "So does that make them immortal?" I jerked my head up, confused, because those words were about to come out of my mouth. Sometimes being a twin was a little creepy.

Cress glanced at us, eyebrows raised. "I keep forgetting you two are new at this." She paused, as though considering how to answer, and then shrugged. "Depends what you think of as immortal," Cress said. "I don't die. I just go back to the start of whatever game I was in. For a long time I thought everyone did that. I learned the hard way that they don't." I was about to ask her what she meant by that when we burst abruptly from the shelter of the trees and onto a drawbridge. We stopped, and I surveyed the scene. The black castle loomed ahead of us, surrounded on all sides by what I think was supposed to be a moat. A deep ravine was cut into the earth in a circle around the castle, but instead of water, thick, gnarled vines intertwined around one another sporting spikes as long as my arm. In front of us was a drawbridge made of rough wooden beams and held together with a clunky chain. The tingling in my feet had started the moment we stopped moving and was building to an uncomfortable crescendo that wouldn't be ignored. I could tell by the way Nash was shifting from side to side that he felt it too. Even Chief was fidgeting, his eyes wide and alert as he took in his surroundings.

"Let's get this over with," Cress said, and together we headed down the drawbridge. We were almost all the way across when the dragons showed up. The first one swooped low, screeching and breathing fire. It was a muted green, and not much bigger than Chief. It snapped its jaws at the dog before belching out a stream of fire that immediately ignited the wood of the drawbridge behind us. The heat hit a second later, blistering at our backs and making my eyes burn.

"Run!" Cress said, breaking away from us to sprint for the dark opening to the castle. I ducked as a bright yellow dragon made a grab for my head with eagle-like talons. Chief let out a snarl and launched himself into the air, catching the dragon by one dangling claw. He yanked it out of the sky and down onto the bridge with a crash. I yelped and jumped sideways out of the way as the oversize lizard landed in a tangle of wings and snapping jaws. Chief gave one powerful twist of his neck and flipped the dragon off the bridge entirely, sending it crashing down to the thorn-filled moat.

"Good dog," I breathed, regaining my feet and stumbling after Nash and Cress through the open castle door. Chief bounded in a second later and a heavy iron grate came crashing down behind us. I looked over to see Cress holding a long, dangling rope that she was expertly knotting around a metal post screwed into the wall. Two dragons collided with the grate, and I scrambled backward as they ripped at the metal with their teeth, shrieking in protest.

"Where's the yellow one?" Cress said, coming to stand beside me.

"Chief chucked it off the bridge," I said.

"Really?" Cress said, turning to look at Chief, who was currently crouched beside Nash, his teeth bared at the dragons. "I changed my mind. I'll take the dog as my payment."

"Not ours to give," I said. "He's our grandfather's dog."

"Hm," Cress said, somewhat grudgingly, with one last covetous look at Chief. "We need to get our clue."

"What clue?" I asked.

"The clue to the whereabouts of Sleeping Beauty's missing spindle. We more than earned it," she said with a jerk of her head at the dragons. She turned to me. "Hold up your right hand." I did what she said, and a second later something hard thunked into my palm.

"What is that?" Nash said, coming to peer over my

shoulder at the thick leather square.

"The clue," Cress said. "Might as well read it."

I squinted down at the square. There were definitely words etched into its surface, but it was too dark inside the gloomy castle to see what it said.

"Oh, for Merlin's sake," Cress muttered, ripping the square out of my hand and going over to the gate, where the dragons were still tugging at the metal, breathing fire like they could melt it if they just tried hard enough. She held up the leather square so that the light from their fires illuminated the etched letters.

"What's it say?" Nash asked.

"I've gotten this one before," Cress said, tossing it aside.

"But what did it say?" Nash said again.

"Oh, just that we need to ask the fairies. Those cards pop up a lot. There's an awful lot of fairies in fairy tales."

"Would any of these fairies know where our grand-father is?" I asked.

"They might," Cress said. "You sometimes get to ask them to grant you a wish, which would be useful here. A few of them are nasty and like to hand out curses disguised as gifts. Once they made a character magical shoes that made him the best dancer in the kingdom."

"That doesn't sound so bad," Nash said.

"He couldn't *stop* dancing," Cress said. "Poor guy eventually threw himself off the roof of his castle so he could go back to start and try again."

"Yikes," I said.

"Yup," Cress said. "But now that we got the clue, we'll have to go talk to a fairy. If we don't, we won't be allowed to draw the next card."

"Do we still need to be touching?" I asked.

Cress shook her head. "No. That only matters right after you pull a card, not if you're fulfilling a clue." The game seemed confusing to me, but I also hadn't played it as many times as Cress, so I wasn't about to challenge her. Besides, we had bigger problems than the logistics of Lost Lore.

"Um," I said, glancing behind me at the snarling dragons. "Not that that wasn't a great time, but how do we get out of here without going through them?"

"Secret passage," Cress said. "There are five of them in this castle. I think the one in the northeast corner will do the trick. Should pop us out right near the Flower Fairy's cottage. She's a bit bossy, but pretty sane compared to a lot of them."

We followed Cress farther into the castle. She knew her way around, taking us through room after room made completely of onyx-colored stones until she came to a chamber full of large portraits. I recognized some of the characters from the familiar fairy tale of Sleeping Beauty and a few characters that I didn't recognize. One in particular was a rather frilly-looking woman with wings. She wore an extravagant green ball gown covered in tiny embroidered flowers, and her face was dimpled and smiling, ringed in a fluff of white hair that reminded me of the round puff of a dandelion.

"Come on," Cress said as she walked up to the portrait and gave it a shove. It slid sideways, revealing a hole in the wall the size of an extra-large pizza. Without any hesitation she hopped into the hole feetfirst and disappeared from view. The portrait of the white-haired fairy swung back into place, covering the hole again.

I hurried forward to catch it before it could close completely, and I swear I heard the fairy in the portrait giggle.

"Come on," I said, purposefully avoiding eye contact with the painting.

"One sec," Nash said. "I'm curious about something."

"Curiosity killed the cat," I said, but Nash ignored me and walked over to a portrait of Sleeping Beauty. He placed his hands on the side of the ornate gold frame and pushed. Sure enough, there was a tunnel behind her portrait too. A quick investigation revealed tunnels behind every single portrait.

"I guess the one you take depends on the clue you get?" Nash said when he was finished.

"Or one of them takes you back to Tunnels," I said. "Those look a lot like the tunnel Cress used to leave Sugar Bugs."

"Hmmm," Nash said, and he walked the perimeter of the room again, sticking his hand experimentally into each of the tunnels behind the portraits until he got to one of a cat wearing large brown boots. This tunnel deflected his hand the same way the tunnel in Sugar Bugs had done.

"Interesting," I said, shifting from side to side impatiently. "But not exactly something we have time for. Can we get on with this now? If we lose Cress we're sunk."

"You go first," Nash said. "Chief and I will follow." I thought about arguing, but it would just waste time that we didn't have. I looked over at the hole and bit my lip.

"Remember what Mom always said," Nash said behind me.

"Eat your vegetables or you're not going to grow?"

Nash snorted. "No. She always told us that being brave didn't mean you weren't scared of something."

"Brave is being scared, and doing it anyway," I said, finishing the familiar line. I took a deep breath and jumped feetfirst into the gaping hole. I was expecting to drop down into a second tunnel, but instead I felt the smooth slope of a slide beneath my back, and I swallowed a scream as I went zipping downward into the pitch-black. I crossed my arms over my chest and leaned back as the slide whipped this way and that, all straight down and all in disconcerting darkness. I heard a yelp coming from somewhere behind me, which let me know Nash was on the same unnerving ride I was.

My stomach lurched sickeningly, and I clenched my teeth, willing myself not to hurl. Right when I thought it was a lost cause, and I was going to lose whatever was left of Snow White's pancakes, I spotted light ahead of me. A minute later I was flying out of the tunnel and into the blinding sunlight. I barely had time to register the surrounding forest before I was dropping through thin air to crash into ice-cold water. A second later Nash splashed down beside me, followed by Chief. We made eye contact underwater before all three of us paddled hard for the surface. I made it up first and gasped in a lungful of air.

Chief erupted a moment later and paddled past me. I turned to see where he was going and spotted Cress waiting for us on the shore. I glanced around, trying to get my bearings. We were in the center of what looked like a picturesque lake complete with a waterfall. If I wasn't still trying my best not to hurl from motion sickness, I'd probably have cared that it was the prettiest place I'd seen in my life. Nash spluttered to the surface next, and together we paddled after Chief.

"You could have warned us," I gasped when we finally made it to shore.

"About which part?" Cress said. "The slide or the water?"

"Either would have been good," I said.

"Why?" Cress said, cocking her head. "Would it have changed anything?"

"Well, no," I admitted.

"All right, then," Cress said. "The Flower Fairy's house is right around the next bend."

"Wait a second," I said, pausing to scrutinize her. "Why aren't you wet?"

"Oh," Cress said with a shrug. "There's a big branch right above the tunnel exit that you can grab on the way out. Swings you right up onto the shore. You just have to know it's there." With that she turned and headed off down a small dirt path that led into the woods.

"I don't like her," Nash said flatly, and I snorted.

"Come on, Chief," I said, thumping my hand against my leg to get the dog's attention. He'd been busy sniffing the rocks that ran along the edge of the lake, and he ignored me. "Chief," I repeated impatiently as I glanced over to where Cress was disappearing into the woods. "Move it, man. We have a fairy to meet."

"Hold up," Nash said as he maneuvered himself down the rocks to where Chief stood. He crouched to inspect the spot that Chief was sniffing. "Get over here!" he called, and I sighed but joined them. I squatted beside Nash and inspected the muck along the edge of the lake.

"Does that look familiar?" Nash asked, pointing to a deep footprint in the mud. The top of the footprint tapered upward into a point while the bottom was a separate defined square.

"Sure looks like it was made by a cowboy boot," I said. "Ace must have been around here pretty recently for that print to still be here."

Pleased with himself, Chief bounded up the embankment and woofed at us, as though we were the ones who had been holding up the show.

"He thinks he's in charge, doesn't he," Nash grumbled as we made our way up the embankment and back onto the path.

"Isn't he?" I said, breaking into a jog to catch up with Cress. We rounded the bend and saw a small cottage in the distance. It was shaped exactly like an oversize tulip bulb and was surrounded by a tumble of flowers barely contained by their white picket fence.

"That looks about right for somebody called the

Flower Fairy," Nash said, stopping so we stood shoulder to shoulder. Cress was nowhere in sight as we walked up to the circular wooden door. Nash was just lifting a hand up to knock when Chief suddenly latched onto his arm.

"Hey!" Nash said, glancing down at the dog. "What's that for?" Chief let out a low warning snarl, and I felt myself stiffen. If Chief was on high alert, then something wasn't right. I glanced around, looking for the danger, but saw nothing that would cause any sort of alarm. Still, something inside me started screaming that we should run. My heart hammered against my rib cage as adrenaline I couldn't even explain flooded my system.

"What is it?" Nash said.

"I don't know," I admitted. "But something feels wrong." I glanced away from the cottage and its quaint garden and scanned the woods. Suddenly Nash dropped like a stone beside me. My yelp of surprise was cut off abruptly by the clunk of a rock colliding with the top of my own head. The last thing I saw before my eyes rolled back in my head was a fuzzy vision of Chief sprinting for the shelter of the woods, something massive and boulder-like hot on his heels.

TWENTY-TWO

I woke up in a cage. I attempted to straighten up from the hunched-sitting position I was in and discovered that I couldn't. My neck let out a spasm of protest as I inspected what appeared to be a very ornate, very oversize birdcage surrounding me on all sides. Beside me, still unconscious, was Nash in his own birdcage, his head lolling to the side, drool dripping out of his mouth.

"Good to see you, boys," said a voice to my left, and I jumped in surprise. It took a second of maneuvering, but I managed to turn my head to the left, where I discovered Ace suspended in a cage only slightly bigger than my own. His knobby knees were tucked up by his ears, and his cowboy boots were nowhere to be seen. The fact that his socks were red with hearts all over them would have been funny in any other circumstance.

"Ace!" I said. "We found you!"

"You did find me," he said, his brow furrowed. "What did you do to this game? I haven't been able to get out."

"We didn't do anything," I said. "Ogden took it. At least that's who we think it was based on Snow White's description. Whoever it was took the game and trashed your office."

"Hm," Ace said, his face dark.

"What happened?" Nash groaned, and I carefully adjusted myself in the cage so I could see him.

"We found Ace!" I said.

"Really?" Nash said, sounding less groggy than a second before. He peered through the bars of his cage at our grandfather, his eyes lighting up as he registered what he was seeing. "We came to save you!" he announced proudly.

"Great job," Ace said dryly.

I turned my head uncomfortably to look around. We were hanging about twenty feet in the air, suspended from a branch by a thick knot of rope. There were five other cages besides ours, and all of them were empty except one. The cage on the opposite side of Ace contained what looked like a tiny woman.

"Is that the Flower Fairy?" I asked Ace.

"Yes," he huffed. "That's Beatrice. Decent fairy as far as fairies go, but utter rubbish at protective magic.

247

You'd have thought she'd have cast some kind of shield over that bulbous monstrosity of a house. Instead, she spends all her time worrying about those flowers of hers. Lot of good a bluebell crop does when the rock giants come a-knocking."

"Where's Chief?" Nash asked.

"I think he got away," I said. My last image of him fleeing something gray and lumpy seemed fuzzy, and I wondered if I'd actually seen it or if my muddled brain had been playing tricks on me.

"What about Cress?" Nash said. "Why isn't she in a cage?"

"Cress?" Ace barked. "What are you two doing with her? You didn't trust her, I hope. You can't trust a Wanderer. Especially not her. Is she the one that got you in here?"

"Sort of," I said. "She told us about Tunnels."

"Tunnels?" Ace said, his face turning white. "How did you find that?"

"Ogden ripped the bookcase off the wall," I said. "I put my hand through your secret compartment when I was trying to get it upright. Why did you have it hidden?"

"Did he get any other games?" Ace interrupted, ignoring my question.

"I don't think so," I said. "The bookcase was still locked. We unlocked it to try to find Tunnels. Cress told us it was the only way to get in here to find you."

"Why would Ogden take Lost Lore?" Nash asked.

"The fact that I can't get out means he didn't just take it," Ace said darkly. "He probably destroyed it or put it into some sort of cat's game trap."

"Why?" I said again. Ace glanced over at me and then away, and I saw a flash of guilt in his eyes. I craned my head around to look at Nash. He was staring at Ace's face, his eyes narrowed. He'd spotted the same thing I had. Ace was hiding something.

"Yeah," Nash pressed. "Why? Why go after you now? You destroyed his game ages ago, right? Why take Mom now? Why take the game? What is it about us Bensons that makes a Wander Lost care about us?"

"Shhhhh," Ace hissed. He shot an anxious glance around the forest, but the only thing near us was a very unconscious fairy. "Don't say that name in a game. Ever."

"Benson?" Nash repeated, and Ace winced.

"Yes!" he snapped.

"Why?" I asked again.

"Because we're bounders," Ace hissed, his voice so quiet I almost couldn't hear him.

"So?" Nash pushed.

"So we can do things even a Wanderer can't, and we can definitely do things a Wander Lost can't." I opened my mouth to ask him why that mattered, but he looked at us, one gray eyebrow arched in expectation. The answer was apparently obvious, if we could just figure out how to grasp it. I thought about everything I knew about being a board game bounder, shutting my eyes as I pictured Ace's expansive shelf of board game treasures he'd apparently spirited out of this game or that. Then I thought about Cress, about her Red Riding Hood cloak, but her apparent ignorance of the world outside of board games. Ogden, of course, could go to the real world from a game, but Ace had said that unlike us, he couldn't remove anything from a game. When Sam hadn't come out of The Pirate's Wrath, Ogden had been allowed to stay in our world, but he'd still taken our mom. What could she do for him that he couldn't do for himself?

"A Wander Lost like Ogden can't take something out of a board game like you can? Right?" I asked, my brain churning.

Ace shook his head slowly.

"But if our mom is in a game," Nash continued, "could Ogden get stuff out of it then? Does having a Benson in a game make that possible?"

Ace nodded, his face grim.

"Does he want something out of this game?" I asked, looking around as though the something might just appear out of thin air.

"Possibly," Ace said. "There are a few useful items from this game that in the hands of a monster like Ogden could wreak real havoc on our world. But I think it's more likely that he wanted me out of the way. As far as he knows, I'm the last of the Bensons."

"He doesn't know about me and Rhett?" Nash said.

Ace shook his head. "If he did, he'd be after you too." Suddenly Ace's rule about not revealing ourselves made a lot more sense. I leaned forward inside my cage, which was a mistake. It swung forward alarmingly, and I let out a yelp of surprise.

The Flower Fairy, Beatrice, woke up with a snort. She sat up, adjusting the bright red horn-rimmed glasses that had been askew on her face.

"What in the righteous roses happened?" she said, ruffling the shimmering wings on her back in annoyance. She had rosy cheeks with oversize dimples and large white teeth that could easily replace the keys on a piano.

"Rock giants," Ace said.

"When will those infernal pests ever learn!" she huffed.

"When will *you* learn to get your head out of your flowerpots and put some protections around yourself," Ace snapped.

"Now don't you strike that tone with me, young

man," Beatrice said, brandishing a thin vine-green wand. "I will brook no lectures from the likes of you." I raised an eyebrow at Nash. It had probably been a hot minute since someone had called our grandfather "young man." From the look on his face, he wasn't a fan.

"Brook?" Nash mouthed at me, and I shrugged.

The disgruntled fairy tapped the metal of her cage sharply with her wand. "Brickle Brack," she commanded, and a second later the bars of her cage transformed into tiny white flowers that immediately fell to the ground. Beatrice, however, hovered in place, her small iridescent wings beating so fast they were a blur. She reminded me of a hummingbird as she turned toward Ace.

"I assume those two are the ones you were so fuss-budgeted about?" she said.

"Yes," Ace said. "Those are my grandsons." I shot Nash a quick look, but he just shrugged. Apparently, this Beatrice character knew about us. Ace saw our look and interpreted it correctly.

"Beatrice is an old friend," Ace said. "I've known her for years. She can be trusted, which, considering she's a fairy, is really saying something."

Beatrice buzzed over to inspect Nash and me, her eyes squinting behind her glasses.

"They look like their mother," she proclaimed. "But what are they doing here of all places?"

"They came to save me," Ace said dryly.

"Oh dear," Beatrice said, her hand on her chin.

"Oh dear later," Ace barked. "Get us out of here before those rock heads come back."

"Right, right. Brickle Brack!" Beatrice said, giving Ace's cage an unceremonious whack with her wand. Just like her cage had before, his turned into a flurry of flowers and he dropped to the ground twenty feet below. He landed in a weird crouch and rolled sideways before regaining his feet.

"Where's my boots!" he bellowed up at Beatrice.

"Never you mind," she said, giving her wand another flick. "Picklety Punk," she commanded. Ace's feet were immediately covered in green polka-dot galoshes. He scowled up at her, but she ignored him as she bustled over to my cage. She had her wand poised to give it a whack, but I held up a hand to stop her.

"I'm not sure I can stick that landing," I said with a jerk of my chin toward the ground.

"Not to worry," she chirped. "Brickle Brack! No big smack!" she commanded, giving my cage a thump. I cringed in anticipation of the free fall, but instead I floated down toward the ground as softly as a leaf falling from a tree.

"I want to do it like Rhett," I heard Nash say, and a second later he was floating down too.

"That would have been nice," Ace grumbled as he rubbed his hip. He looked utterly ridiculous in the knee-high green boots, but I decided not to point it out. We had bigger issues than his footwear.

"What's a rock giant?" I asked, deciding not to ask about Cress. She was a sore subject for Ace, that was obvious.

"I'm guessing that," Nash said, his voice tight as he pointed at something behind us. I turned to see a hulking gray creature standing next to a tree that was barely taller than he was. The mystery of how those cages had been hung so high was suddenly clear, and I swallowed hard. The creature was lumpy, as though a child had been told to mold a giant out of Play-Doh and had given up halfway through. Instead of hair, broken bits of gravel stuck out at odd angles over its square head, which sat directly on broad boulder shoulders. The giant surveyed the scene, taking in his newly escaped prisoners before letting out a bellow of rage. I took an unconscious step backward into Nash, who stumbled and fell.

"Well, I best be going!" Beatrice said from above us. I looked up to see her zipping away in the direction of her house.

"Fairies," Ace muttered darkly before turning to spit in the grass. Before I could ask if we should run, there was an ear-piercing bark and Chief came flying out of the woods to stand between us and the giant.

"Chief!" Ace barked. "No! You're no match for that brute. Get back here." Chief must not have heard him, though, because he dropped his head and lowered his body into an aggressive crouch as he prepared for attack. Before Ace could shout another warning, the dog launched himself at the giant. The giant swung a massive arm back, ready to clobber the dog. Suddenly there was a yell from somewhere behind us, and I felt a rush of air as something went flying past my right ear in a tight spiral. It hit the giant square in the chest, sticking hard into the rock with a sharp twang that made my ears ring. The giant froze instantly, and Chief collided with its chest before bouncing off like a pebble hitting a window. He whined and rolled, regaining his feet to crouch with a snarl again. The giant didn't move. I squinted, trying to make out the thing stuck in its chest. Was it a pine cone?

"You're welcome," said a voice behind us, and we turned to see Cress. She was standing with her arms crossed, looking smug, and I glanced from her to the giant and back again. She turned, catching sight of Ace for the first time, and froze. Her expression changed

255

from haughty confidence to dread in an instant, and she took a step back.

"Ace?" she gasped, glancing over at us. "Your grand-father is Ace?!"

"That's a problem?" Nash asked, his voice echoing my own confusion.

"Don't tell me you two are Bensons," Cress said, her voice tight and higher pitched than I'd ever heard it before. She looked from Nash to me and back again and nodded. "I should have seen it," she said to herself. "You've got the same pinched, high-cheekbone look to you."

"Um, thanks? I think?" I said.

"You're Natalie's kids," Cress said, her voice drop-ping into a whisper I could barely hear.

"Um, yeah," I said, glancing over at Nash, but he just shrugged. It seemed like everyone knew our mom. I wondered how many games she'd trekked through by the time she was our age. Even Flanny had known who she was. Cress stared at us both for a second as though she'd seen a ghost. "Have you seen her?" I said. Now that all our cards were on the table, I figured I might as well ask.

"No," Cress said, her brow furrowed. "Is she lost too?"

"We don't need her help," Ace said gruffly. "That

one will help you right off a cliff." Cress didn't say anything, but she pressed her lips together into a grim line as she looked from us to Ace and back again.

"What was that thing you threw at the giant?" I said, glancing back at the frozen giant.

"I don't know," Nash said, "but I want one."

"I think I know what that is," Ace said, narrowing his eyes. He turned to Cress. "Where did you find it?"

"Wouldn't you like to know," Cress said as she regained her composure. At that moment the immobilized giant teetered forward, unstable on its frozen feet. "Oh no you don't!" Cress yelped, catapulting herself over Nash's prone figure to shove past Chief. She reached the giant just as it pitched forward completely. Faster than I thought possible, she yanked the thing out of the giant's chest before rolling to the side and out of harm's way. The ground shuddered under our feet as the giant made impact.

Nash walked over to cautiously examine the top of the giant's gravel-covered head.

"She killed it," he murmured.

"It's sleeping," Ace said, coming to stand beside him. He gave the giant's head a shove with his green boot, and I heard the slightest whiffle of a snore.

"Might as well be dead," Cress said, coming over to stand by us. "No prince is going to kiss that thing."

"You never know," Ace said wryly. "There're some exceptionally odd princes in this game." I ignored him. I was too busy studying the thing Cress was holding in her hand. On closer inspection I could tell that it wasn't a pine cone. It was made of wood, long and lethally sharp. She held the sharp end pointed down and well away from her, in the same way you'd hold a knife, or a turtle you were worried was going to bite you.

"Wait, is that what I think it is?" I said.

"Depends," Cress said, cocking her head. "Do you think it's Sleeping Beauty's spindle? *The* spindle that can knock you out cold for a lifetime? That spindle?"

"Is that why you disappeared?" I asked. "Because you were looking for that?"

"I'm not sorry," Cress snapped defensively. "I've been looking for this thing forever, and I had an opportunity to use a Play a Hunch card, and Play a Hunch cards are super rare in this game! Besides, how was I supposed to know a rock giant was going to show up! I thought those things were hibernating this time of year!"

"Help you right off a cliff," Ace repeated under his breath, and Cress winced as though he'd slapped her. There was more to this story, but it was going to have to wait.

"Let's get out of here and go home," I said, looking

down at the rock giant. He was snoring softly, but the thought of him waking up again was enough to give me nightmares.

Ace turned to us, a pained look on his face. "I can't," he said.

"What?" I said. "Why in the world not?! What about . . ."

Ace held up a finger, cutting me off. "Don't tell me about Tunnels. I've been doing this longer than you've been alive. I know all about that game. But since I'm not a Wanderer I can't leave here and go to a different game through one of those blasted holes. The only way for a Benson to access Tunnels is through the physical game. Besides, even if I could get to Tunnels, there isn't any way to get back to our world through that game. You two will be fine since you got here through Tunnels, but since I came in through Lost Lore, I have to go back out through Lost Lore. No shortcuts, I'm afraid."

"But Ogden has the game," Nash said.

Ace nodded. "If he simply locked it in a cat's game trap, there's a chance I could get back. He'd have to take it out of the trap, of course, but if he destroyed it . . ." He let his words trail off and I saw his eyes flick over to Cress.

"The game's not destroyed or we couldn't have

gotten in," Cress said, and there was a hard edge to her voice that I didn't think had anything to do with her dislike of my grandfather. "You might not even know this little fact, Ace, but after the last copy of a game is destroyed, the door to it in Tunnels seals shut. If that happens, it will be impossible for anyone in this game to leave. Including us."

TWENTY-THREE

"Impossible to leave?" I repeated in disbelief. "Are you sure?"

Ace nodded. "Come on," he said. "Follow me back to Beatrice's house. I'll explain. Besides, I need to figure out what she did with my boots." Cress hesitated, and he shot her a look. "You too," he said gruffly. She looked like she wanted to argue, but instead she huffed and followed. Ace led us back through the woods to the tulip bulb house, where the sound of someone singing, badly, was floating through the window. We entered the small picket-fenced yard and the smell of flowers was so overwhelming that I sneezed. Bees were buzzing happily from flower to flower, and butterflies flitted here and there on their paper-thin wings.

"Disgusting, isn't it?" Cress said.

"What?" I said, surprised. I could think of a lot of

words for Beatrice's garden, but disgusting wasn't one of them.

"The perfection of it all," Cress said. "Drives me nuts about games like this." She reached out, grabbed a bunch of daisies by the stems, and gave them a sharp twist. The flower stems bent in half, cracking along their fragile middles, and the daisy heads drooped toward the ground. Cress inspected her handiwork and then lifted a booted foot and stomped on the flowers twice. She gave a nod of satisfaction before turning to me.

"I think you better tell me everything," she said. "Start at the beginning. What exactly happened to your mom?"

I glanced over to make sure Ace wasn't in earshot, and then I launched into the story, starting with our mom not showing up to pick us up, and our confrontation with Flanny and her miniature horse in our grandfather's office.

"I know Flanny," Cress interrupted. "I like her. I can't believe you almost told her how to get out of her game, though. She's going to be too big for her britches next time I pop in and expect me to pay her instead of the other way around." She shook her head ruefully before motioning for me to go on. So I did, with a few interruptions from Nash to fill in important details that he thought needed to be included. Cress listened, nodding her head here and there until I explained who it was that had taken our mom.

"Whoa!" Cress said, holding up her hand. "A pirate?! Captain O?! You never mentioned he was involved in this mess. You're sure that's what Snow White said his name was?"

"Snow White fell asleep," Nash said dryly. "But process of elimination points to Ogden. I mean, pirates aren't exactly a dime a dozen these days." Cress flinched at this, and for a second her overly confident facade slipped. Nash noticed too, and I saw him narrow his eyes at her.

"Have you ever met Ogden?" I asked. There was something about the way she said his name; what had she called him? Captain O, with an awed reverence, that made it seem like she had.

"Oh, I've met him all right," Cress said. Her face clouded over with a strange expression before she flapped her hand at us to continue. Nash finished up the story, and Cress sat back on her heels to look at us. I half expected her to demand her payment and leave, despite Ace's instructions, but instead she studied us for another moment before turning and stomping into Beatrice's house.

"Bea!" Ace bellowed, and I jumped, whirling to see what giant monster was after us now. Instead, I saw Ace standing beside Beatrice's circular front door, his hands propped on his hips as he surveyed the planters she had set on either side of her welcome mat. They were cowboy boots. Ace's cowboy boots to be exact. Each of them was filled to the brim with dirt while a thick tendril of green vines and pink flowers spilled happily out of the top.

"What is it now?" Beatrice said, bustling out with a flutter of wings. She inspected Ace's angry face staring at his defiled cowboy boots and then gave her hand a dismissive flip. "You look better in green polka dots. I have no regrets!" She turned away from him and dropped her red glasses so she could peer over them in my direction.

"What did you do to my flowers?" she cried. I glanced behind me at the crumpled daisies, debating what answer wouldn't result in this tiny fairy turning me into a frog.

"Don't get your wings in a bunch!" Cress called from inside. "It was me."

"I should have known," Beatrice said with a stomp of her foot. She whipped out her wand and pointed it directly at me. I leaped out of the way as she gave it a flick. "Higgilty Piggilty Pie," she said. The flowers snapped back to attention, fully restored, and she gave a nod of satisfaction before going back inside. Ace's face was bright red as he ducked to follow Beatrice through the low doorway, Chief at his heels. Nash was already inside, and I closed the small door behind me as I entered.

Everyone except for Beatrice and Chief was seated around a battered wood table. Beatrice was at a squat potbellied stove stirring a large pot of something that was bubbling merrily, while Chief stretched out on the colorful braided rug in front of the fireplace. There was a Chief-shaped indent in the rug, as though it was a spot he frequented often, and I glanced over at Ace and noticed that the wooden chair he sat in had the letter *A* carved into it in script. Something here wasn't quite adding up. Had he been in this game to look for our mom? Or had he been paying a visit to Beatrice? Beatrice tapped her spoon sharply on the side of the pot, and I jumped. The entire place smelled like heaven, and my stomach let out an angry gurgle. A moment later she flicked her wand and six bowls came sailing off a nearby shelf to land in a perfect spiral in front of us. Beatrice was at our side a moment later, large black pot propped precariously on her hip as she dished the steaming stew onto the plate. She was about to dish it into mine, but Ace's hand shot out and snatched the bowls from in front of me and Nash. He flipped them over onto the table and glared at Beatrice.

"They can't eat the food in a game. You know that," he snapped.

"Oh poo," she said, brushing his hand aside so she could ladle some stew into our bowls. "Just because you ate my food and decided you liked visiting me, doesn't mean it's bad luck to eat the food."

"What does it mean, then?" Ace snapped, his cheeks flushing a bright pink.

"It means I'm delightful company, and you're a grumpy, lonely old man who likes my stew," Beatrice said. She jerked her chin at me and Nash. "Eat up," she commanded. "It's no good cold."

Nash and I both looked at Ace for confirmation, and he flapped a hand at us to go on, obviously giving up on this particular battle. Beatrice gave her wand another flick and a soup bowl went sailing over to a very happy Chief.

"Talk," I said to Ace as I lifted the first spoonful to my lips. "You're really stuck here? Forever?" I was going to go on, but what I'd just tasted finally registered with my brain, and I shut my eyes in appreciation. I had no idea what was in the brown stew, but it tasted better than anything I'd ever eaten. I shoveled another bite into my mouth and chewed, realizing for the first time how hungry I actually was.

"Lost Lore is a lovely place to live," Beatrice said

indignantly. "Once you get past the poisonous trolls, rock giants, evil fairies, nymphs, and singing princesses."

"Ugh," Cress said with a shudder, "singing princesses." She took another bite of her stew and gestured to it with her spoon. "Woolly mammoth?" she asked. Beatrice nodded, and Nash and I both froze mid-bite. I considered my spoon for a second, decided I didn't care, and took another bite.

Ace raised his shoulders up and dropped them with a heavy sigh. "I don't make the rules of board game bounding, boys. I always knew that Ogden would get his revenge on me someday. I thought it was by taking your mother, but apparently that wasn't enough. You two need to get out of here and go home. Take Chief with you. Call the authorities from the cabin and have them come pick you up. Forget all about this world," he said, waving his hand to include the cottage. "Forget about board game bounding." His words felt like a punch in the gut, and I heard Nash inhale sharply beside me.

"Forget about board game bounding?" Nash said. "You can't be serious. This isn't something you forget about."

"And what about Mom?!" I said. "You expect us to just forget about her? To leave her trapped in some game for the rest of her life?"

"Being trapped in games isn't so bad," Cress murmured so softly I was pretty sure I was the only one who could hear her.

Ace winced. "Don't forget her," he said. "We never forget the ones we love." Cress choked on a bite of her stew and Beatrice thumped her hard on the back.

"You can't mean that we should just give up," Nash said, ignoring Cress and Beatrice completely as he stared at our grandfather, searching his face for something.

"Everyone loses a game sometimes," Ace said. "It's better to do it with grace. Pitching a fit won't change anything."

"I don't lose games," Cress said, and Ace shot her a look.

"You don't know enough," Ace said to us.

"I can second that," Cress said around a mouthful of stew. "Now the dog," she said, jerking her head at Chief. "He would be just fine." Chief lifted his head up to look at Cress before plopping it back down onto Beatrice's worn rug.

"We *can* find Mom!" I said. "We found you, didn't we?"

"You'd be dragon dinner if it weren't for me," Cress muttered. Beatrice promptly rapped her on the head with the wooden soup ladle she still had in her hand. "Ouch!" Cress said, rubbing her head and glaring at the fairy. "What was that for?"

"For my flowers," Beatrice said. "And the sass."

"You don't even know what game she's in," Ace said. "It's like looking for a needle in a needle stack."

"Don't you mean a needle in a haystack?" I asked.

"No," Ace said. "I mean a needle in a needle stack."

"If you need someone to process a haystack, I know a girl," Beatrice said. "Not bad as far as princesses go, but very weird about people's names."

"We're good," Nash said, "but thanks."

"Seems to me these boys deserve a chance," Beatrice said. She'd abandoned her bowl of stew and was bustling about with a teapot on the stove, and it almost seemed like she was talking to herself instead of us. "You certainly wouldn't have let an old man tell you what to do when you were young and fresh."

"Hush," Ace snapped, but Beatrice ignored him as she carefully poured steaming mugs of something bright green into chipped enamel mugs.

I leaned over to inspect the leaf-green liquid inside Ace's cup. It was fizzing slightly and letting off a faint spiral of steam that curled up in a perfect corkscrew before disappearing. It was because I was looking at Ace's cup so intently that I saw the liquid inside suddenly shudder. A second later there was a rippling tremor under our feet, causing the tea set on the table to rattle alarmingly.

"Grasshopper gumbo," Ace snarled, jumping to his feet. Cress was already heading for the door.

"If those rock giants smash my petunias, I'm going to turn them into pebbles so small their mothers won't even recognize them," Beatrice fumed, following Cress. Nash was still sitting at the table looking confused, and I hauled him up by the arm and out the door. In the clearing in front of the cottage stood ten rock giants, their eyes trained on the tiny tulip house with such ferocity that it made my blood turn to ice in my veins.

"Something tells me that they found their buddy sleeping in the woods," Ace said.

"I think that's my cue to move on," Cress said, and before we could stop her, she pulled a card out of her pocket and read.

"Jack was nimble, Jack was quick, fly south to discover the candlestick," she read out loud. Dropping the card, she took off into the woods. A single rock giant broke off from the group to chase her, but the others stood frozen like the rocks they were made out of and stared at us.

"She left without getting paid," I said as I watched her disappear into the trees. "That doesn't really seem like her."

"Paid?" Ace asked, jerking his head over to look at us. "What did you two offer her?"

"This," I said, pulling the Ziploc bag out of Nash's pocket. "Cress said it's from some Midas guy or something."

Ace jumped in alarm at the sight of the stone, but his reaction was nothing compared to Beatrice's. She whirled to face our grandfather, her hands on her hips, rock giants seemingly forgotten.

"*You're* the one who took the Midas stone?!" she said. "Do you know the traffic jam you caused? All those bumbling players can't get past the Witch Alley now! So whose door do you think they knock on when they can't figure it out! You know they have to pay the woman with their weight in gold, and the only way to do that is by finding the Midas stone!"

Ace winced. "Did I forget to mention that?"

"Bigger fish to fry . . ." Nash murmured under his breath.

"I'll turn your grandfather into a big fish," Beatrice sniffed.

"The boy's right," Ace said. "We can talk about that later."

"How about we talk about the fact that Cress just took off with the only weapon that can take those things down, didn't she," Nash said, gesturing to the woods where Cress had disappeared from sight.

"Or did she?" Beatrice said slyly. She pulled the spindle out from between the folds of her dress and smirked. "I'll teach her not to go stepping on people's flowers," she said.

"This is why no one trusts fairies," Ace told her disapprovingly. One of the rock giants across the way stomped a foot, making the ground under our feet tremble. "But," he said, reconsidering, "well done."

"One spindle and nine giants," Nash said. "I'm horrible at math, but I'm pretty confident that it doesn't add up in our favor."

"Boys," Ace said, his voice tight. "I need you to listen carefully and follow my instructions."

"Okay," I said. Nash nodded, and even Chief moved between Ace and me, his heavyset shoulders pressing hard against our legs. I put a hand down onto his head and let it rest there.

"In my back pocket is a card," Ace said, his eyes never leaving the giants in the meadow. He was whispering, his voice low and urgent. "I need you to grab it, but I need you to make sure you're holding on to each other before you read it. Oh, and one of you needs to have a good grip on Chief."

Chief, hearing his name, looked up at Ace and whined a question.

"Don't look at me like that," Ace told him. "You know what has to be done." Chief whined again, and

Ace finally tore his eyes away from the giants to look down at his dog.

"You're a good dog," he said. "And I'll miss you too." His voice caught on the last word. I watched the exchange and knew I should be feeling something. Sadness. Anger. Panic. But I felt frozen, as though I was watching a scene from a movie. It sounded like Ace was saying goodbye, but my brain was refusing to accept that reality. The tallest giant across the way let out a roar before grinding its rock teeth together menacingly. "Now," Ace said. "Do it now."

I felt Nash grab on to my shoulder, and I reached down to get a grip on Chief's collar. The rock giant bellowed again, and as though it were some kind of signal, they charged.

"Now!" Ace bellowed again as the ground under our feet shook and rumbled, pitching us off-balance. I somehow managed to keep on my feet and reached for Ace's back pocket, where I could just see the edge of a white card. I pulled it out. The giants were closing in on us, and Beatrice was yelling something as she launched the spindle at the closest one. I tore my eyes away just long enough to read the card.

"LOSE YOUR LOOT AND GO HOME!" I read out loud. The words had barely registered before I felt a hard yank on my spine, and everything went black.

CRESS

I should never have tried to go back in, not after what happened. I should have stayed far, far away, but there is something about the game you originated from that pulls at you. It was a tug that I ignored for years, happy with this new life I'd discovered, this second chance I had been given. I tried to tell myself that it didn't matter that I'd gotten this life in trade for someone else's life but, of course, it did. That reality tainted this new life, every bit of it. I hadn't wanted it without him. I hadn't wanted it without my friend. But now that I had it, I wasn't going to waste it.

That tug had gotten more and more persistent with each day, until I had found my way through the tunnels to the door that I swore I'd never go through again. I'd run my hands over the familiar carvings, tracing my fingers down the ridges of The Royal Run, *her sails flung wide to catch the wind. I'd felt my way down the* door, tracing the outlines of treasure chests and thick chains, my fingers going over the shapes of sea monsters and sailors whose names I knew by heart. Then I'd tried to open it, only to discover that it didn't open anymore. It was sealed shut as firmly as though it had been glued. It was then that I knew Ace had destroyed it. That knowledge had both freed me and wrecked me.

The tug was pulling at me again now, harder than I could ever remember it. Maybe it was because I'd just been talking about The Pirate's Wrath with Ace, or maybe it was because the door was close, but my feet felt like they were moving of their own accord. I'd escaped Lost Lore through the first available tunnel, grateful that the rock giant was too big to squeeze into the tight space, and come out only one tunnel over from the door to The Pirate's Wrath. I'd only ever visited the door one time. It had been too painful to see it and not be able to open it. I'd never thought that I'd want to go home, but somehow, knowing that I couldn't still hurt.

My feet took the familiar path until I saw the door illuminated in my headlamp. I tucked Sleeping Beauty's spindle into a belt pouch and approached it warily. I stared at the door, my door, my heart hammering as each image brought back a wave of memory, some good, most bad. My life inside that game felt like it belonged to someone else. It did. It belonged to the girl

I used to be. The girl from that game owed the Bensons a debt, a debt that I'd failed to pay. I'd run away. Again. Just like I had the day that it happened. I'd turned my back and run like the yellow-bellied coward that I was. The weight of what I owed the Bensons sat on my soul like an anchor, and I wondered if that weight could eventually sink me. My eyes flitted across the carvings to land again on The Royal Run; *its large cast-iron anchor was carved in excruciatingly accurate detail on its port side. It used to be my job to reel in that anchor. My hand flexed at the memory of the bloody blisters that used to cover my palms, and just like my feet, my hands seemed to move on their own to stroke the long mast of* The Royal Run. *I could almost smell the briny salt of the ocean. I shut my eyes and inhaled, wondering if some of the smell of the sea had gotten embedded in the wood of the door. A moment later, the door gave way under my hands and opened.*

TWENTY-FOUR

I opened my eyes in Ace's office and sat up gingerly. Everything hurt. My bones felt like one of those rock giants had been sitting on me, and my muscles were tight and angry as I eased myself into a sitting position. The office looked just like we'd left it, with the exception of the chocolate. Someone, and I was suspecting Snow White, had cleaned up every last smudge of the stuff. Next to me Nash groaned and sat up. Chief lay beside him, his head on his paws, his eyes sad.

"What in the world?" Nash said. "How did we get back here?"

"Welcome back!" trilled Snow White, and we both jumped in surprise and then winced in pain. She was peering down at us, her head cocked sweetly to the side, a platter full of blueberry muffins the size of cantaloupes stacked artfully on the platter she was holding.

"How did we get here?" I said.

She shrugged. "Muffin? I made them for those adorable little digger moles, but they left as soon as you showed up!" She pouted out her lip, seeming sad about the trade.

"Thanks," Nash said, grabbing a muffin in each hand. My stomach snarled, and I reached for one too, only to discover that I was still holding the card I'd removed from Ace's pocket.

"Lose your Loot and Go Home," I read for the second time. The card shuddered once in my hand and then disintegrated into a small pile of yellow dust. I glanced up at Snow White. "Is this a card from your game?" I asked. Snow White looked down at the pile of dust and shook her head.

"Wherever it was from, it worked," Nash said.

"Yeah," I said. "But why didn't Ace use it on himself?"

"He probably tried, and when it didn't work, he realized he was stuck," Nash said. "So he gave it to us. Do you think he's okay? There were a lot of giants."

"I hope so," I said. "Beatrice seemed like she had a handle on things."

"Now what?" Nash said. "Do we do what Ace told us to do?"

"You mean call the police and tell them to come

pick us up?" I said. "Pass."

"Ace is right, though," Nash said. "We don't have a clue where to start looking for Mom, and we don't know enough. Cress took off, so we don't even have her help anymore." I nodded. There was something about the Cress situation that felt off, but I couldn't put my finger on it.

"Those moles were ever so enjoyable," Snow White mused to herself as she picked at one of her giant muffins. "They were delightful conversationalists. Nothing like those horrible pirates."

"Wait, what did you just say?" I asked.

"Which part?" Snow White said. "About the moles? Their names were Gerald and William. They were so nearsighted they could barely see, poor dears, but so painfully polite you'd never know that they hadn't been out of their tunnel before."

"Not the moles," I said. "The part about the pirates. You said pirates. Plural. You never said there was more than one."

"Oh yes," she said, her eyes wide. "There were two of them. Both horrifyingly ugly."

"That's impossible," Nash said. "The only pirate that got out of The Pirate's Wrath before Ace destroyed it was Ogden."

Snow White blinked at us, wide-eyed. "He must

have made a friend."

"Vicious pirates don't make friends," Nash said.

"No," I said, shaking my head as the pieces of the puzzle slowly started coming together. "I bet it's another pirate from The Pirate's Wrath."

"Earth to Rhett," Nash said. "That's impossible. Ace destroyed the last copy of that game. Remember? If he's stuck inside Lost Lore, then Ogden's pirate buddies are stuck inside The Pirate's Wrath."

"What if someone remade the game?" I said, my brain churning.

"The last I checked, remaking old board games wasn't high on anyone's list," Nash said. "No one even really plays board games anymore. Like Ace said. It's a dying art. Everyone plays video games now."

My jaw popped open as I stared at my twin.

"Why are you looking at me like I just sprouted an extra head?" Nash said.

"Say that again," I said.

"What? That I sprouted an extra head?" Nash said.

"No," I said, shaking my head. "What did you say everyone plays now?"

"Um, video games?" Nash said.

"That's it!" I yelped. "Remember what we noticed earlier? About the board games?" I stumbled over to where the pile of disheveled board games still sat in front of the open bookcase, and started sifting through the pile.

"Dwarves sometimes lose touch with reality," I heard Snow White tell Nash in a conspiratorial tone. "Usually, they're just hungry, though. Or sleepy. Or grumpy!"

I ignored them as I flipped over box after box, looking for the game I'd seen earlier. Finally, I found the right one, flipping over a lid to reveal the cartoon illustration of a burly Viking standing at the helm of a massive ship. The game was simply called Pillage.

"Look familiar?" I said, holding it up to Nash.

"Should it?" Nash said.

"It's called Pillage," I said, waiting for a flash of recognition. It didn't come. "This is a video game," I explained.

"No," Nash said slowly, as though I really had lost my mind. "That's a board game."

I rolled my eyes in exasperation. "I know that. But I know for a fact that this is *also* a video game. I've seen the commercial for it."

"Oh yeah!" Nash said. "I remember that one! They shoot those flaming arrows at the Viking ships, right? It looks awesome. Also, violent."

"What are the odds that a board game and a video game have the same name?" I said.

"Slim to none?" Nash said. "I mean, I'm sure there

are copyrights or whatever on those games. So if there's a video game by the same name, then it's someone that turned the board game into a video game."

"So here's my question," I said. "If someone remade The Pirate's Wrath into a video game, would it work the same as a board game? Like could a Wanderer go into it?"

"I'm not following you," Nash said. "Spell this one out for me."

"I think I know where Mom is," I said.

"No, you don't," Nash said.

"I think I do," I repeated. "She's in *The Pirate's Wrath*."

"Impossible," Nash said, shaking his head. "Ace destroyed the last copy of that game, remember?"

"Oh, I remember," I said. "But then two pirates showed up to steal Lost Lore. Two."

"Okay," Nash said slowly as he tried to follow my train of thought.

"If someone remade The Pirate's Wrath, they could send Mom in, and get someone out. Right?"

"I mean, in theory," Nash said. "You think Ogden sent her into a remake of The Pirate's Wrath to get one of his buddies out?"

I shook my head. "I think his buddy was an added bonus. I bet he wanted back into the game to get something else out."

"I'm not following you," Nash said. "You're going to have to spell this out for me."

"Remember what Ace said? Or, I guess, didn't say?"

"Wow," Nash said. "You are truly terrible at this. The more you talk, the more confused I get."

I flapped an impatient hand at him and shut my eyes. My brain hurt, but it was all starting to make sense. I opened my eyes.

"Ace said that board game bounders, that's us, can take things out of a game. A Wander Lost like Ogden can't. He can go in and out of games, but he can't take anything with him. Remember? Ace said it was lucky because otherwise Ogden could have gotten his hands on all sorts of dangerous weapons or artifacts."

"Okay," Nash said. "So you think he used Mom as a sort of key to get something out of his game?"

I nodded. "I think that as long as she's in there, Ogden can go in and get stuff out."

"What do you think he's trying to get out?" Nash asked. Instead of answering, I pulled out the directions to The Pirate's Wrath and studied the gem-studded skull and crossbones.

"Treasure?" I said, looking up. "He may be in our world, but gold is gold, right? Maybe he needs it for something."

"Money," Nash said, nodding. "That tracks. The bad

283

guy always wants money."

"Maybe that's the reason Ace destroyed his game," I said. "So Ogden couldn't go back in for his treasure?"

"Maybe," Nash said. "Although his son dying in the game seems like a pretty solid reason too."

I bit my lip. "If Ogden remade the game into a video game, that means other people can play it, right?"

"I'm not the video game guy," Nash pointed out. "That was your obsession."

"Obsession," I said, nodding my head. "I *was* obsessed, and those were just regular old video games. I wonder what is going to happen to the people who play a video game with a Benson inside it."

Nash's eyes widened. "Now that's a horrible thought. But I think you're getting ahead of yourself. How in the world do we find out if someone even remade it into a video game?"

"Seriously?" I said. "We haven't been in the middle of nowhere that long. Did you forget about a little thing called the internet?"

Nash blinked at me in surprise. "Um, yeah," he finally said. "I kind of did."

"Snow White," I said, turning to the princess. "Am I right in assuming that you cleaned the entire house while we were gone?"

"Yes," she said, smiling brightly. "Everything except

the bathroom." She wrinkled her nose. "I don't do bath-rooms."

"Right," I said. "Did you see a computer anywhere?"

"A Com Put Ter?" she repeated. "Is that a kind of flower?"

Nash groaned. "Come on," he said. "Ace has to have one somewhere." The cabin was small, and it didn't take long to search the place from top to bottom. I refused to believe that Ace had been living without any kind of modern-day technology, although after the first fifteen minutes I was almost convinced. We did locate Geronimo Jones the Third under Ace's bed, and Snow White about lost her mind at the sight of some-thing small and furry. She immediately started singing to the confused guinea pig, who seemed unsure about the whole situation.

Another few minutes of searching produced an old battered black laptop sitting camouflaged among the clutter and books on the small desk in Ace's bedroom. It took a full half hour to find the charging cord for it.

"This thing is older than we are," Nash said, wrin-kling his nose in disgust as he booted up the ancient laptop.

"What are the odds he has internet in here?" I said.

"Slim to not a chance," Nash said.

"Okay," I said as the laptop slowly buzzed and

beeped itself to life. Behind us I could still hear Snow White singing, although it sounded like Geronimo had started chirping and squeaking along with her.

When the laptop finally woke up completely, I was shocked to see three little bars in the corner of the screen.

Nash thrust his arms into the air triumphantly. "We have Wi-Fi!" he crowed.

"One of the dwarves got that once," Snow White called from the other room. "He just put some ointment on it, and it cleared right up."

We ignored her, and I watched over Nash's shoulder as he opened up a search engine and typed in *The Pirate's Wrath*. There were a few hits with images of the original board game, and Nash immediately clicked on one. Like the instruction booklet, the box was octagonal in shape. Gold script wound across the top, complementing the gold clasps on the corners that made the entire thing look like a treasure chest. The skull on the front seemed even more ominous than the one depicted on the directions, and I sucked in a breath.

"Whoa," Nash said.

"I second that whoa," I agreed. "Go back. What else comes up for the game?"

"Bingo," Nash said a second later as he clicked on a link. Up popped an announcement for a video game company called Reboot. From a glance it was obvious that remaking old board games into modern-day video games was their main business, and at the very top of the page was an image of the original board game for The Pirate's Wrath right next to the slim boxed video game with the same haunting image of the skull and chain on the front.

"Look," I said, leaning over to point at the top of the screen. "It's not released yet. It says *Coming Soon*."

"That's good news, right?" Nash said.

"Definitely," I agreed. "Scroll back to the top." Nash obliged, and I narrowed my eyes. "Click on the *About Us* tab," I instructed. Nash did as he was told. The screen changed, displaying a picture of the founder of Reboot. The second I saw him I felt a shiver run down my spine. The man was broad-shouldered and tall, with thick curly hair pulled low into a bun. His power suit was black with a red tie, and expertly tailored to fit his large frame. He'd look like any other businessman, except for the scar. It was long and thick, running perpendicular from the top of his hairline, over the mottled skin where an eye used to be to end at the top of his cheekbone. The effect gave him a pinched and snake-like appearance that made my insides crawl.

"Do you think that's him?" Nash said. "Do you think that's Ogden? He doesn't look like a pirate."

"I'm sure he figured out pretty quickly that walking around like an extra on the *Pirates of the Caribbean* ride wasn't super inconspicuous. But there's one way to find out. Hey!" I called over my shoulder. "Snow White! Could you come here a second?" A moment later she bustled into the room, Geronimo Jones perched on her shoulder like some kind of trained parrot. I peered at him and blinked in surprise when I saw that he was now wearing what looked like a tiny polka-dot apron.

I shook my head, forcing myself to refocus. "Hey," I said, moving aside so she could see the computer screen. "Can you look at this a second?"

"Why, that's one of the pirates who came in through the window!" she trilled. "Is that a magical portal that shows you what you wish to see? My stepmother had a mirror that did something like that!"

"Yeah, it's magical all right," Nash muttered. Chief trotted in then, looking glum. He came to a sudden stop when he spotted the picture on the screen. His lip rose in a silent snarl as the fur along his back stood up in an angry ridge.

"Well, that seals the deal," Nash said as we stared at the furious dog.

"That's all we needed to know," I said to Snow White and Geronimo. "You two can go back to doing, um, whatever it is that you're doing." They disappeared, and I turned back to Nash and Chief.

"I'm not seeing things, right? Geronimo was wearing an apron. Wasn't he?"

Nash nodded. "He also had his nails painted. Red. I always thought he liked green the best."

"So Ogden started a video game company?" I said. "That seems ambitious for a board game character."

"I mean, he's had a lot of years to figure it out," Nash said.

"I wonder what took him so long to remake The Pirate's Wrath," I said. "Look at all these other games that have been out for years." There in the sidebar was an image of *Pillage*. It had been released a full two years before. There were other games that I recognized from our grandfather's shelf, and I realized with a chill of recognition that I'd even heard my classmates mention a few of them.

"Holy shirts and pants, he has a profile," Nash said, scrolling down even further. He cleared his throat and read. "Dennis Ogg has a passion for bringing old, forgotten games into the twenty-first century. He has scoured the globe to find the rarest board games ever produced and hires the best programmers in the business to bring them to life. His employees say that he has an uncanny knack at visualizing what board games would look like in three dimensions, and a creative genius that is unparalleled in the industry."

"Creative genius my foot," I muttered. "He just finds old games, goes in to scope them out, and then tells the designers what to do. That's cheating."

"Is it, though?" Nash said. "I mean, people don't usually make rules against doing stuff that is supposed to be impossible."

"You're right," I admitted. "Still *feels* like cheating, though. Dennis Ogg? He just reversed his name? Too weird."

"Shhhh," Nash said. "Listen. Dennis Ogg is most excited for the release of his newest game, *The Pirate's Wrath*. He crafted the game completely from memories of his favorite childhood game that is sadly no longer in existence. Ogg made a country-wide search for it, offering rewards up to ten thousand dollars for even incomplete games until he was able to assemble a partial copy. The video game version of the forgotten classic is set to launch at midnight on September twenty-eighth at Ogg's flagship location in Plainfield, Indiana."

"Hold up," I said. "What day is it?"

"Maybe Wednesday?" Nash said. "I've lost all sense of time since I've been here."

"Ask Google," I said.

"It's the twenty-seventh," Nash said as we read the

date outlined in bright blue at the top of the screen.

"It's five o'clock," I said, consulting the alarm clock perched next to Ace's bed.

"How far are we from his store?" Nash said, and then held up a hand to silence me before I could say anything. "Never mind," he said, "I got it." He opened up the website our mom used for directions and typed in the name of the store. The computer popped up a box asking if we wanted to use our current location, and Nash clicked yes.

"Good to know something knows where we are," he muttered as the website quickly triangulated our position on the map. "Well, that's closer than expected," Nash said, leaning forward to peer at the screen. "Do you think that Ace knew he'd settled into a cabin less than an hour from his mortal enemy?"

"If I had to guess, I'd say no," I said.

"We need to get to that store before they launch the game," Nash said.

"I know it's only an hour away," I said, pointing to the small red line connecting our location to the store. "But that's drive time. If we have to walk this? That's going to take us a day. Also, that sounds awful." Nash sagged in disappointment before perking up a second later.

"Ace has a truck," he said. "And he can't exactly use

it at the moment, so he won't care if we borrow it." I raised an eyebrow at him and waited. "Fine," he said. "He'd care. But he's not exactly here to drive us, is he? And unless you want to saddle up one of those cows, we don't have a whole lot of other options."

"Do I need to remind you that we aren't sixteen?" I said. "If the police pull us over, we get taken into custody immediately. Without Ace or Mom to bail us out, we get thrown into the foster care system. Or worse, the juvenile detention center since driving without a license probably qualifies as a crime."

"Do you have a better idea?" Nash asked in frustration.

"Maybe," I said. "Hey!" I called behind me. "Snow White! Could you come here again?"

"You have *got* to be kidding me," Nash said.

"Yes?" she said, peering around the doorframe. Geronimo was still on her shoulder wearing his apron, but he'd acquired a tiny straw hat.

"How old are you?" I asked.

"Eighteen," she said.

"Perfect," I said. "How would you feel about learning to drive a truck?"

TWENTY-FIVE

Ace's keys were in a wooden bowl by the door, and within ten minutes we had one very confused princess behind the wheel of the truck. She'd refused to leave Geronimo behind, and he sat perched on her shoulder wearing a tiny pair of goggles. If we survived this whole experience, I was going to have to ask Snow White where in the world she was finding a guinea-pig-sized wardrobe. Nash explained the basics of driving a car. Snow White nodded as he explained brakes and steering, and the importance of staying on your own side of the road. It was a pretty good lesson considering Nash had never driven a car a day in his life. Meanwhile, I dug through Ace's drawers for something Snow White could wear that would be a little less conspicuous. We needed her to look less like a fairy tale princess, and more like a babysitter our mom had hired to drive us to the launch of a video game. I settled on a pair of Ace's blue overalls, cuffed at the ankles, and a red button-up shirt. She changed into the new clothes without protest, and while it definitely helped, she still looked like she should be walking around Disney World taking pictures with tourists.

Snow White proved to be a quick study and seemed to enjoy driving around Ace's gravel driveway. The fact that she backed into his mailbox and clipped the front fender on the gate was to be expected. We didn't have time for her to reach expert status, though, and we climbed in for the drive to Plainfield.

Nash had written down directions from the map website, and he seemed pretty confident that he could navigate us there. I thought about pointing out that the closest he'd ever come to navigating was holding Mom's phone while the GPS barked out directions but decided against it.

Once we'd done everything we could think of to prepare, including locking up Ace's office and the mess of board games we still hadn't had time to sort out, we were off.

"I've never been on such a grand adventure," Snow White said as she pulled the truck out of the driveway and onto the road. I put my hands on the dashboard and nodded through gritted teeth. She had a tendency to stomp on the gas and then on the brake, causing the truck to lurch rather than roll. Nash sat right beside her on the bench seat of the truck, and Chief lay at our feet, looking more than a little concerned. The only creature in the truck that seemed completely at ease was Geronimo, who occasionally squeaked or chirped in encouragement.

Thankfully the backroads of Indiana were pretty quiet, and we got through the first half hour without any major catastrophes. The hardest part was keeping Snow White focused. She wanted to pull over and personally greet every cow, horse, or chicken we happened to pass. She was also very confused about why she had to stay on her side of the road, preferring to drive in the dead center whenever possible or zig and zag between the two. When we passed the sign for Plainfield almost an hour later, I thought about getting out to kiss it in the same way a sailor kisses dry land after surviving a shipwreck.

The town was quiet, most businesses were closed, and I found myself peering in the glowing window of the small houses as we passed. Families were huddled together on the couch watching TV or sitting at kitchen tables doing homework, and I felt a pang of jealousy. We'd had that once. Our mom used to sit with us every night while we tackled math worksheets and book reports. Helping, harassing, and encouraging in turns, and I'd thought it was the most obnoxious thing in the world. Why did she have to care so much? I'd taken all that lovely normal for granted, and I wondered if I'd ever get an opportunity to appreciate it the way I should. I felt a lump in my throat, and I swallowed hard, hoping against hope that my hunch was right. That Ace was wrong, and that we'd get her back.

My mind flitted back to Ace, stuck in Lost Lore, and I glanced over at Snow White. How could we tell her that she was never going to get to go back to her beloved board game? How could we tell her that she was stuck here forever? Also, if she *was* stuck here forever, did that mean we were stuck with *her* forever? That thought was pretty horrifying all on its own. Although, I had to admit, she was proving useful. Nash navigated her through the town's dark streets, past stores, restaurants, and fast-food places until we were about a block from Reboot.

"Pull in over here," Nash instructed, and we braced ourselves as Snow White ramped the curb with Ace's tires and came to a clumsy stop in a school parking lot. Nash reached over and put the truck into park, and I felt myself sigh in relief. We'd made it. And we'd made it in one piece. It felt like some kind of miracle.

"That was fun!" Snow White said. "Much better than a horse."

"Debatable," Nash said. He turned to look at me. "Am I green? I feel like I should be green after that. I think I left my stomach on William Street about an hour ago."

"You're not," I confirmed. "We can pick up your stomach on the way back. It's probably somewhere near mine." Snow White had started humming something, and Geronimo was making odd little squeaks in harmony to it. The combination was really hard to think around. "Can you stay here?" I asked Snow White. "Don't talk to anyone, and don't unlock the car doors for anyone but us."

She nodded a confirmation, not bothering to stop her humming, and it wasn't until I got out of the car that I remembered that historically she wasn't really good at the whole don't-talk-to-strangers bit.

"No fruit," I said, popping my head back in the truck. "Don't open the door. Even for fruit." Snow White looked like she nodded, and I sighed and shut the door.

"Fruit?" Nash said. "News flash. No one walks around peddling poison apples in Plainfield, Indiana."

"News flash," I spit back. "We're about to go break into a store where a board game character re-created his destroyed board game in video game form and then trapped our mom inside it. I'm going to say that just about anything is possible, even in Plainfield, Indiana."

"Solid point," Nash admitted. Chief let out a quiet

297

woof, and we glanced over at him. He'd climbed out behind us, not seeming at all interested in staying in a truck with the singing princess and her harmonizing guinea pig. Once he had our attention, he trotted off through the playground of the school, obviously expecting us to follow. He was heading in the direction of the store, so we complied. There was a slight breeze, and the swings on the playground were creaking as they swung back and forth as though propelled by ghost children. I shivered and hurried to keep up with Nash.

"Do we have a plan?" he asked.

"No," I said.

"Cool." He nodded. "Just checking." Chief slowed down as we passed out of the school's playground and into an adjacent parking lot. We were approaching a strip mall from the back, and I wrinkled my nose as I caught a whiff of the dumpsters that sat stacked in a row behind the store like small, stinky soldiers. I could hear a low hum of voices, and the parking lot was filling up with cars despite the late hour. Kids and teens carrying folding chairs and small coolers were walking around to the front of the buildings, where I could see a line already queuing up for the release of *The Pirate's Wrath*. I glanced down at my watch. It was almost nine o'clock, which meant we had three hours until the release of the game.

"Do we need disguises?" Nash said. "What if Ogden recognizes us?"

"How?" I said. "He doesn't even know we exist. If he did, he would have come out to that cow pasture when he took Lost Lore."

"Right," Nash said, deflating. "I just always wanted to wear a disguise. I think I'd be good at it."

"The best disguise right now," I said, "is game-obsessed teenager." I held out a hand to the throng of kids passing us, completely wrapped up in a debate about the benefits of extra lives vs. extra levels in games. "Come on," I said. "The front's going to be locked until midnight. There's no way we will be able to slip in unnoticed with this crowd. People who wait in line for hours tend to get really grouchy when you cut in front of them. Let's see if we can find our way in through the back." Chief was already a step ahead of us, sniffing at the nearest dumpster. For a second I thought he might have found something useful, but then he lifted his leg on it.

"Nice," I said. "Good manners there, Chief." There were five storefronts in the strip mall and five corresponding doors leading to the back alley where we were standing. We needed to figure out which store was Reboot from the back, which, thanks to the dumpsters sitting beside each of them, wasn't going to be too hard. The first store looked like it was probably a restaurant of some kind, and based off the smell of rotting food coming from the dumpster I was pretty confident with that guess. The second was a pet store, the third was a dry cleaner, but the fourth and fifth doors were a bit of a mystery. Neither of them had any markings on them, and the only difference between the two were their colors. One was black and one was red.

"Of course they'd both be pirate colors," Nash muttered.

"Well, only one way to find out," I said, walking over to the black door's dumpster and flipping up the lid. Inside was a pile of garbage bags, and I reached down and ripped the closest one open. Inside were empty shampoo bottles, small strips of foil covered in purple goo, and hair. Lots and lots of hair.

"I'm going to bet that's a salon," Nash said, wrinkling his nose at the hair. I was already moving over to the last dumpster in the line. I flipped open the lid to see similar industrial-sized black trash bags. This one wasn't as full as the salon dumpster, and I had to jump and lever myself half into the dumpster on my stomach to reach one of the bags. My feet kicked in the air, and I struggled to keep from toppling in headfirst. Nash's hands grabbed my ankles a second later, and I was able to finally lean down far enough to get a good grip on the slippery plastic. I gave it a good rip and out came empty boxes of candy, used tissues, empty fast-food cups, and small glossy boxes. I used my sweatshirt to cover my hand since the boxes were all covered in what looked like melted slushy, and flipped the closest box over. There, smiling up at me from the shiny cover, was a Viking with the word *Pillage* in a graceful arc above his head. "Bingo," I whispered.

"Find anything?" Nash whispered. I didn't respond right away; I was too busy staring at the cover of *Pillage*. The corner of the box was bent and warped, like it had been damaged in shipping, which explained its presence in the dumpster, but it was the image of the Viking on the cover that drew my attention.

"Are you going to move into this dumpster?" Nash grunted. "Hurry it up. I'm getting some weird looks." In response I tossed the box behind myself so it sailed out of the dumpster. It turned out that was a giant mistake. Nash immediately let go of my ankles, probably in an attempt to catch the flying box, and I fell headfirst into the dumpster. I landed on the layer of trash at the bottom of the container and scrambled to find my feet, completely grossed out. I grabbed the rim of the dumpster, ready to lever myself back out, when something stood up outside the dumpster, and it wasn't the brother I was fully prepared to ream out. It was a very large, very angry-looking Viking. Apparently, Nash had entered *Pillage*, and I was now going to have to deal with the behemoth that had taken his place.

TWENTY-SIX

The Viking's face was partially obscured by a metal helmet that came down over the top half of his face, and he was wearing a thick gray shirt under leather armor studded with tiny bits of bone. He was holding what looked like a fancy axe, and the moment he saw me he launched it at my head.

I ducked back into the dumpster, and the axe flew over my head before making contact with the brick of the building. The Viking bellowed in anger as he reached into the dumpster. His beefy hand closed around my neck, and he launched me in the same direction he'd thrown the axe. I flew through the air, the world somersaulting around me so fast I wasn't sure which direction was up. I hit the pavement with my shoulder and hip, and rolled. The Viking had a second axe and was approaching me with it held high over his head. His intention was crystal clear. He was

302

going to split me open from top to bottom and ask questions about why he was in a strip mall parking lot later. That's when Chief showed up. He launched himself at the Viking from behind, sinking his teeth into the massive shoulder muscle that was holding up the axe. The Viking yelled and twisted, the axe falling from his hands to clang loudly on the asphalt. Operation Poke-Around-the-Dumpsters had gone from quiet and sneaky to very loud very quickly, and a small herd of kids and teenagers had gathered to watch.

"Is that Erik the Evil!" someone called out. "He's my favorite player! Look! He's even got his axes!"

"I didn't know the release was going to have a pop-up performance!" said someone else.

"Where are the pirates?" said a third. "I thought this game had pirates?"

"Maybe they come later?"

"Sweet, that actually looks like real blood! The trained dog is a cool addition. I think I saw him in a movie once."

"Is this a diversion to get us to lose our spot in line?" asked someone else.

I ignored it all as I scrambled backward on my hands until I felt the reassuring solidness of the building behind me. Erik the Evil was bellowing as Chief got tossed here and there like a furry rag doll. I couldn't believe this was happening. When I'd thrown that box, I'd never imagined that Nash would catch it and instantly end up inside the game. I'd handled the game and stayed put. Why hadn't he? It was then that I remembered grabbing the box with my sweatshirt to avoid the slushy mess. Nash hadn't had a buffer between him and the box, and he'd apparently been sucked into it like water down a drain. Well, that was an obnoxious development. Whatever happened to open sesame?! Were video games somehow different from board games? Easier to fall into somehow? I didn't think so. I'd spent years playing video games, and I'd never accidentally ended up in one. Then again, I thought as my hand went reflexively to my neck, I'd never been wearing a board game piece from my great-great-grandfather's board game around my neck. Did this mean Nash was on a Viking ship somewhere? How in the world was I supposed to get him back out?

The crowd was starting to cheer and take pictures when the door beside me suddenly burst open. Three men came out of the store; two were in bright orange shirts that said *REBOOT* in block letters, and the third was a security guard. The security guard stopped in his tracks when he saw the eight-foot Viking battling a massive dog. His body language made it clear that this was *not* what he'd signed up for. Meanwhile, the crowd was getting bigger as spectators filmed the show with their phones. The men had left the door to Reboot open, and I slipped in behind them. I slammed the door shut and threw the metal lock, saying a silent prayer that Chief wouldn't get hurt. For a second my mind flitted to my twin, but I pushed the thought away. There was nothing I could do for Nash at the moment except pray he got out of the game and back here before the Viking did any permanent damage. My heart hammered against my ribs in an angry staccato as I took in my surroundings. I was in a storage room. The walls around me were lined with shelves holding gaming consoles and stacks of glossy games. There were also bins of movie-theater-boxed candy, crates of soft drinks, and collectible video game memorabilia.

The sounds of chaos coming from the other side of the door were getting louder, and I felt something crash into it on the other side. I stayed where I was, frozen to the spot. The adrenaline of moments before was fading fast, and my legs were starting to shake underneath me. I had to move. I had to go find *The Pirate's Wrath* and get Mom out. I had to figure out what Ogden was up to. But it was taking everything in me not to pass out or puke.

The sound of approaching footsteps finally prodded me into action, and I managed to stumble away from the door and behind a shelf of games moments before someone came striding into the storage room.

"Melvin!" bellowed a deep male voice. "Greg?! Where in the blazes did you two go? Doors open in two hours, and that display case isn't going to stack itself!" I swallowed hard. The man apparently had no idea that Melvin and Greg were currently trying to calm down a raging Viking in the parking lot behind his store. I peered out from behind the shelf to get a look at the man, and my breath caught in my lungs. It was Ogden. He was wearing full pirate garb in preparation for the launch, and he more than looked the part. His black hair was no longer in the bun he'd sported for his profile picture, and it hung around his shoulders in greasy twists. His black pants were cuffed and threadbare, and the white shirt he wore was bloodstained and tattered. To the waiting crowd, he was a store owner playing a role for a new game's launch, but I knew better. I'd bet anything that those clothes were the same ones he'd worn the day he'd come out of his game. The door to the store banged open and another man entered. He too was dressed head to toe in pirate gear, complete with a long sword on his hip. He was leaner than Ogden, with a patch over one eye and a hunch to his shoulders that gave him a crumpled look.

"What be happening?" he growled.

"What *is* happening," Ogden corrected him in annoyance.

"I thought I be allowed to talk the way I always be talking tonight?" the other pirate objected. "You can't expect a man to talk different when he's back in the clothes he belongs in."

"Forget it, Slim," Ogden said, scowling as he surveyed the seemingly empty room. "I'm missing two employees and a security guard."

"Slain or slaughtered, I'd wager," Slim said.

Ogden growled low under his breath. "More likely they thought they'd take a break before the store opens. I'll have to call in reinforcements to keep those brats in line."

"I'm happy to keep them in line, Captain," Slim said, drawing his curved blade with a smile. "One or two of them tadpoles loses a hand and they won't be so keen to push and shove their way in here."

"Absolutely not," Ogden said. "We need them to buy the game, and we need them to play the game. They can't do that if you go slicing off appendages."

"Slice off appendages?" Slim said, baffled. "Whatever be ye talking about? I don't want to cut off no appendages, just hands. And maybe a foot. I loves a good foot."

Ogden rolled his eyes skyward as though searching for patience. He apparently didn't find any because he turned back to Slim, his arms crossed over his massive

307

chest. "They have to play," he hissed. "Because that's how we make our bloody money. Every game I make has to be played, or they won't buy the next one, or the next one. We need them to waste their lives staring at a screen, immersed in the heady world of our games until their very lives are sucked away one minute at a time."

"I thought we makes that money stuff by bringing out the treasure." Slim sniffed.

"We do," Ogden said. "Lord knows we need it after the amount of money I put into creating the game. The best designers don't come cheap, and everything about it had to be absolutely perfect for it to work. I'm headed for financial ruin if we don't get that treasure out, but we need those tadpoles, as you call them, to play the game or that treasure in *The Pirate's Wrath* won't keep regenerating, will it? We won't have anything to find. Besides, the more games in circulation, the less chance there is of ever having the game destroyed again. It's the only game we can bring things out of, I've explained this to you. Without a Benson in the game, all I can do is visit. I can't take anything back out with me."

"Why don't we just kidnap another of them Bensons," Slim said with a smile. "That way you can get some useful things from some of them other games yous visited. I'd fancy a dragon or a troll."

"I would," Ogden said. "But there aren't any more. The woman and Ace were the last of the wretched bunch. I may use the old man if I can figure out a secure way to remove him from Lost Lore, but that's a problem for another day. Right now I need to know where my blasted employees wandered off to."

"Is there time to go back for a visit to the old *Royal Run* before the store opens?" Slim asked, sounding forlorn. "I be missing our ship, Captain. It smelled like a hog's underbelly, but it's home."

"You smell like a hog's underbelly," Ogden said. "Didn't I tell you to shower?"

"I won't be getting wet for no good reason," Slim said, sounding aghast. "You want me to catch my death of the consumption?"

Ogden sighed and shook his head. "Hopefully the crowd thinks it's just part of the ambience."

"Ambience?" Slim repeated. "That some sort of an illness?"

"Was I this much of a buffoon when I came out of the game?" Ogden asked himself. "You're more headache than you're worth, Slim. If I could have chosen someone to come out when I sent that woman in, it wouldn't have been you."

"Sorry, Captain," Slim said. Ogden surveyed the empty room again and then stomped back through the door to the front of the store. Slim didn't follow. He stood in the empty room muttering to himself as he dug something out of the inside of his leather vest and shoved it inside his cheek. He spit, still muttering to himself, and I held my breath, worried that he'd hear my hammering heart. He started puttering around the storage room, picking up this and that to inspect it. He pocketed a few items with a furtive glance toward the door Ogden had just gone through. He stopped at a large pallet of cardboard boxes. He withdrew a wicked-looking sword from his belt and jammed it into the top of the box. It was obvious that he'd never opened a duct-taped box before, and he hacked at the cardboard, pulling back chunks until he'd exposed whatever was inside it. He pulled out a small octagonal object, and I peered around the corner to look. It was a copy of *The Pirate's Wrath*. Like the original board game, it had been packaged to look like it had shiny metallic clasps on the corners. This disappeared into Slim's oversize vest, and I marveled at the amount of stuff one man could steal in less than three minutes. He was either brave or stupid. If Ogden caught him, he was going to learn what a lost appendage really meant.

"Slim!" Ogden yelled from the front of the store. "Something's going on out back. Handle it!" Slim spit again and headed toward the rear of the store. He threw the bolt I'd just locked and opened it. The sound of a rampaging Viking, an overexcited crowd, and a barking dog came roaring inside. Slim bellowed, pulled his sword, and ran out, leaving the door open. I was up and moving the second he was gone, running for the box he'd just opened. I reached in and grabbed the top copy of *The Pirate's Wrath*. The second my hand made contact with the game, I felt a yank on my spine, and everything went black.

TWENTY-SEVEN

I knew immediately that I was on a ship. The wooden floor beneath me was pitching this way and that with such ferocity that I barely managed to stay on my feet. The smell hit me next, an overpowering stench of rotten fish, old sweat, and mildew. I coughed and staggered as the floor tipped in the other direction.

I was in another storage room, but this one couldn't have been more different from the orderly shelves and crates of the Reboot store. Wooden barrels were lashed haphazardly to the walls, while a handful of leather sacks slipped across the floor untethered. Empty glass bottles rattled after them while full ones smashed into the barrels and burst open. My stomach was rolling and pitching along with the floor, and I had to force myself not to think about getting sick. I needed to get out of here and fast. There was an arched door at the far end of the room, and I grabbed the knob. Nothing happened; the door was locked. I looked for Nash, just like I always looked for Nash when things got tough, but for the first time in my life, Nash wasn't here. I was alone.

I shut my eyes, forcing myself to block out the image of the pitching floor and the rolling bottles and the smell. What would Nash do? What would Ace do for that matter? My brain felt scrambled, and the room just kept rolling this way and that like the world's worst amusement park ride. Panic was tightening itself around my ribs like a boa constrictor, and I gulped at the rancid air. I tried to shove the feeling aside the same way I'd shoved aside the thought of getting motion sickness, but it refused to be shoved. What would Nash do? What would Ace do? What would Cress do? The questions felt like they were stuck on repeat, going around and around in my head like a helicopter spiraling toward the ground in a tailspin.

Ace's lesson came floating back to me. I could imagine him leaning over, his long bony finger in my face as he admonished me that *you can never forget that it's a game.* I snapped my eyes open. This *was* a game. How had I forgotten that I was in a game?! So I did what I'd done in every game I'd gone into: I jammed my hand into my pocket. There *was* something there, but it wasn't a set of dice, or a spinner, or a stack of cards like I'd expected. I blinked down at the video game controller. This wasn't just a game. It was a video game.

I refocused on the small claustrophobic room and really looked at it. It felt real, almost too real, like if I went back to the real world it would seem like a faded copy of this one. The lines between the game and reality felt dangerously small, and I realized how easily I could slip over that edge.

I took a deep breath and braced my feet against the nearest barrel. I was going to have to be the hero of this story, whether I wanted to be or not. My mom was somewhere in this game, and I wasn't going to find her trapped in the world's smelliest storage room.

There were no dice to roll, no spinner to spin, no cards to pull, and as far as I could tell, I wasn't going to have to wait my turn. I squinted at the controller in the dim light. The buttons were labeled A, B, C, and D. There was only one way to find out what each one did, and I braced myself as I hit button A.

No sooner had I hit it than I felt my arm rip to my side, clench into a fist, and whip out in front of myself again. It was exactly the move I'd make if I had a giant sword on my hip. But, of course, I had no sword, so I stood there in a sword-fighting stance, hand held up in front of my face, with nothing in it. Awesome. It turned out that button B made me swish that non-existent sword from side to side, while button C made my arm go up and down in a hacking motion. The whole thing made me feel like a puppet on a string, and I didn't like it.

Like it or not, I had to play the game if I was going to find my mom. Glancing around, I saw a thin metal rod sticking out of one of the busted barrels. It was no sword, but it was better than nothing. Tucking it in the belt loop on my left side, I approached the locked door for a second time. I held the controller in front of myself and hit A. For the second time, my hand whipped to my side. This time there was more than thin air to grab, and my fingers gripped the metal rod and smashed it into the door. The wood broke into small shards that crumbled at my feet, and I was out. I tried to bolt from the room, only to find that my feet were frozen in place. With a sigh, I put my thumb on the controller and pushed the joystick forward. I moved. At first my steps were jerky, and I lurched forward in sudden bursts that made my already queasy stomach roll angrily.

I was a quick study, though, thanks to my previous video game experience, and soon I was moving down the hallway of the ship with some sense of normalcy.

There were doorways lining the hallway, and I repeated my maneuver with the metal bar, crashing down each one that I passed. The first three held similar contents to the room I'd just left, but the fourth was stacked floor to ceiling with treasure. I'd have loved to explore that one, but I kept moving, making my way down the hallway until I came to a ladder leading upward. It took a second to figure out the combination of buttons I needed to hit to climb the ladder, but I managed it.

I emerged from the hull of the ship and into the bright light of day. The sea around the ship was full of huge, rolling waves, explaining the pitching sensation I'd felt belowdecks. I was also surrounded on all sides by pirates.

TWENTY-EIGHT

This was Ogden's crew, I realized as I took in the ferocious men and women surrounding me. They were dressed the same way Ogden and Slim had been in the store, wearing ragged shirts, faded and patched pants, and leather boots that came up to their shins. All of them had swords at their sides and suddenly my metal rod felt incredibly stupid. I took this all in in a second and was just trying to mentally figure out what buttons I'd need to hit to go back down into the belly of the ship when I heard someone scream my name.

"Rhett!" called a female voice. For a heart-wrenchingly hopeful second, I thought it was my mom. I jerked my head to the side, scanning the deck wildly even as the pirates pulled their swords and rushed toward me. A moment later I felt someone grab me from behind, lifting me off the ground and into the air. I yelped, barely managing to keep my grip on my controller as I flew through the air.

I was swinging over the deck of the ship like some kind of deranged bat, my shirt hiked up so far around my neck it was practically choking me. I looked up, and to my utter shock saw Cress. She was wearing pirate gear, her hair tied back in a red bandana. A large sword was buckled at her waist along with a wide variety of smaller knives, and what looked like a pistol. She was holding a rope in one hand and the neck of my shirt in the other as she swung us past the edge of the ship and out over the open ocean.

"Can you swim?!" she yelled down. She let me go before I could answer, and we both went catapulting toward the rolling waves below. The water closed over my head, and I tried to kick for the surface. My legs didn't respond, and I felt my lungs constrict in panic. I was sinking, fast, my clothes pulling me deeper by the second. I tried to pull myself up with just my arms, which is when I spotted the controller still clutched in my hand. In desperation I started pushing buttons and wiggling the joystick, and like magic, my legs went into high gear, pummeling me up to the surface so fast that I popped out of the water like some kind of deranged dolphin.

"Phew," Cress said, swimming over to me. "If you couldn't swim that would have been the world's worst rescue. Pull you right out of the frying pan and throw you into a fire." The pirate ship we'd just vacated was pulling around in a wide arc, a swarm of angry pirates at the helm waving swords in the air. A second later there was an earsplitting boom and something landed five feet to our left with a colossal splash.

"Wasting good cannon-shot on the likes of us!" Cress bellowed. "Ye be bigger fools than the mothers that didn't drown ye at birth!"

"Wow," I said. "That was harsh."

Cress eyed the controller in my hand. "Is that the thing that let you swim like that?"

I nodded.

"Good," she said, grabbing on to my shoulder with one hand while she pointed ahead with her other hand. "Swim us that way and make it snappy if you don't want to die." I hit two buttons and moved the joy-stick forward, and we were off. My legs were a blur, propelling us through the water faster than humanly possible. Cress pointed the direction we needed to go, all the while holding on to my shoulder with a pinch-ing death grip and hurling insults behind her at the quickly disappearing pirate ship. I lost track of time, my focus on maneuvering the waves and pushing the right combination of buttons that would keep my legs moving in the right direction. I almost didn't see the island until we were a few feet from shore. I released the buttons on the controller, and we coasted to a stop in a foot of water. Cress immediately bounded onto shore, wringing out her sopping-wet shirt.

"Where did you come from?" I asked.

"What do you mean?" she said. "*The Royal Run*. Same as you."

"How did you get into *The Pirate's Wrath*?" I said.

"Tunnels," Cress said. "The day Ace destroyed the game it sealed itself shut. But I checked it after I left Lost Lore, and it had opened back up."

"Where is your controller?" I said, holding up my dripping-wet one. "How come you get to move around without using this thing."

Cress studied me for a second and then huffed out a sigh. "Because this be my game." She paused and shook her head. "Sorry," she said. "You can take the girl out of the pirate game, but you apparently can't take the pirate out of the girl. What I meant to say was, this is *my* game. You don't need a spinner or dice or whatever that thing is when it's *your* game."

"Your game?!" I spluttered. "How in the world is this your game? I thought you beat your game! That's how you became a Wanderer!"

"I did beat it!" Cress said, sounding furious. "I got

out, and I vowed never to come back. But I pay my debts, Rhett Benson. Don't let anyone tell you that I don't!"

"I'm confused," I admitted. There was a loud boom in the distance, and we both turned to see *The Royal Run* making its way at a steady clip toward our island.

"There's no time for long explanations," Cress said. "Do you want to find your mom or not?"

"Of course," I spluttered. "Do you know where she is?"

Cress nodded grimly. "I know," she said. "Follow me, and make it snappy. The moment those brutes make landfall, they're going to be on us like fleas on a dog." With that she took off at a sprint into the underbrush bordering the beach. I followed, the controller in my hand feeling as much a part of me as my own arms. I ducked tree limbs, hurdled rocks, and leaped over streams as we made our way deeper and deeper into the island's jungled interior. The boom of cannon fire was getting louder by the second, and I wondered how long we had before a pack of angry pirates landed on the beach. Cress seemed to be making her way toward a large outcropping of rocks, and I did my best to keep up. Finally, she skidded to a stop. I bent over, one hand on my cramping ribs, as I tried to inhale enough air for my greedy lungs. We were standing beside the entrance to a small cave half hidden behind a bramble of blackberry bushes.

"She's in there," Cress said.

"How do you know?" I said, bending over to peer into the dark hole in the side of the rock that was only about three feet high by two feet wide.

She huffed in exasperation. "This is my game, remember? I know a few things."

I was about to go in when I stopped and turned around, crossing my arms. "Wait a minute," I said. "How do I know I can trust you? Last time we almost became rock giant dessert because you decided to go after the spindle instead of helping us."

Cress narrowed her eyes at me. "This is different," she said.

"Why?" I asked.

"Like I said, I owe the Bensons, and I don't like owing anyone," she said.

"Why would you owe my family?" I said. There was a loud boom in the distance, and we both jumped.

"We don't have time for this!" Cress said.

"Make time," I said flatly. I wanted the story, and I wanted it before I climbed into the coffin-sized hole in the rock.

Cress glared at me, and I glared back. There was another loud boom, and I could hear the sound of yelling pirates faintly in the distance.

"Fine!" Cress. "I owe your family because I'm the

reason your uncle Sam never made it out of this game."

"What?" I said, dropping my arms to my sides in surprise.

"I met Sam the first time he came to The Pirate's Wrath," Cress said, her words coming out in a jumbled rush. "He noticed me. I wasn't a main character in this game, and it was the first time someone had ever done that. I don't know why he picked me to be his friend, but he did. He told me all about board game bounding, and he took me with him into other games. It was the first time that I realized there might be a way out of this life that I hated."

"You hated being a pirate?" I said.

"I hated being a second-rate deckhand," Cress spit out. "I hated being treated like a dog that everyone on board that boat got to kick whenever they felt like it. When I met Sam, I realized that if I just figured out how to win my game, I'd be free. Sam promised to help me win it. He read the Pirate's Wrath instruction manual, and he told me things. Things that your grandfather would have never approved of him telling a lowly board game character like me." When I continued to stare at her in confusion, she huffed and dug around in one of the leather pouches at her side. After a moment she produced a small white piece of paper and thrust it at me. I took it, but part of me already knew what it was. Feeling numb, I reached back into my own pocket and

323

pulled out the manual for The Pirate's Wrath, ignoring Cress's sharp intake of breath at the sight of it. Flipping it open to the missing page, I slid her page inside. It fit like the last piece of a puzzle.

"Sam gave this to you?" I said.

Cress nodded. She swallowed hard. "Because he was my friend. But I'm a bad friend to have."

"Why? What happened?" I asked.

"I made a mistake," Cress said, her voice cracking on the word *mistake* as she fought back tears. "Ogden had caught sight of Sam during one of his visits, and he cornered me. He threatened to cut off my hands and imprison me in a cat's game if I didn't tell him who Sam was. He thought I was a traitor and was telling his enemies about the inner workings of his ship. I was ignorant. I thought that Sam was like me. I thought, stupidly, that if something happened to him, he'd just go back to start. He never told me that he'd die. I didn't even really know what that concept meant. I'd only ever seen people walk the plank one second and end up back at the start of the game the next second."

"You didn't realize he'd die," I repeated. I had no idea what it felt like to have an out-of-body experience, but it had to feel similar to this. Cress shook her head, tears streaming down her face.

"I didn't know," she said. "So I did what Ogden wanted. I told him everything. I told him about how characters in games could trade places with people like Sam. I didn't know that if Sam died, Ogden would become a Wander Lost. Maybe Sam didn't tell me that on purpose, or maybe he didn't know. I can't really be sure. Either way, I told Ogden about the Bensons, and he believed me hook, line, and sinker. Probably because a few of our crew members had swapped places with Sam and had been raving about a dream they had where they spent hours trapped in a strange office." Cress swiped angrily at the tears on her cheeks, and I watched, my heart hard and heavy, because I knew how this story ended.

"So Ogden figured out that to stay in our world, all he had to do was make sure Sam was killed in his," I said.

Cress nodded, wiping at the tears as they slid over her cheeks. "Sam brought your mom to meet me," she choked out, "and it was the first time that Ogden went to your world. He must have given orders about what to do if he ever disappeared, because when Sam and your mom showed up, they were ambushed. Sam didn't make it out," she said. "I never got to talk to your mom. I never got to tell her how sorry I was."

"But you figured out how to win your game," I said. "Because Sam had given you the last page of the instruction manual." There was a boom that made the ground under our feet shudder, and I cringed as the sounds of rampaging pirates making their way through the under-brush got louder.

"Exactly," Cress said, and she reached out and plucked the manual from my hand, waving it in front of my nose. "I know this thing better than you know yourself. So if I tell you that your mom's in there, she's in there. So go get her out."

I nodded, already turning toward the cave. "And Rhett!" Cress said. "Don't return to this game. Not ever. It's no good."

"You could have come out of your game," I said instead. "You could have come to our world and told her. Explained somehow."

Cress shook her head. "You can only go to your world from your own game. The second I left The Pirate's Wrath, it became impossible for me to go to your world. Then Ace destroyed The Pirate's Wrath, and that door closed forever."

"Did you want to?" I said, surprised.

Cress shook her head again. "No. Now go!" She pulled the sword out of her belt and turned toward the sound of approaching voices. "I'll do my best to buy you some time!" I ducked into the cave. Explanations were going to have to wait until after I saved my mom.

TWENTY-NINE

The cave tunnel was small, forcing me to bend practically in half as I ran. The controller in my hand felt like an extension of my arm, and thanks to the small light shining from it, I managed to zig and zag around boulders and rocks without any difficulty. The place reminded me a lot of Tunnels, and I wondered if this was the way Cress had reentered her game. I took a sharp right and came to a locked door. There were odd symbols carved into its wooden surface, and I peered at them, trying to make out what they were. It appeared to be a row of small birdcages, just like the ones the rock giants had used to capture us in Lost Lore. Inside each cage was a cat. I looked back down and grabbed the door handle, not surprised at all to discover that it was locked. I rattled it angrily.

"Who's there?" someone called from the other side,

and my heart lurched. I knew that voice.

"Mom!" I yelled. "Mom! It's me!"

"Nash?" she said.

"Rhett!" I replied, not even the least bit bothered that she'd assumed that my brother would be the one who rescued her. "I'm going to save you!" I said, even though I had no idea how I was going to do that.

"Get out of this game," Mom called, her voice high-pitched and scared. "If they find you, they'll lock you up in here too."

"I'm not leaving without you," I said. I started hitting buttons on the controller, desperate for any combination that would help me break down the door. I jumped, grabbed for a sword that wasn't there, and banged uselessly to no avail. It was then that I heard the pirates. They must have been closer than Cress and I had realized because the sound of angry voices reverberated off the walls. I hurled myself into the door in desperation as the sounds got closer, but all I managed to do was bruise my shoulder. I stood back, panting, as my mom pleaded with me to save myself.

"Get out, Rhett! Take your brother and go! I'll find a way out. I promise. Just go!"

I gritted my teeth, wishing that I hadn't lost that metal rod. The doorknob stared back at me, its large gaping keyhole looking like a smirking mouth, and I felt the distinct urge to give the thing another kick.

I blinked. A keyhole. I jammed my hand into my pocket and froze. I'd left the instruction booklet to The Pirate's Wrath in Cress's hand. The sound of a pirate bellowing in frustration snapped me back into action, and I dug deeper, finally pulling out the skeleton key that I'd found on the floor of Ace's office. Could it be? I shoved it into the lock. With a neat click, the door swung open, and my mom came rushing out. The sound of the approaching pirates was getting louder by the second. My mom grabbed me, pulling me behind the open door so that we were wedged between it and the cave wall, the door to the cat's game prison cell standing wide open. We crouched hidden from view just as the pirates rounded the bend. My hand was squeezing the controller so hard that my knuckles had turned white, and sweat trickled down the back of my neck.

"Why's the bloody door open?!" one cried.

"He got the prisoner!" said another.

"Are you sure? Maybe she's just hiding in there."

"Ogden's going to kill us," said a third.

"He can't kill us if he's not here," said someone else. The pirates all shuffled and shoved until they were inside the prison, all the while yelling at one another. The second the last one stepped inside I hit three buttons on the controller. My body moved faster than seemed humanly possible to slam the door shut behind them with a clang. My mom was at my side a second later to turn the key that was still in the lock.

"Let's get out of here," I said.

"Agreed," she said, taking my hand. Together we shut our eyes, and I felt the familiar pull at my insides. We were going home.

I opened my eyes in the Reboot storage room just in time to see Slim and a heavyset pirate I'd never seen before disappear. A second later a very sweaty Nash came bursting in the back door. He looked like he'd been rolled down a cheese grater, and his clothes hung off him in muddy strips. Chief was at his heels, hobbling on three legs while the fourth dragged behind him. As soon as Chief was through the door, Nash slammed it shut behind him, blocking out the sound of the Reboot employees' frantic efforts to direct the crowd around to the front of the store. He turned, his eyes wide and frightened as he took in the storage room. He gasped when he caught sight of who I was standing next to, dropped something from his hand with a loud, metallic clang, and launched himself at us.

"Mom!" Nash said, throwing himself into her outstretched arms. She hugged him back, tears streaming down her face. I gently pushed Nash to the side so I could join the hug, and I felt tears oozing from my own eyes. I wasn't sure what heaven was like, but I'd guess it was a lot like hugging a loved one you thought you'd never see again.

"You did it!" Nash crowed, shoving my shoulder in his excitement. "You found Mom!"

"He did," Mom said, smiling through tears at the two of us. She blinked, seeming to really see Nash for the first time, and her mouth turned down at the corners as she took in his appearance. "What happened?" she said.

"Vikings," Nash said with a grimace. "Give me a rock giant any day."

"Vikings? Rock giant?" Mom said, her face turning white as a sheet. "When I get ahold of your grandfather, I'm going to . . ." She never got to tell us what she was going to do to Ace, because at that moment Ogden came stomping into the storage room.

THIRTY

"I'm going to hang you from the ceiling by your toenails, you lazy sack of shark spleens!" Ogden shouted, stopping short when he saw the three of us.

"Captain O!" Mom said, her face hard as she shoved Nash and me behind her.

Ogden looked from us to our mom and back again, his forehead crumpled in confusion as though he were trying to figure out a complicated math equation but things just weren't adding up. He curled a lip to reveal blackened teeth, and I took a step back, bumping hard into the crate of games behind me.

"Didn't know there were any more Bensons running around, but these two brats resemble that brother of yours like mirror images."

Mom stood up straight, her shoulders back and her chin up, and faster than I'd have thought possible she'd reached out and grabbed a broom that was leaning up against a nearby wall. She brandished it in front of her, and based off the look on her face I had every confidence that she'd be able to pound him to a pulp with it without breaking a sweat. Ogden seemed less impressed as he casually reached over and pulled his sword from its scabbard.

"You brought a broom to a sword fight," he said. "So very Benson of you." Behind me the crates of *The Pirate's Wrath* pressed against the back of my calves, making them tingle. What now? I'd managed to find my mom, but in Cress's words, I'd grabbed her from a frying pan and thrown her into a fire. An image of Cress in her full pirate garb popped into my brain, and I wondered if I'd ever see her again.

Ogden pulled his sword back and swung hard for Mom's head. She flicked the broom up into both hands to block the blow. The sword hit the broom handle with a sharp crack, snapping it in two. Mom leaped backward, knocking Nash into the crate of video games. He fell, his hands outstretched, and he disappeared the second his fingers touched one of the exposed games. A moment later a pirate appeared in the exact spot he'd just vacated. This man was the opposite of Slim, built wider than he was tall, with lumpy muscles covering his arms and shoulders. Large, swirling black tattoos raced up his arms from his wrists, intertwined around his stubby neck, and curled around his ears and onto the top of his bald head.

"Captain!" he said, catching sight of Ogden. "What be the meaning of this?!"

"Excellent," Ogden said, smiling so widely I could see the gold caps on his molars. Mom muttered something under her breath before grabbing my sleeve and yanking me away from the crate of games. "Take off the game piece," she hissed. I reached up and grabbed the small wooden piece and pulled; the leather shoelace Ace had used stretched and snapped. "We need to get your brother's off when he comes back," Mom whispered. I nodded. She'd just confirmed my theory about the game pieces. I couldn't believe that Nash had disappeared like that again. Video games apparently had a much stronger pull than board games, and I remembered the terrifying moments in the belly of the ship where I'd completely forgotten that I was in a game. Had that happened to Nash? Was he stumbling around in *The Pirate's Wrath*, unaware of the mess he left behind? I quickly jammed the broken shoelace into my pocket and felt my fingers brush up against something slick and plastic. I had forgotten that I had the Midas stone in there. I closed my hand around the Ziploc bag encasing it and squeezed.

A loud thump and crash suddenly came from the front of the store followed by raucous cheering. One of the overeager teens had apparently managed to break down the front door, unwilling to wait until the official midnight launch to get their hands on *The Pirate's Wrath*.

The voices of squealing and chattering teenagers poured into the back storage room as an apparent free-for-all broke out on the floor of Reboot. Ogden's attention wavered. I pulled out the Midas stone and held it hidden behind my back just as the muscular pirate lunged for Mom. She sidestepped smoothly, her leg jutting out like lightning as she used both hands to flip him hard over her hip. He landed with a resounding whump on his back. It was an impressive move to say the least, and I glanced over at my mom, eyebrow raised. A second later the pirate disappeared, and Nash was back, standing in the middle of the room looking bewildered. Ogden had him before I could even shout a warning, his sword pressed hard against the thin skin of his neck. The knife sliced neatly through the string holding his game piece, and I saw it tumble to the floor.

"Let him go!" Mom cried, stepping forward, her hand outstretched.

"Oh, I will," Ogden said. "I'll let him go over the

side of a ship in shark-infested waters, just like I let your brother." Mom let out a strangled cry, and Ogden's grin got even wider. "Of course, you two are free to join him," he said. "I may even visit the old ship to watch."

I kept my hands behind my back, opening the top of the Ziploc bag with one hand. I felt my mom trembling beside me, her breath ragged, and I knew she must be remembering what had happened to her brother.

A second later the door to the storage room burst open as a flood of people pushed inside, shouting in excitement. Ogden's head whipped around as an especially excited teenage girl jumped on his back, her cell phone held out in front of her. "Selfie with a pirate!" she squealed as Ogden let out a roar of outrage. I waited until the girl was clear of Ogden to pull the stone out from my pocket. Nash saw it, his eyes going wide as he realized what I was planning. We looked at one another. Nash flicked his eyes up to Ogden and then to the stone and I nodded. I opened the bag wide, careful not to touch the stone, and held it poised to launch out of the bag.

"Nash!" I called loudly above the fray. "Catch!"

Ogden's head whipped toward me, and he let go of Nash to intercept the object that I hurled toward them. Nash ducked, rolling sideways out of the way as Ogden's hand closed over the Midas stone. He turned instantly to solid gold.

"Whoa," said a teenage boy beside me. "Talk about your special effects."

The video game launch had turned into a mob scene, with people helping themselves to the games and candy sitting in stacks on nearby shelves. I ripped off my T-shirt and used it to gingerly pick up the fallen Midas stone before it could turn anyone else to gold. I looked up to see Nash holding a copy of *The Pirate's Wrath* in his hand.

"What are you doing?" Mom asked, her voice tight.

"We can't just leave him here," Nash said. He glanced around at the floor. "Where's my game piece?" We looked around, but Nash's makeshift necklace was nowhere to be seen. Nash was holding the game in one hand, while his other hand was pressed firmly to the golden statue that used to be Ogden. I saw his plan in an instant. He might not have his game piece, but I had mine. My mom apparently figured out his plan a second later and opened her mouth to protest, but it was too late. I ripped my game piece on its shoestring out of my pocket and threw it over my head. That done, I lunged for Nash, grabbing him and the game at the same time, and the room around us immediately disappeared.

THIRTY-ONE

I opened my eyes in *The Pirate's Wrath* as we splashed down into the ocean. I looked to my left to see Nash fumbling madly in his pocket for a controller as the statue of Ogden plummeted down into the dark depths of the sea. I didn't bother looking for a controller, I didn't want to play this game. I wanted out of it. Reaching over, I grabbed my twin by the shoulder and the game piece around my neck with my free hand, and shut my eyes. The familiar yank and twist came a second later, and I opened my eyes back in the storage room with Nash at my side, his hands still shoved into his dripping-wet pockets. I blinked in surprise at the person who had materialized next to Nash.

"Cress!" Nash said, wiping water from his eyes. "What are you doing here?"

"Cress?!" Mom said from behind us, her tone

338

completely at odds with Nash's eager, excited one. She was looking at Cress as though she'd just seen a ghost, her face losing all color in an instant.

"Natalie," Cress said, dipping her head at my mom. Her eyes widened a second later when she caught sight of the pile of *The Pirate's Wrath* sitting stacked on the crate behind her. My mom turned to see what had caught her attention, and her expression darkened.

A second later she'd picked up the Viking axe that Nash had dropped and swung it up over her head in both hands. She brought it down with a sharp crack onto the first box, cleaving it and the games inside in two.

"Whoa!" said a teenage boy, stopping to watch as she took out the next box. "Is that the axe of Vanguard the Viking?"

"If Vanguard had one eye, a giant scar across his cheek, and the personality of an angry wildebeest, then yes," Nash said. Mom reared back again, hacking into the second box, a look of grim determination on her face.

"Is that lady destroying all the new games?" someone said. "I'm writing such a bad review about this place. What a rip-off." I ignored the concerned murmurs of the bystanders as I watched my mom split another stack of games in two. She was right. We needed to destroy *The Pirate's Wrath* as well as the rest of the games Ogden had created. I had no idea what he'd meant by sucking the life out of the players who played them, but it hadn't sounded like a good thing.

"Not fast enough," I said, biting my lip as I turned to survey the storage room that was currently overrun with teenagers helping themselves to Reboot's merchandise. One of Ogden's employees chose that moment to burst in through back door, his mouth hanging open as he took in the utter pandemonium. That's when I noticed the little red box to the left of the door.

"What are you doing?!" Nash yelled as I darted through the crowd, weaving between the sweaty bodies of boys attempting to carry out stacks of fifteen games at a time. I finally reached the back wall, and its small, innocuous red box. I slammed my elbow into it, shattering the thin plastic cover, and ripped down the white handle. Immediately a fire alarm went off. Everyone in the back room froze for an instant, bewildered, and then the sprinkler system went off. Water streamed in icy swirls from the ceiling, dousing the kids and their free games and equipment in seconds. There was a second burst of screaming and hysteria, and everyone tried to exit the building at the exact same time, shoving and pushing as they made their way out of the front and back exits of the storage room. Meanwhile, Mom continued her single-minded destruction of the *Pirate's Wrath* boxes, although the torrential downpour of the sprinklers was doing more damage than her axe. As I watched her career into the next box, I had a feeling that this was probably healing something inside her that had been broken ever since she lost her twin. Cress stood next to Nash, a look of grim approval on her face.

"You can stop now," Nash said, putting a hand on Mom's arm. Water was streaming off all of us, and I could hear the blare of sirens in the distance. She gave it one more cathartic whack, splitting the last box of games into small shards.

"We need to go," I said, glancing around at the trashed and almost bare storage room. If we got caught in this mess, it was going to be incredibly hard to explain.

"Right," Mom said, shaking her head. "Sorry. Let's go." We headed for the open door in the back at a trot, the water still streaming down from the ceiling in a torrent. We emerged into the cool night air, and I let out a sigh of relief.

"Come on," Nash said. "We left Snow White back this way."

"Snow White?" Cress said. "Uh-oh."

"What?" I said.

Cress winced. "Let's just say we had an incident

involving her apple that she probably hasn't forgotten."

"Wait a second," I said, stopping in my tracks. "Where's Chief?" Nash, Mom, and Cress all stopped as I turned back. The door to Reboot still stood open, and I could just see Ace's massive dog inside. The sirens were getting closer by the second, and I knew that any moment now fire trucks and police cars would be all over this place.

"Chief!" Mom called. "Come!" The dog either couldn't hear her or was choosing to ignore her, because he didn't even flick an ear in our direction.

"Get them to the truck," I told Nash. "I'll get Chief and meet you there." Nash hesitated, but then he snapped out of it, grabbed Mom's arm, and started pulling her across the parking lot toward the school's playground. Cress ignored my orders and stayed right at my shoulder as I charged back into the storage room. I was worried that Chief had somehow gotten trapped, but as soon as I was back inside, I saw that wasn't the case. He was crouched, his shoulders hunched, as he stared at a large metal box bolted to the wall. At first glance I thought that it must be the store's safe, a place to keep the extra cash or valuables they didn't want to leave out, but it didn't have a keypad or a large dial with numbers on the front like I'd seen on the safes my friends had in their basements.

"Come on!" I said to Chief, grabbing him around the collar. "We have to get out of here."

Chief wrenched himself out of my hands and returned to his position in front of the box. This time instead of staring at it he whined and pawed at it, his motions frantic.

"Whatever is in there, he's not leaving without it," Cress said.

"We have to!" I said, my heart hammering as the sirens got louder and louder by the second. Cress disappeared from my side as I ran my hands over the sides of the box, searching for some sort of latch or lever that would pop the thing open. She returned a second later.

"Stand back," she said. I did, pulling Chief back with me, as she took the double-sided axe my mom had been using moments before and hefted it above her head. She brought it down with a crash. The metal box didn't even dent. Cress dropped the axe, rubbing her arms as she winced in pain.

It was then that I noticed the markings. Pressed into the metal was an etched row of tiny golden birdcages, each containing a very angry-looking cat. They were the same markings that had been on the cave door that had trapped my mom. "Cat's game," I murmured. I suddenly knew what was inside that box.

I picked up the axe Cress had dropped. "Good luck," Cress muttered. I was about to start hacking at the soggy drywall behind the safe, thinking that if I could just disconnect it from the wall, I could drag it out of there, when I noticed something. On the top right-hand corner was a small brass disk attached to the safe with a screw. I slid it aside to reveal a keyhole. For the second time, I pulled the key out of my pocket and slipped it in. I felt the mechanism inside the box unlock and yanked the door open. Inside, just like I knew it would be, was Lost Lore.

The sound of shouting voices suddenly echoed from the front of the store, and I snatched up the box just as Cress grabbed me in an attempt to haul me out the door. I resisted just long enough to rip my key back out of the door before sprinting after her. Chief came with us this time, hobbling on his three good legs, as we ran.

The parking lot was a blur, the flash of sirens lighting up the surrounding trees in bursts. Due to the crush of cars trying to exit the parking lot, the emergency vehicles hadn't been able to make their way into the back alley, and we hit the adjacent school's playground at a dead sprint. Ace's truck was running, this time with our mom behind the wheel, and I jumped into the truck bed, followed by Cress. Chief attempted to make the jump but his bad leg caused him to miss the mark. Cress's hand shot out, grabbing his collar, and together we hauled him inside the truck bed as Mom careened out of the parking lot, Ace's diesel engine roaring. I clutched Lost Lore to my chest as we took a turn and Reboot disappeared from sight.

THIRTY-TWO

The drive back to Ace's cabin was one that I knew I'd never forget. I lay in the bed of the truck, the road rumbling beneath me, staring up at the stars. On my right Cress was doing the same thing, and I wondered what she thought of my world. She'd never been able to get to it before, and I wondered if it lived up to her expectations. On my left, Chief sat with his head and paws firmly positioned on Lost Lore, as though someone might try to take it from him at any moment. In the truck cab I could hear our mom laughing as she chatted with Nash and Snow White. I felt equal parts exhausted and exhilarated. I was alive. Mom was back, and we'd get Ace back soon enough. The world felt right in a way I'd never really experienced before.

My eyes were just getting heavy as we pulled in to the gravel driveway of Ace's cabin. Mom put the truck in park and climbed out of the cab, peering over the side of the truck bed at us.

"Do I still have a Benson boy back here?" she said.

"You do," I said, sitting up stiffly. Cress hopped out of the truck, looking around herself with wide-eyed interest.

"Cress," my mom said, her tone holding none of the warmth it had possessed when she'd said my name. "I think you and I need to talk." Cress nodded, sliding her bandana off her curls and looking down at the ground. Without a word she slipped the instruction booklet for The Pirate's Wrath out of her pocket and handed it to my mom, who took it gingerly.

"I'm sorry about Sam," Cress said. "Sorrier than you'll ever know. If I could go back and change it, I would." She grimaced, shaking her head. "I guess that was my problem. I got in the habit of thinking that when things went wrong you could just go back to start and try again. Sam shouldn't have trusted me."

Mom studied Cress for a moment. "I forgave you a long time ago," she said, and sighed. "Just like I had to forgive myself."

"What?" Cress said, her head jerking up. "What are you talking about? You didn't do anything wrong that day."

"Oh, but I did," my mom said. "I knew that Sam

347

was playing with fire by going into that game, and I let him go anyway. I didn't tell my dad. If I'd told him what was going on, he'd have stopped it. He'd have found a way to protect Sam. That's the guilt I have to live with, Cress, but I knew that I had to forgive myself before I let it crush me."

"Without Cress's help, I'd never have found you," I pitched in.

"I repay my debts," Cress said, her face still fierce.

"Thank you," Mom said, and she put an arm around the girl's tight shoulders and squeezed. Cress seemed frozen, not sure what to do with this show of kindness, but then she relaxed, nodding her head. Mom turned to Nash and me, eyebrows raised. "I suppose I owe you two an apology as well."

Nash said no at the exact moment that I said yes, and Mom laughed. "Forgive me?" she asked, taking us both under her arms and squeezing.

"Yes," I said, and I did.

"And will you forgive me for all the times I said you were nuttier than a port-a-potty at a peanut festival?" Nash said, grinning up at her impishly.

"You said that?!" Mom said.

"No," Nash admitted. "But I sure thought it a lot."

"Fair enough." Mom laughed. Even Cress laughed, the corners of her mouth quirking up. She was still

348

dressed like the pirate she was, and I wondered if it would be rude to offer her a change of clothes. Snow White beat me to it, though.

"Oh, my dear!" she said, gliding over to pick up one of Cress's sleeves in disgust. "You look like something the cat dragged in."

"What's that supposed to mean?" Cress said, crossing her arms over her chest.

"She's right," Mom said, putting a hand on both girls' backs as she led them toward the cabin. "Let's get washed up and get some food." I sighed, happy to follow them all into the cabin. After feeling like the world was on my shoulders for the last few days, I suddenly felt like a kid again, happy to have someone else in charge for once.

At two in the morning, we all settled onto the couches in the living room as though it were the most normal thing in the world. Snow White had Geronimo Jones wrapped in a blanket like a baby and was rocking him back and forth while he snoozed happily, and Mom had found Cress a pair of black leggings and one of Ace's old sweatshirts to wear. On the coffee table in front of us sat Lost Lore.

"Do you think he's still with Beatrice?" Nash asked.

I shrugged. "I kind of got the impression that she was his girlfriend," I said.

349

"Really?" my mom said, raising an eyebrow. "Dad has a girlfriend? Who's a fairy?"

"Either way, I think I'm going to look there first," Nash said.

"*You* are doing no such thing," Mom said. "I will be the one going in after my father. You two have had enough excitement for one night. Besides," she said, her face clouded over, "I have a bone or two to pick with him."

"I'd hate to be Ace," Cress muttered in my ear, and I nodded.

"You two stay here and keep whatever comes out busy until I get back," Mom instructed. We nodded. "Open sesame!" she said, knocking on the cover of the game. She was gone a second later. In her place sat a very handsome but very confused-looking man.

"Charming!" Snow White said, dropping Geronimo to the floor as she threw herself into his arms.

"Snow?" he said as he took in the overall-clad princess and the shabby cabin with its threadbare couch and wood-paneled walls.

"Don't worry," I said, "you won't be here long." I stood up as Snow White started singing to him about her deep and abiding love.

"Could be worse," Nash said. "Could have been a rock giant."

"Are you sure that would have been worse?" Cress said, wrinkling her nose in disgust. She walked over to where Ace's office door stood open and took in the mess of board games we'd crammed haphazardly back into the bookcase.

"Thanks for your help," I said, coming to stand beside her.

She snorted. "I wasn't much help," she said. "I almost got you killed multiple times, remember?"

I shrugged. "I feel like that's just par for the course in board game bounding."

"What about those video game things Ogden made?" Nash said, coming to stand beside us. "If they're all from old board games, are they dangerous?"

"They are a different beast, that's for sure," I said with a shiver. All the games in the store had probably been destroyed thanks to the sprinkler system, but I could still picture all those kids running out with their arms loaded with their stolen contraband. What was going to happen to them? Were they going lose themselves in the game like Ogden intended? I knew firsthand how slippery that slope was, and I hadn't been playing a game created by Ogden.

"At least we destroyed all the copies of *The Pirate's Wrath*," Nash said. "That's something."

"We?" I said.

"Fine," Nash said. "You and Mom. That fire alarm idea was pretty brilliant." He paused, considering. "Well, except for the part where it *actually* called the fire department."

"I may not have thought the idea through all the way," I admitted. I glanced back over my shoulder to where Snow White and the prince were cuddled up on the couch next to Lost Lore. "Do you think Mom's okay in there?"

"Oh, she's more than okay," Cress said. "Don't you know?"

"Know what?" I asked.

"About your mom," Cress said. "She's a legend. The greatest player to ever go plunking around in a game. Sam used to brag about her all the time. It's why I begged him to bring her into the game so I could meet her. Why do you think Ogden's crew didn't manage to catch her on the day they caught Sam? Slicker than snot, that one," Cress said. I remembered the way Mom had handled that broom in Reboot and nodded. There might be more to her than I'd ever given her credit for.

"Our mom," Nash said. "You're sure you're talking about *our* mom."

Cress nodded. "Living legend."

"That's just weird," I said.

"Agreed," Cress said with a shrug. "But life's kind of weird."

Snow White chose that moment to start singing in harmony with Geronimo, who'd extricated himself from the blanket to perch happily on her shoulder.

"You can say that again," I agreed.

"Should we pick this mess up before they get back?" I said, jerking my chin at Ace's office. They agreed, and together we worked side by side sorting out the pieces and board games into their correct boxes. The tedious task was made a lot more interesting by Cress, who seemed to have done at least one or two adventures in each of them and regaled us with stories about everything from giant octopuses to slugs that oozed glitter.

We were just sliding the last box onto the shelf when there was a scuffling sound from the living room. We darted from the office to see Ace and Mom standing over Lost Lore, crying as they hugged. Snow White and Charming were gone and in their place sat Beatrice, white puffball hair standing on end as she surveyed her surroundings.

"How in the wide world did you get in here?" Ace said, turning to look at her.

"Now how in the blue blazes would I know that?" she snapped, jumping to her feet and brushing off her bright green dress.

"Geronimo Jones the Third," Nash said. "Geronimo's gone. He was on Snow White's shoulder."

"Interesting," Ace mused. "Usually, animals can

only swap with animals. At least that's how it's always worked for Chief." He turned to Beatrice, eyebrow raised. "Not sure what that says about fairies, but I don't think it's a compliment." Beatrice made a face, and Ace chuckled.

"Does that mean Geronimo Jones is gone for good?" Nash asked.

"Good riddance," said Mom.

"Mom!" Nash said.

"Sorry!" she said, holding up her hands in defense. "He wasn't my favorite pet, though."

"She has a point," I said, placing a hand on Chief's head.

"Well," Ace said, taking off his hat to run a hand over the top of his head as he looked at his daughter. "I'm sure you're wanting to get the boys as far away from me as possible, but do you reckon you could stay for supper first?"

"If by supper, you mean breakfast, then I think that sounds lovely," Mom said. "And I don't know if we'll be leaving any time soon. I have a feeling you've opened Pandora's box with these two." Cress had hung back, leaning against the office door with a look on her face that I couldn't quite understand.

"Cress," Ace said, nodding toward her. "Hoping you'll stay around for a bite to eat as well."

"Really?" Cress said.

Ace nodded, his hands shoved into his jean pockets. "Really."

It was by far one of the oddest meals of my life, but it also felt like the best meal too. Beatrice helped Mom make pancakes and eggs, and Ace fried up bacon on a big cast-iron skillet. As I watched Beatrice laugh with Ace, I had a feeling that no one was going to go hunting for Geronimo Jones the Third any time soon. Meanwhile Nash and I sat next to Cress on the couch, talking. Cress's life outside The Pirate's Wrath had been an interesting one to say the least. She waved her hands animatedly as she discussed the dangers of leprechauns and their gold, and I smiled. She looked just as at ease on our grandfather's threadbare couch as she'd looked perched in that licorice tree on the first day we'd met her. She seemed different now, though. Happier, lighter, as though the guilt of Sam's death had been lifted off her shoulders at long last. Soon it was my turn, and I told them about figuring out that Ogden's key opened not only Mom's prison door but the safe in Reboot.

"The same key opened a lock in a game, and a lock in our world?" Nash said skeptically. "That seems like a stretch."

I shrugged. "Ogden must have dropped it."

"Can I see this key?" Ace said. I nodded, fishing

around in my pocket for the key that had come in so handy and held it up.

"Bless my barnacles," Cress said, "it's the Golden Key."

"The what?" I said.

"The Golden Key," Ace said, plucking it from my hand. "Ogden didn't drop this that night, my boy. I did."

"You?" I said.

Ace nodded. "I keep my keys around Chief's neck for safekeeping, but you had Chief in the field. The Golden Key is one I found in Lost Lore years ago and kept in case something ever happened to Chief."

"Will someone please tell me what the Golden Key is?" Nash said, sounding exasperated.

"It's the key from the very last fairy tale the Grimm brothers ever told," Cress said. "It unlocks any door, and if you want to win Lost Lore you have to find it." She crossed her arms over her chest and glared at Ace. "I've been looking for it for years," she said. "Would have been nice to know it was long gone."

"The Midas stone and the Golden Key?" Beatrice squawked. "You're the biggest thief of them all, Ace Benson, and that's the honest truth."

"Speaking of that stone," I said as I pulled it from my pocket, careful to keep it covered in its T-shirt wrapping. Ace took it carefully from my hand and put it into a new Ziploc bag. Everyone breathed a sigh of relief as he sealed it shut.

"You need to return that to Lost Lore," Beatrice admonished.

"I will," Ace said. "Eventually."

Nash cleared his throat and changed the subject. "You may have found a cool key," he said. "But did you go toe to toe with a Viking as big as a house?" I rolled my eyes at my twin and smiled. Leave it to Nash to try to one-up a magical key. He grinned, regaling us with his Viking encounter, which sounded hair-raising, and Cress added her own insights about the games. Then it was my turn to tell about the video game version of *The Pirate's Wrath* and my trial and error in learning how to use the game's controller properly.

We eventually sat down to eat, and I glanced around the table. One fairy, currently AWOL from her board game, one Wanderer that didn't age, our grandfather, our mom, a dog the size of a bear, and my twin brother. Despite the odd assortment of characters, I couldn't help but feel like I was eating a meal with family. A strange family, but a family nonetheless. I sighed, taking a bite of my pancakes. Cress was right. Life was pretty weird, but I was beginning to think I liked it that way.

AUTHOR'S NOTE

Dear Reader:

Did you notice the quote at the beginning of this book? I'll wait. Go look.

Did you see it? Do you know who that is? Let me give you a hint . . . Golden Ticket. Giant peach. Snozzcumber. Miss Trunchbull. If you still have no idea what I'm talking about, you clearly haven't been using your childhood correctly, and it's high time to go read every one of Roald Dahl's books. Well, except for *The Witches*. That one still gives me nightmares, but if you're into creepy things . . . go for it. Roald Dahl was one of my favorite authors as a kid. He crafted these incredible characters who made me laugh while simultaneously keeping me on the edge of my seat. I still remember my pure delight upon discovering the mixed-up way that the BFG talked about everything from Bonecruncher the giant to whizzpoppers. In fact, I probably channeled a little BFG magic into the creation of characters like Flanny and Beatrice. I was almost done writing *Wander Lost* when I stumbled across this Roald Dahl quote, and it felt like finding that elusive missing puzzle piece under the couch. Click. Mr. Dahl was absolutely right. Life IS more fun if you play games!

In retrospect, writing a book about board games was probably always in the cards for me. Growing up, my cousins and I used to have epic Monopoly games that lasted for weeks. Some of my favorite memories of my childhood were of sitting around a small pop-up card table on a rainy day, bargaining myself into possession of the purple properties, and holding my breath as I skated past a hotel-laden Park Place. Like books, there is something just a little magical about board games. Maybe it's the way they make people laugh or the conversation that happens over rolled dice, but the memories made with games seem to stick around. They offer something that modern-day technology doesn't—connection. The real-life, shoulder-to-shoulder, hands in a popcorn bowl, laughing so hard your drink comes out your nose kind of human connection. The good stuff.

I got the idea for this book while I was driving, and I typed *Middle grade book. Fall into board games* in the Notes app of my phone. (If my mom asks . . . I did this safely, at a stoplight.) It was a jumbled, sloppy, incomplete sentence that made my English teacher heart cringe a little, but it did the job of catching a spark of imagination so I could examine it later. Then, like all good ideas, I forgot about it for a few years. In fact, if my phenomenal editor hadn't asked me to dredge up a list of book ideas for her, I probably never would have found that particular idea again. Ideas are funny like that. Sometimes you capture them and use them right away, and sometimes they wait patiently in whatever spot you happened to stick them until you're ready for them to make their debut in the world.

Of course, when I initially had the idea, I conveniently forgot that if I ever *actually* used it, I wouldn't be able to use any preexisting board games. When I did finally process that I couldn't send my characters cavorting through Candy Land or Clue, I was more than a little disappointed. Copyright can really get in the way of having fun sometimes, let me tell you. So not only was I creating the brand-new world of a book, but I was also inventing board games as I went along. It's harder than it sounds. It turns out that there are A LOT of board games out there, and no sooner would I think up something amazing and original than Google would prove me wrong. Google can be a real buzzkill too.

When I pitched the idea for this book, it was all about board games. When my publisher jumped on board, they had one request: make it about video games instead. At first, I said no. Absolutely, positively no. I'm not a fan of the addictive hold technology has on my kids' generation, and writing a book about video games felt like going against the themes I wove into books like *Float* and *Vanishing Act*. In both of those books the characters learn that real-life friends and adventures are *infinitely* better than anything a screen has to offer. I was stumped but stubborn. After a lot of emails and back-and-forth discussions with my incredibly patient publisher, we came to a compromise. I could write a book about board games (hurray!), but there also had to be a video game element. I agreed. After letting this story roll around in my head for months on end, I knew I couldn't leave the characters in imagination limbo. They had a story to tell. A story full of danger, adventure, lost fairy-tale characters, gigantic bugs, an ornery guinea pig, and two brothers figuring out where they fit in the world. So I wrote a rollicking adventure in board games, and I made the video game the domain of the bad guy. (Insert evil villain laugh here.)

Until next time, Reader, keep reading, and maybe go dust off a board game. You won't be sorry.

Sincerely,
Laura Martin

ACKNOWLEDGMENTS

This book wouldn't have happened without my amazing editor Tara Weikum's willingness to trust me when I said I wanted to write a book about board games in a climate where video games are king. It was a leap of faith that I will forever be grateful for. A big thank you to my agent, Jodi Reamer, for sticking with me even when I was stubborn, and for your patience as we figured out a way to make this story work.

For my best friend, the guy who's been in my corner since I was eighteen. Thanks for being the serious to my silly and for keeping your feet firmly on the ground so mine could be in the clouds, imagining dragons and giant bugs. For my four kids, who love a good board game and made me trust my gut that a board game book is still completely relevant even for the technology generation, and for my mom, who flew in and took over my life for a week so I could make the deadline on this book. My village is a really good one, and I'm so grateful for it.

And finally, for my creator. Thanks for blessing me with a double dose of imagination, even if that meant cutting out any ability in math whatsoever. God must have known that I'd be born into the generation that carried a calculator around in its pockets! Forever thankful for the bigger plan He has for my life, and that it includes writing stories like this one.

Ephesians 3:20
Now to Him who is able to do immeasurably more than all we ask or imagine, according to His power that is at work within us, to Him be glory.